DEAD TO ME

HIDDEN NORFOLK

BOOK 13

J M DALGLIESH

HP

First published by Hamilton Press in 2023

ISBN (Trade Paperback) 978-1-80080-941-3
ISBN (Hardback) 978-1-80080-738-9
ISBN (Large Print) 978-1-80080-862-1

EXCLUSIVE OFFER

DEAD TO ME

PROLOGUE

If the truth be told, this is a strange day. Upon reflection, it has been building for a while now and she should have known. There was the underlying tension hanging in the air over the last couple of days. The walking on eggshells, hoping not to be the one to trigger the anger, to be the one who causes everything to go off like it had done so many times before. Each step taken in the short walk home from school has felt heavier as the weight of what she might be walking into feeds her anxiety. Although anxiety is the fear of an uncertain outcome, the therapist told her. This isn't uncertain. This is happening again, and it is very, very real. You're not alone, Mum. You're never alone.

The shouting has stopped. It's been at least five min-

utes. Too soon to allow a sense of relief to settle in though.

Hopping off her bed, she crosses the short distance between it and the rear-facing bedroom window, gently easing the net curtain aside to improve her view, but careful to stand back and keep out of sight. Daft really, seeing as this is her bedroom and the only person who would be moving the curtain would be herself. The gentle breeze passing through the cracked window whistles momentarily. Glancing at her bedroom door, the chair still wedged underneath the handle to prevent anyone from entering unbidden, she feels safe.

He is there, standing in the garden in the sunshine, hands on his hips, a look of mild consternation on his face. Other than that, broadly emotionless… as always. What did he expect to happen? It was like watching a living statue, but one so beleaguered that it wished to decay, collapse and disappear from existence like many of those depicted in the books he loved to read. Fascinated by life as it was several thousand years ago… but far less interested in what was happening in front of his eyes.

There's the shouting again. A scream and a crash. He flinches. The statue actually flinches! A positive sign? Perhaps.

Locking her in the orangery probably wasn't a good idea. Another pane shatters and a wrought-iron chair clatters to the patio. Her dad turns to his right as two figures approach. Police officers. A man and a woman. She is a fair bit shorter than him, blonde hair tied into a ponytail beneath her funny little hat, at the nape of her neck. They glance nervously towards the orangery, taking in the situation. Dad looks apologetic, like butter wouldn't melt. Mind you, he's probably at a loss at how to explain this one. Then again, he is a man skilled at fashioning excuses to explain away all manner of bumps, bruises and random injuries, all seemingly occurring through unfortunate and unavoidable mishap. Even the school seemed to buy into his nonsense. He's plausible if nothing else.

One of the officers is walking away from her Dad now, a large walkie-talkie pressed to her lips. The other one is still standing with him. I wonder who called them? It wouldn't have been him, that's for certain. *It will blow over. Don't worry.* That was pretty much his stock phrase. That and, *I'm sorry.* He says it so often these days it's hard to feel any genuine passion contained within the words. If he is truly sorry, then he needs to work on his delivery because it has all the contrition of a puppy caught shredding a newspaper. The puppy couldn't stay either. *Too much work on top of everything else we have going on,* he said.

The policeman moves towards the orangery, ducking as something's thrown at him. I can't see her though. I hope she's alright. One of these days she won't be, and what will we do then?

Stepping away from the window, she goes back to her bed and clambers in, pulling the covers over her and burying her head in the pillow. The screaming has started again. It will last for hours. It always lasts for hours. The fear of what might happen to her Mum is followed by a selfish thought, one that makes her feel guilty the moment it pops into her head. She always feels bad when her subconscious throws it at her, but it is a concern repeatedly raised. *This is my future… and I don't want it, but how can I get out?*

She draws the covers overhead, trying to drown out the screams from the garden. It makes little difference. It never does.

CHAPTER ONE

THE AIR FELT THICK this morning. A bank of fog drifting in off The Wash had settled along the coast, stubbornly refusing to allow the morning sun to burn it away. In a few hours the sun would be sitting low in a blue sky but, for now at least, it was a hazy circle barely visible though the gloom. Every footfall sounded, almost as if it was reverberating in the moisture hanging all around him. It felt cold as well. Not unusual for mid-November, but this wasn't any normal onset of autumn. Not this year. Daily averages were still well into double figures up until two days ago. An abnormal seasonal shift, the local weather presenter had said. He'd heard others call it an Indian summer, as if that made it better. Norfolk was basking in spring-like temperatures, plants still flowering rather than hibernating, while across the pond in the USA, vast swathes of the country were freezing in temperatures at the other end of the scale.

The dog barked. Looking along the line of the twisted and bent chain-link fence, he saw Barney, his ever-present sidekick waiting patiently at a point in the fence where the base had come away from the concrete pillar it was fixed to, curling up barely a foot high off the ground.

He smiled.

"Well, you might fit through there, Barney, me old mate, but what do you expect me to do?"

The dog stood, wagged his stumpy tail, barked once more and slipped through the gap before turning to face him with an expectant expression. It was large enough for a West Highland Terrier, but not for an adult.

"I'm not coming that way!" he said, slipping his fingers through the links at chest height and shaking the fence. The metal was cold and damp to the touch but, despite the give, it stood up to his efforts at dislodging it. The main gate was tied together with a thick chain and reluctant as he was to use bolt cutters, there was no way he was getting through easily. Taking a deep breath, he tested the fence with both hands, judging it would hold his weight, before clambering up, using the top of the post to brace himself as he reached the summit. The ageing boundary marker wobbled under his weight and, for a brief second, he wondered if it was about to give way under the stress, but the rusting brackets held firm and he levered himself over and dropped to the ground with a thump.

Breathing heavily, he looked around. Mature pine trees surrounded the compound, their younger siblings growing within it. There was other vegetation too, all growing in and around the rusting hulks of twentieth century castoffs. Taking out his mobile, he set the camera function live and started taking pictures.

"Okay, you want more proof," he said aloud, "then I'll give it to you."

Barney trotted along next to him as he moved deeper into the compound. Some of the old cars were stacked on top of one another, no doubt by some machinery that was no longer present, but no more than two high. The majority of the vehicles had no windows and had been stripped of parts for salvage, but for some reason the core of the chassis or bodywork had never been processed, instead just left here exposed to the elements.

"Look at that!" The dog looked where he was pointing at a red car, once shiny metallic paint but now a faded, drab pinkish colour far from its hey-day. "I've not seen an old Rover like that for years," he said as if Barney could understand him. "That was probably last used in *The Sweeney*!" The dog set off to investigate while he took another picture. The ground underfoot was a mix of local shingle, mud and an awful lot of dying weeds and vegetation that were desperately trying to re-establish control of the area. Interspersed between the vehicles were shards of glass and plastic, bits that'd dropped off the old cars while they were stacked for processing.

"None of this should be here. It's bloody criminal."

Barney started barking, but he ignored it. Even for a Westie, Barney was yappy. He was a lovely companion, but excitable and quite annoying. Spotting a pool of oil beneath one car, he crouched and took another snap. If he gathered enough evidence, then maybe the council would be forced to acquire the site and clean it up. The sound of an approaching car made him look up. He saw the beams of twin headlights approaching through the fog. It was travelling at speed and momentarily he was concerned the driver might not see his own car parked up half on the verge and plough into it, but the driver lifted off the accelerator and passed without incident.

Barney was still at it.

"Give it a rest, would you?" he called, and the dog quietened down for a moment before starting up again. It was probably a deer or something on the other side of the fence tormenting him. The breeze picked up, driving a chill through him and ruffling a tarpaulin off to his left. He looked at it, tied between the trunks of two trees growing at the edge of the compound and sloping down at an angle where the corners were fastened to stakes in the ground, folding across the front to create a makeshift door overhang. It was here where the blue tarpaulin had worked loose and was flapping in the breeze. It struck him as odd; something akin to a den children would cobble together.

The dog was still going. He sighed, slipped his mobile into his pocket, and went in search of the creature, taking the most direct route, turning side on to slip between two lines of vehicles. Barney appeared in front of him, excitedly bounding away once he was certain to be followed. Stepping clear of the last car, he turned to his left and saw Barney ten feet away barking at the rear of another car.

"All right, I'm here. What's all the fuss about?"

He stopped. This displeased the dog who turned to face him, tail twitching, still barking incessantly. Tentatively walking forward, he was no longer hearing the dog, his eyes focussed on the arm dangling from the boot of the car, streaked in dried blood, the hand hovering a few inches from the sodden ground beneath it where a patch of earth was stained dark red. A crow cawed from a branch somewhere in the nearby forest, a call picked up by others. It seemed like they were announcing the discovery.

Looking around, he could see nothing but the haze of the damp fog. Backing away from the car, he called the dog.

"Come on, boy. Let's go."

Barney cocked his head quizzically.

"Come on! Now!"

Reluctantly, the dog trotted after him as he picked up the pace back to the main road. Something caught his eye, startling him as he saw a figure standing off to his right watching him. He gasped, backing away while reaching for his mobile. Fumbling to unlock it with numb fingers, he glanced back to his right, but the figure had been absorbed into the mist. Was it even there?

Dialling 999, he clamped the phone to his ear and stared back into the fog. Barney stood in front of him looking in the same direction, growling. He hadn't imagined it. There was someone there.

"I'm calling the police!" he shouted with as much confidence as he could muster, which wasn't a lot. He could hear the fear in his voice. "They'll be here any minute."

Barney looked up at him, his ears erect and in tune with their surroundings.

"They're coming, little man. They're coming," he said as the call handler answered.

"999, which emergency service do you require,"

the efficient voice asked calmly. He needed to hear that because he was far from calm.

"P-Police… please. I've found a body."

The call was transferred to the police, and he waited, eyes nervously scanning his surroundings, back pressed firmly against the fence.

CHAPTER TWO

Tom Janssen sipped at his coffee. This one was a little too bitter for his liking and there was something about the milk that he found odd, but he couldn't quite figure out what it was.

"How do you like the new pods?"

He looked over at Alice, hurriedly packing Saffy's school bag with everything she was likely to need that day.

"Different."

She stopped, two hands in the bag trying to make room for everything, glancing up at him. "Different good or different bad."

Tom's brow creased as he took another sip. "Just different."

Alice exhaled deeply and smiled. "Is that what I should say to Mum later?"

"It's a lovely gift..."

"But?"

"But nothing," he said. "However—"

"However is a fancy *but*, Tom Janssen."

"However," he continued, "I do prefer the old machine."

"Which is noisier, more of a faff and makes a mess all over the counter. That machine?"

He nodded.

"Yes. But I wouldn't advise saying that to your mum."

Alice shrugged. "She would take it well, I think."

Tom arched his eyebrows. "Without doubt. When are you seeing her today?"

"Once I've done my morning shift," Alice said, letting out an exasperated sigh and pulling the PE kit out of Saffy's bag. "It's no good. She'll have to take two bags." Alice glanced at the clock and swore. "Where is she anyway?"

"Do you want me to chase her up?" Tom asked, getting up from the table.

"No, I'll do it." Alice took one step towards the hallway and shouted, "Saffy! It's time to go!"

"I could call in at the hospice later."

Alice looked at him. "Could you?"

He nodded.

"That'd be great, thanks."

"Not a problem," he said, picking up his coffee

cup. Alice turned back to the door, ready to shout even louder only for her daughter to walk into the kitchen clutching a pencil case and a schoolbook.

"What have you been doing?" Alice asked.

"My homework."

It tripped so easily off the tongue, it seemed like the only possible, and very obvious, answer.

"At this time? Why didn't you do it yesterday after school?"

"Because… you know… reasons."

Tom turned away to hide his smile. Saffy was precocious and getting more so as time went by. Alice noted Tom's reaction but remained steadfast in her disapproval.

"Are any of those reasons…" she shrugged, "good ones?"

"I was exhausted," Saffy said, pursing her lips. "You've no idea the pressure I'm under."

"Saffy," Alice fixed her with a stern look, "you're barely nine years of age."

"Which just goes to show you how advanced I am for my years," she said, reaching past her mum and putting the pencil case and book into her bag. Alice rolled her eyes. "Sophie says her mum told her that I should be put up a year."

"Did she now?" Alice asked, glancing at Tom who smiled. "And who is Sophie?"

"The new girl who started this term."

Alice frowned. "I'm not sure I know her."

"Yes, you do," Saffy said inspecting the contents of her school bag. "She's the one whose mum you said must put her make-up on with an airbrush."

Tom mock grimaced. "You said that?"

Alice flushed. "I may have… but I didn't think I said it aloud."

"There's not a lot of room in here, Mum," Saffy said, frowning deeply. "I think I should take a second bag."

"Very astute," Tom said. Alice glared at him. He smiled playfully. "Just saying."

"Hashtag," Saffy said, grinning up at Tom.

Alice put both hands on her daughter's shoulders and steered her towards the hall. "I swear the two of you have your own language sometimes."

"It's true," Tom said. "We made it up so we can plot behind your back without you realising."

"I believe that I really do," she replied. "Saffy, get your coat and put your shoes on, and don't forget your trainers for sports. And as for moving up a year, don't be so quick to sacrifice your childhood. You only get to have one."

"It never stops, does it?" Saffy said, leaving the kitchen.

"What doesn't?"

"The demands on my time."

"Oh, it does, young lady," Alice called after her. "In about thirty years from now." She looked at the clock again and then checked her watch, clearly hoping the former was wrong. "I'm running so late."

"Do you want me to drop Saffy at school?"

"No, it's on my way. Aren't you due into the office by now?"

"Cassie is leading the morning briefing today. She doesn't need me standing over her."

"Oh, is your dynamic DS looking at a promotion?" Alice asked, opening the cupboard under the stairs and pulling out a small backpack before putting Saffy's clothing inside.

"She denies wanting it, but I think she'd comfortably make the step up. Provided she can curb her inner tendency to vent her unfiltered consciousness. Besides, the new detective chief superintendent is starting today, so Tamara and I will be busy."

Alice stopped what she was doing. "Do you think you'll have time to make it to the hospice?"

Tom came over to her, putting his cup down next to the drainer and put his arms around her, drawing her into him. "I'll make time," he said, kissing the top of her head as she laid it on his chest.

"Can I come and see Gran too?" Saffy asked from the doorway. "I miss her."

"Not today, sweetie," Alice said. Seeing Saffy deflate, she quickly crossed to her, kneeling down so they met at eye level and squeezing the little girl's upper arms. "But I promise, I'll take you in on the weekend. Good enough?"

Saffy acknowledged that with a nod and a half smile. "The nurses always share their biscuits with me."

"I know," Alice said, glancing down at Saffy's feet. "Now, for a genius, you do have a habit of putting your shoes on the wrong feet."

Saffy looked down and frowned. "I thought they felt strange." She made a performance of walking out into the hall to sit on the stairs and swap the shoes over. Tom chuckled.

"Is there anything you need me to do?" he asked.

Alice pointed at Russell, their terrier.

"He needs a walk. If you have time?"

Tom looked down at the dog who knew they were talking about him. He inclined his head, ears pricked.

"What do you say Russell, shall we go out for a walk?"

Russell barked and came to sit at Tom's feet, looking up expectantly.

"Whenever you're ready," Saffy said from her place, standing in the doorway. Alice leaned over and kissed Tom.

"I'll see you this afternoon. Around two?"

"Two o'clock," Tom said, tapping his finger to his forehead. Saffy ran across the kitchen, threw her arms around Tom and he scooped her up as if she were a rag doll, although she was getting bigger, and he was certain there would come a time when he couldn't do it any longer.

"See you later, Daddy."

Tom gave her a kiss and put her down. Alice handed Saffy her bag as she passed, making for the front door. Alice followed, looking back at Tom over her shoulder, smiling, and he could see moisture in her eyes. The adoption wasn't official yet but from the moment they'd agreed it, Saffy had referred to him as her dad and it never failed to lift him whenever she did. He hoped that would never wear off. He waved to Alice, drawing breath. It'd been a rollercoaster of a few months since they'd brought their wedding forward, due to Alice's mother's aggressive cancer, they'd been in a holding pattern, waiting for the hammer to drop before they could move on with their lives, living very much in the moment. It felt that period was coming to an end quite soon. What would come next, or how long it would take to make that step, was yet to be determined, but they relished any lighter moments that came their way. Becoming an official family was one such moment to celebrate no matter what else was going on.

Tom's mobile rang.

"Hey, Cassie, missing me already?"

"Change of plan, I'm afraid."

He noted the seriousness in her tone as well as the sound of the breeze coming down the line. She was outside.

"A body's been found… and it's messy," she said flatly.

Tom looked down at Russell who appeared to understand his fate as he lay down forlornly resting his head on his paws.

"Send me the location." He hung up. "Sorry, little man." Dropping down on his haunches, he stroked the dog's head, hearing his mobile beep with a text message notification. Russell offered him a pitiful look, vainly hoping for good things to happen. "I guess a quick lap around the block won't hurt, will it?"

Russell leapt up, scampered into the utility room and emerged moments later with his lead clenched tightly within his jaws.

"Ten minutes, no more," Tom said, wagging a pointed finger at him and glancing at the clock. "Why do I talk to this dog? There's no way he understands me."

Russell barked impatiently. Tom wondered if he was wrong about that last thought.

CHAPTER THREE

Tom found the access track to the scene just off Bircham Road on the approach to the village of Fring, a little way south-west of the larger village of Docking. PC Dave Marshall was leaning against his patrol car, parked up on the grass verge alongside a line of trees lining this stretch of road. Tom pulled up alongside and lowered his window, Marshall ducking to meet his eye.

"Morning, sir."

"Morning, Sheriff," Tom said, addressing him by his nickname. Whether the constable liked this name, Tom didn't know, but everyone addressed him by it. "Where's Cassie?"

The constable looked over his right shoulder and pointed beyond the trees. "Head along the track and the access to the compound is just on your right."

Tom looked in that direction, surprised to hear anything described as a compound this far out of any major settlement in what was an ostensibly agricultural part of the county. Marshall read his mind.

"I know, weird isn't it? It's just out of sight, shielded by the trees. I've driven past here thousands of times and had no idea it was even there. It doesn't look like it's been used in years, mind you."

Tom nodded his appreciation and drove along the track. It was made up of earth, with no material used to harden the surface like gravel. Evidently it was used to access the fields beyond the trees but not by any heavy machinery, otherwise the track would likely have been torn up. As it was, it was bumpy but passable in an average car. He didn't have far to go, however. The line of trees extended barely fifty feet and before he passed them, the entrance came into view.

There were several CSI vans already parked along the perimeter and Tom saw both Cassie's car and the one belonging to Dr Fiona Williams, their on-call forensic medical examiner. Another constable stood at the entrance to the scene. Tom pulled up and got out of the car, scanning the scene as he walked to the entrance. It looked like a scrapyard but a very dilapidated and uncared for one, which took some doing, bearing in mind what was stored there.

PC Kerry Palmer welcomed him with a warm smile.

"Good morning, sir."

"Hi, Kerry," he said looking around. He could see the compound stretched away from him in a rectangular shape with a perimeter fence encompassing the entire site as far as he could see, although the view was hampered by trees and vegetation pressing against the boundary on all sides as well as growing unchecked within. He roughly counted thirty to forty old vehicles, spying rusting agricultural machinery as well as old cars. The chain-link fencing gave the site a semblance of purpose for without it, it would look like a fly-tipping site on a monumental scale. "Point me in the right direction, if you don't mind?"

"Yes, sir. If you head towards the rear and bear right as if you're going back to the main road."

Tom looked and Kerry was right, the compound appeared to angle back into the trees towards the rear of the site, almost in a P shape. He nodded his thanks and made his way towards the back, taking care where he placed his feet. In contrast to the track, the inner compound had a mix of old shingle concrete and gravel dropped to patch holes appearing in the ragged surface. The shingle cement mix of concrete was a popular construction method for surfacing in the fifties and sixties. It was cheap and the materials plentiful. However, despite its hardiness, after this many years of exposure to the elements it was prone to cracking and breaking up in patches where the cement bond was failing. In such places, gravel had once been used to fill such holes, only now Mother Nature was making a good job of breaking it up by herself, and any further attempts to preserve the surface clearly hadn't been made in years.

The forensic technicians were busying themselves processing the area around one particular car. Cassie, standing at the nearside rear of the rusting hatchback, spotted Tom's arrival and stepped away from Dr Williams, clipboard in hand and making notes, to greet him.

"Morning," she said grimly. "You've timed it well; the photographs have been taken and we're ready to pull him out of the car. Just waiting on you."

"Morning," he said, checking his footing and following an assigned path to allow him to get closer without damaging any possible forensic trace evidence on the ground.

"A local man called it in this morning," Cassie said as Tom came to stand on Dr Williams' shoulder, peering into the boot. The body was curled up in the foetal position, facing away from them. Tom could see blood pooling on the surface beneath the body. There was no boot lining or carpet to absorb the liquid and it had been flowing throughout.

"He wouldn't have been killed elsewhere," Tom said absently.

"Very good, Detective," Dr Williams said. "You could make a success of your career if you can keep that up."

Tom offered her a sideways smile. "I figure he wasn't transported here in this car either," he said, angling his head to the side and glancing along the length of the car. It couldn't have seen a road for decades. The shell of the vehicle was all that remained; wheels and fittings, both internal and external, had been removed. All that was left was the body of the vehicle. Neither of which bore any resemblance to a working vehicle. "Killed nearby, do you think?"

"Without doubt," Fiona Williams agreed. "The amount of blood lost would indicate the heart was still pumping around the time he was dumped in there or pretty close to it."

"How long has he been here?"

The doctor screwed up her nose, mulling it over momentarily.

"Rigor has been and gone… so that implies a minimum of twenty-four hours since death occurred. Looking at other factors, taking into account recent weather and overnight temperatures, I should imagine you're looking at a window of thirty to thirty-six hours. Once we get him out and I have space to do a liver test, then we'll be more accurate, but I think I won't be far off."

Tom looked around, hearing a car passing on the road to his right, visible just through the trees.

"Cause of death?"

Dr Williams chuckled. "I have an idea, but let's get him out first."

Tom nodded and Cassie signalled to the crime scene techs to come over and move the body. They stretched out a tarpaulin on the ground nearby, laying a body bag on top of that. Tom and Cassie moved back to allow them the space to work.

"Who found the body?" Tom asked, glancing around and taking in the remoteness of the location.

"He's over there with Danny."

Tom looked to his left and saw a slight man standing beside Detective Constable Danny Wilson. The newest member of the team was busy taking notes of their conversation, clearly irritated with the man's Westie which was straining on the leash and climbing Wilson's leg.

"Who is he?" Tom asked Cassie.

"A local. He's been applying pressure on the council to have this place dealt with."

"Dealt with?"

"Yeah, cleaned up… all these rotting hulks cleared, the ground returned to nature or something like that. He's likely one of the knit-your-own-sandals brigade."

They walked over to the pair, DC Wilson greeting Tom with a broad smile.

"Hello, sir. I'm just taking down a statement from Mr Bowles here."

"Yes," Cassie said with a knowing look, "we can see… and it is your job."

Tom was aware of Wilson's desire to please, always keen to explain how productive he was being. Whether that was due to him wanting to impress his new inspector or if that was just his way remained to be seen.

"Mr Bowles," Tom said, "what time did you arrive here this morning?"

"I left home at six-thirty. I always take Barney out at that time, every day. I live a quarter of a mile away," he pointed behind him, "on the outskirts of Fring."

At the mention of the creature's name, the dog turned its attention away from Wilson to his owner and then to the newcomers. Cassie ignored it and so he stood on his hind legs, resting his paws against Tom. Tom reached down and made a fuss of the dog.

"Lovely looking dog," he said, scratching him behind the ears.

"Thanks."

"You were inside the compound?"

Bowles shifted his weight nervously between his feet. "Yeah, I know it's trespassing and all that, but… I've taken pictures from beyond the fence, but the council said it didn't give them enough reason to act." His voice elevated in pitch. "I just thought… if I came inside…"

"It's okay, Mr Bowles. We're not concerned with that."

"No, of course not," he said, his gaze drifting over to where the body was carefully being lifted out of the boot of the car. His complexion turned pale, and he swallowed hard. "I… never expected to see anything like that in here."

"No. I imagine it was quite a shock."

Bowles nodded vigorously. "What happened to him?"

"That's what we're here to find out," Tom said. "What can you tell us about it?"

"Me?" he said, fearful. "Nothing. Why do you think I would know anything about it?"

Tom saw Cassie suppressing a smile to the man's right as his discomfort grew.

"Why not just tell me what you saw, Mr Bowles."

"Oh… right, yes of course. Well, I climbed over the fence… Barney came through a damaged section. I didn't do it. It was like it already." Tom smiled and gestured for him to continue. "Yeah, well, anyway… I was taking pictures, gathering evidence for the council. This place is an eyesore and should be cleared. It's a travesty to allow it to just rot away in such a lovely part of the world."

Wilson coughed loudly.

"Why don't you tell DI Janssen about the person you thought you saw—"

"I did see him!" Bowles protested. "Or… I think I saw him."

"Who did you see?" Tom asked.

"A figure… like some sort of spectre floating in the mist!"

"Floating?" Tom asked.

"Or standing… I couldn't really see. I was a bit overwrought with finding the dead body, you see?"

"Where did you see him, this man you're speaking of?"

Bowles looked past Tom, pointing towards the perimeter fence. They all followed his hand, pointing to where the entrance gates were located. It was a distance of fifty feet or so.

"Did you get a decent look at him?" Tom asked.

"No, can't say I did."

"The fog is lifting now, but how thick was it at the time?" Wilson asked.

"Dense. It was hard to make out. I mean, it was a bloke, I'm sure of that but I couldn't say a lot more. He was watching me."

"Did he say anything?" Tom asked. "Move towards you—"

"No, no, nothing like that. He was just standing there, watching me. It creeped me right out, I can tell you."

"But you're sure it was a person?" Tom asked.

"Without doubt."

"Have you ever seen anyone out here before; hanging around, a random car parked out here… anything like that?"

"No, I can't say I have. Sorry. This guy was a proper weirdo though… just standing there. I'll bet he's your man."

"Our man?"

"Yeah, the killer. Why else would he be out here?"

"You're out here," Cassie said straight-faced.

Bowles looked nervous again. "Yes, but I'm walking my dog… and doing community-spirited work. You don't think that I… I mean, I wouldn't—"

Tom placated him with a gently raised hand. "No, Mr Bowles. Don't worry. Perhaps you could finish giving DC Wilson your statement and then we can get you away home."

Bowles nodded, smiling at Wilson. Fiona Williams caught Tom's eye and he steered Cassie away. Together, they crossed the short distance back to where the FME was kneeling beside the deceased. As they reached her, she stood up and removed the mask covering her mouth and nose. The dead man lay on his back. A person who has been dead for some time, particularly one who died during a traumatic event can look older than their years but, even so, Tom guessed this man was in his early thirties. His black hair was sporting a spattering of grey, and the devil's forks were showing signs his hair was receding at a glacial pace.

He was tall, perhaps topping six feet, but if not then it was close. His leather bomber jacket was unzipped, and he wore a tight-fitting white T-shirt beneath it over indigo blue jeans and a pair of well-worn Chelsea boots. Tom could see he was athletic, not necessarily muscular but lean with muscle definition around his lower abdomen, chest and neck. The veins on the latter were raised. The jacket he wore was a soft leather, smooth and supple allowing the width of his shoulders to be visible. This man worked out fairly regularly. Either that or he had a manual job requiring significant use of his muscle.

The white T-shirt, jeans and the jacket were stained with blood, presumably his judging by how much was visible in the car itself.

"Thoughts, Fiona?"

The doctor cocked her head, grimacing. "Well, it's certainly interesting."

Tom could tell the deceased had been in quite a fight; likely a fight for his life, and one that he'd lost spectacularly. The T-shirt had multiple holes in it, most were barely an inch in diameter. Fiona pointed to his chest.

"Multiple wounds to the chest as well as the lower abdomen. Easily into double figures."

"A knife?"

She nodded. "That would be my guess. The wounds appear circular at first glance, which might indicate gunshots…" She looked around them. "Which I guess would be possible to go unnoticed out here, but the lack of any exit wounds tells me they are stab wounds."

Cassie frowned. "Can't you tell the difference?" Fiona looked at her as a teacher would an unruly pupil asking a deliberately daft question. "Of course, I know the difference, Cassandra, but once the incision has been made and the blade withdrawn, the elasticity of the skin which holds its shape is broken and the wound opens further, stretching into a circle—"

"Similar to a gunshot?" Cassie asked.

Fiona nodded. "Correct. However, if you take thumb and forefinger, squeeze the two sides of the wound back together then it reveals more of a slit, which is what one expects from a knife wound. Believe me, the mistake has been made the world over from time to time."

"Sorry," Cassie said. "No offence."

"None taken, DS Knight."

"Forgive me, Fiona," Tom said, "but that isn't particularly interesting."

"Bear with me, Tom. With this number of injuries, I would be very surprised if even half of them weren't sufficient to kill him on their own, either by puncturing a primary organ, or two, or nicking an artery perhaps. What's interesting me though is up here," she said, taking her pen and leaning over the deceased, gesturing towards his eyes with the tip. "The petechiae that are visible here around both eyes. That's haemorrhaging indicative of—"

"Asphyxiation," Tom said, glancing sideways at Cassie.

"Exactly."

"Now… that is interesting."

Cassie's frown deepened. "He was stabbed multiple times and then strangled?"

"Or the other way around," Fiona said, inclining her head as she stood upright. Shrugging, she then shook her head. "Or both at the same time. I'm not a forensic psychologist, but for what it's worth in my opinion, this number of stab wounds… none of which appears to be aimed at any particular point of the body, nor are they delivered with any semblance of control, suggesting more of a frenzied attack than a planned assault."

"Which is very different to a case of strangulation," Tom said, "in the main." He focussed on the neck. A powerful man, or at least one with thick neck muscles, was not an easy target when it came to strangulation. To kill someone in that particular manner was never as easy as it appears in television or literature. The neck is strong and when compressed, the muscles push back. Strangling someone, someone conscious and able bodied, takes a significant amount of time, minutes rather than seconds, and in a fight situation it is even harder.

"There's no indication that a ligature was used, no abrasions from a cord or a length of rope. No texture or patterns either. They might show up under a lab analysis but, as of now, I would suggest he was strangled in the crook of the arm."

Dr Williams lifted her right arm and bent it at an angle as if she had someone in a headlock, pulling her arm into her body.

"There are marks to the neck, but not the impressions that would be left by manual strangulation by hand. You can see this reddening of the skin," she pointed for their benefit, "here and here. I would expect this to have developed into bruising if the victim hadn't died or had lived longer. The passage of blood was restricted, driving it closer to the surface."

"Any defensive injuries?" Tom asked.

"Plenty," Fiona said. "Scratches and abrasions to the knuckles, a few minor lacerations indicative of the victim moving to try and avoid slashes or blows. He made a pretty good fist of it, by all accounts. I dare say whoever he was scrapping with will likely be fostering some wounds of their own."

"With a bit of luck, we'll get some trace evidence from the victim," Cassie said.

"It'd make a welcome change, wouldn't it?" Tom said with a wry smile. "Fiona, I know it's speculation, but should we be considering the possibility of multiple attackers here?"

Fiona shrugged. "That's beyond my remit, Tom. I dare say the pathologist will have something to say on it."

"He usually does," Cassie said under her breath.

"Sir, do you have a moment?"

Tom turned to see a forensic technician beckoning him over. He gestured for Cassie to come with him, thanking Fiona for her insights.

CHAPTER FOUR

"We found this in the mud," the technician said, handing Tom a transparent evidence bag. "It was found on the ground a few metres away from the car the body was left in."

Donning a pair of nitrile gloves, Tom opened the bag and took out the contents, a brown leather wallet. It was distressed, showing signs of age, with a button clasp that had long since ceased working. Cassie hovered at his shoulder as he opened it, peering inside. There were no cash, credit cards or receipts present, unusually, which suggested it had been cleared of its contents. There was a sleeve with a plastic window, the perfect size for a driving licence, but it too was empty. However, behind this was another pocket, not clearly visible unless you were looking for it, and within this one Tom found a slip of cardboard tucked away out of sight. He teased it out. It was a business card, dog-eared and faded, for a bar in Sheringham. Tom recognised the name although it wasn't one of his personal haunts. He reversed it in his hand and showed it to Cassie.

"Well, that's a place to start, at least,' she said.

"We've got something else of interest, sir," the tech said, leading them to a patch of ground close to the centre of the compound, approximately ten metres away. The crime scene investigators were marking out an area roughly three metres in diameter. Tom and Cassie held back, evidently he'd found something significant. The tech directed one of his colleagues to lay down numbered markers and came to stand with Tom who shot him an inquisitive look.

"Do you see the churn in the ground here?" he said, pointing to the immediate area one of his colleagues was now taping off. "I think this is where they were fighting."

Tom scanned the ground in front of them. It was clear that there had been activity in the area recently. Where there were soil deposits you could see where it'd been recently disturbed. Similarly, gravel deposits had been turned over, the darker stones not yet bleached by the sun were now atop the others. Weeds and long grasses were flattened or damaged. It was quite noticeable if you paid attention.

"I think there was a fight going on here," the tech said, gesturing in a circular motion with his hand. "The combatants trading blows and circling one another. You can see where their heels were dug in, pushing back or launching strike and offensive… counter-offensive," he said, pointing to specific areas. "You can tell from the heel patterns and subsequent movements."

"Can you tell how many people?" Tom asked.

The tech shook his head. "Not at the moment, there are too many movements on top of one another, but if you can give us a bit of time, we'll map it out and you never know, we might even be able to work out a bit of strategic choreography for you."

"That'll be great, thank you."

"No promises, though," he added as Tom made to leave. Tom turned and arched his eyebrows. The tech shrugged, "I just want to manage expectations."

"Noted," Tom said.

Cassie had already made her way back to where the deceased lay. When Tom reached her, she was on her haunches inspecting the man's boots.

"Found something?" he asked.

"These boots are leather soled. No treads."

"Good quality?"

"Yes, four to five hundred pounds, I should imagine, based on the brand."

"Specialist?"

"Hardly, but one with a royal warrant."

"I didn't know you were a fashionista?" Tom asked.

Cassie chuckled. "I'm not, but I know quality when I see it. He's had his use out of them though. The jeans are branded as well. Not cheap. Likely over a hundred quid a pair. And the choice of footwear is curious too."

"Why?"

"I wouldn't choose to wear them if I thought I was going into battle."

"Caught unawares, you reckon?"

She shrugged. "If you thought you were likely to have a ruck, wouldn't you be prepared?"

Tom had to admit she had a point.

"Look at his boots."

"Caked in mud," Tom said.

"Particularly up the back from heel to above the ankle."

"Dragged?"

She nodded, glancing back at the suspected fight location and then pointing at the boot of the car. "Dragged to the car unconscious and dumped inside."

"So why was he here?"

She shook her head. "Seems an odd place to be, doesn't it?"

"Especially dressed like this, in this weather," Tom said.

"Meeting someone here, perhaps?"

"Or followed them."

"Whatever the reason, I reckon he got way more than he bargained for."

Tom looked over to where he eyed a makeshift shelter of sorts. A sheet of tarpaulin was purposefully tied to form a canopy, draping across the front which he figured was an entrance point. He gestured towards it.

"Have you checked that out?"

"Not yet," Cassie said. "The techs have been too busy on the victim and the groundworks."

"Come on, let's take a look."

"No one will shout at us as long as we don't touch anything," she said.

The flap at the front blew back and forth on the breeze, Tom eased it aside and peered into the gloomy interior. It was as he suspected, a makeshift shelter. The sides were constructed with old wooden pallets wedged against two trees on one side and two of the rusting cars stacked on top of each other. To the rear, fallen tree branches were strategically placed to secure the wall in place. Lining the interior were a multitude of broken-down cardboard boxes, stacked against one another to form a windproof barrier. The roof of the shelter, barely chest high on him, forced Tom to stoop low to survey the interior. The roof was also formed from old cardboard boxes protected from the rain by the large blue tarpaulin sheet.

The interior was just over a metre wide and almost three deep giving an occupant room to stretch out. More pallets and cardboard made up the floor, on top of which were several sleeping bags and a heavily stained and discoloured duvet. The shelter felt remarkably insulated against the cool breeze blowing the damp fog around the exterior. It wasn't exactly homely, but someone had gone to great lengths to make the space habitable, at least in the short term.

"A home from home for the homeless?" Cassie asked.

"I should think so," Tom said, pursing his lips. Still wearing his gloves, he tentatively entered seeking any signs of blood or clothing that might relate to the attack on their victim. An old metal tin was wedged at the rear between two pallets, behind the head of the sleeping bag. He took it out. It was battered, rusty where the paint had flaked off in places, painted green on the sides with a white band across the top along with the brand imagery. The wording was still legible in most parts. It was an old cigarette tin, of a brand which had long since disappeared as Tom didn't recognise it. Roughly twelve centimetres long, slightly less wide and barely eight deep, it was a curious find. It was lightweight but he could hear and feel movement inside.

Putting it down, he allowed Cassie to take a few pictures with the camera on her phone before he eased the lid off. It squeaked on its hinges as he revealed the contents. Inside were a few photographs, some in black and white and any colour images were faded with muted sepia tones overpowering the original hues. None of them was recent. An old man with white hair swept back from his head, sporting thick-framed black glasses popular back in the early sixties, and holding a walking stick featured in one. There was a gathering, black tie by the look of it, but this man was the focus of the shot. Judging by the clothing worn by people in the background it suggested his thoughts were correct and it was taken in the late fifties or early sixties. Flipping it over, Tom found a handwritten note simply reading 'Granddad.'

A woman sitting on parched grass, leaning on her outstretched arms behind her, legs laid out before her, crossed at the ankle, was the next image. She had big, permed dark hair, and sported horn-rimmed glasses. Again, there was no date, and nothing was written on the rear. The next picture was of a younger woman, dark hair stretching to the shoulder. She was smiling at a toddler standing on her lap, a mother holding a child by the waist maybe. The toddler was a girl, a pink ribbon tied through her hair, grinning at the person holding the camera. On the reverse were two letters, L and K, along with a year, 1976.

Showing it to Cassie, she took more pictures.

"Sentimental keepsakes?" she asked.

He nodded, putting the picture back and picking out the only other item left in the tin. It was a locket on a delicate gold chain. The clasp was quite stiff, and Tom was careful not to damage it as he opened it. Inside were two pictures facing one another. They were black and white. One was of a man. If it was the same elderly man in the black and white photo, Tom couldn't tell. This image was of a much younger man, dark haired and not in need of glasses. Not for this picture at any rate. The other image was of a little girl, perhaps six or seven years of age. There were no identifying names or dates to be seen. The locket itself was carved with an elaborate swirl pattern, gold and darkened due to its age. Tom was no judge of the quality of the item, but it must have held some level of attachment to the owner. "Looks like it," he said, glancing at Cassie.

"Do you think whoever is dossing here is the spectral figure that Mr Bowles saw earlier?"

Tom inclined his head. "Quite possible," he said looking around. "We'd better have forensics look at all this lot. It might be related, or not. Who knows?"

"Well, if they're not involved, then there could

be a chance they witnessed what actually happened to our victim."

"Good point." Tom thought on it for a moment. "It might be worth getting some uniform bodies out here to have a look around."

"With all of us here, he'd likely be long gone, surely?"

Tom nodded, gently closing the lid on the tin. "Perhaps." He held the tin aloft before placing it down on the sleeping bags. "Although, if this is all their worldly possessions, then they might struggle to leave them behind."

"Probably nicked them anyway!"

Tom shot her a dark look. She held up a hand by way of apology.

"Sorry, but you know what I mean. He's not living in luxury here. Why keep something like that locket? If he hasn't stolen it, why wouldn't he have sold it for… I don't know, food and stuff?"

Tom smiled. "Some things are more valuable than money. Cass. Come on, let's get the forensic team in here."

They left the shelter, Cassie crossing to the compound to let the techs know they had another area to process. Tom took the opportunity to look around, meandering through the rusting hulks of once-roadworthy vehicles. There wasn't much else of interest within the perimeter fence. Whatever operation had worked out of this place, it had its day a long time ago. It was as if someone had locked up one day and never come back. It was a time capsule of sorts. That thought piqued his curiosity and Tom stopped, scanning the exterior fencing as far as he could see from his vantage point.

Heading back to the main gate, he found Kerry Palmer still standing there, ensuring no unwanted locals ventured upon the scene for entertainment. Not that Tom imagined many people passed this way. He knew of a bridleway that ran through here nearby. Alice had taken them riding once and he was confident they'd passed by here. Perhaps local dog walkers used the track to access the fields as well but, aside from that, this was a remote location.

"Hi, sir," Kerry said, smiling warmly.

"Were you one of the first responders?" Tom asked.

"Yes. Mr Bowles was pretty shaken when we arrived."

"Still is, I think," Tom said, looking around. The fog had lifted further, and he could see it receding across the open expanse of farmland into the distance. "Did you see anyone hanging around or passing by when you arrived?"

She shook her head, brow furrowed in concentration. "No, sir. It's been proper dead." She grimaced. "Sorry, no pun intended."

He smiled. "What about since? Anyone come by to have a nose around?"

Again, she shook her head. "I'll expect that later. People will have heard the sirens and seen a police presence, but no one has ventured down the track. Maybe Sheriff is putting them off, down on the main road," she said with a smile.

"It'd make me drive on," Tom said, and Kerry laughed. "I'll check with him though." Tom looked past her, and Kerry followed his eyeline to the gates behind her. She stepped aside as he took a step closer, inspecting the chain hanging from the gate. "Were the gates open when you got here?"

"No, sir. They were secured with that padlock."

Tom saw a heavy-duty lock hanging from a thick chain; the latter cloaked in a veil of reddish-brown rust, still solid enough to secure the compound but it must have been exposed to the elements for years, if not decades.

"You broke the chain to gain access?"

"Yes, sir. We used a set of bolt cutters. Mr Bowles climbed over the fence, but we didn't fancy doing that."

Tom smiled. "I don't blame you." He studied the padlock itself, taking it in the palm of his hand. It was in good condition. Not quite new, but it hadn't been in use anywhere near as long as the chain, which he found curious.

"What is it, sir?" Kerry asked.

Tom shook his head. A crow cawed from somewhere in the nearby trees, drawing Tom's attention skyward. "Probably nothing. While you're here, keep an eye out, would you?"

"Looking for anyone in particular, sir?"

He shook his head. "Just anyone who takes an interest."

"Will do, sir."

Detective Constable Wilson approached, and Tom noticed him shoot a brief but winning smile in Kerry's direction. She returned his with a coy one of her own, turning straight faced when Tom caught her eye.

"I've taken Mr Bowles' statement and contact details. Am I all right to let him head off home, sir?"

Tom nodded. "Perhaps you could take him personally."

Wilson frowned, briefly glancing at Kerry.

"I can, sir, yes."

"Good. Keep him talking."

"You think he's not told us everything?"

Tom shrugged. "He'll relax now he's leaving the scene. There may be details that will come to the fore on the way home."

Wilson's eye drifted to the dog sitting at its owner's feet, slobber dripping from the corners of its mouth, the paws damp with mildew and caked in mud.

"Right you are, sir," he said, failing to mask his irritation. He smiled at Kerry as he turned away, heading back to the waiting witness beckoning him forward with a flick of the hand.

Once he was out of earshot, Tom caught Kerry's attention.

"What do you make of the new addition to CID?"

She was noncommittal. "Seems okay… as far as south folk go anyway."

Tom smiled. South Folk, the origin of the county name of bordering Suffolk as opposed to those of the north, the North Folk. Local rivalries still played into conversation, always had and probably always would. If Wilson stayed in Norfolk long enough, then he might one day be considered a local; provided he stayed for thirty or more years anyway.

CHAPTER FIVE

Tom entered the ops room back in Hunstanton, DC Eric Collet glancing up from his desk and tilting his head towards Tom's office before he had a chance to greet him. Tom looked across the room spotting DCI Tamara Greave escorting a smartly dressed man back into ops. This had to be the new detective chief superintendent. He'd forgotten this was their new boss's first day. Tamara saw him and guided them in his direction. Eric smiled awkwardly and returned his focus to the files on his desk. The motion conveyed a lot.

"Tom," Tamara said cheerfully as he strode across to meet them. "May I introduce Detective Chief Superintendent Cole."

"Sir," Tom said, offering his hand. The officer took it in a vice-like grip.

"Tom Janssen," Cole said, shaking his hand assertively. "Pleased to see you again."

Tom was surprised. To his recollection they'd never met, and he had a good memory for faces, if not names, and Detective Chief Superintendent Cole was a striking individual. Almost as tall as Tom, only more slightly built and wiry, Cole was naturally hunched at the shoulder. Were he to pull himself fully upright then he might measure taller than Tom, which was an occasion that rarely occurred. Tom figured honesty would serve him best.

"I'm sorry, sir, have we met?"

"I saw you speak at a federation event..." Cole said, his brow furrowing in concentration. "Last year, I believe it was. You were speaking about modern policing in rural areas."

"Ah... yes. That was last year, sir."

"It was a decent presentation, Tom. Impressive."

"Thank you, sir."

"It'll be interesting to see what you've done with your thoughts in this area." Cole glanced around the ops room. "Whether or not you've been able to put those ideas into practice."

Tom saw Tamara direct her eyes downwards briefly, pursing her lips.

"We do our best, sir," Tom said.

"Indeed. Innovation is the key to managing more with less," Coles said. Tom narrowed his eyes, unsure of the intimation but feeling there was one. Cole fixed his gaze on him, as if reading his expression. "Wouldn't you agree, Tom?"

"I'm sure it plays a role, sir."

"Quite right."

"Along with experience and perseverance."

Cole bit his lower lip, holding Tom's attention and then nodded.

"Indeed."

"I'm sorry I wasn't here to welcome you to CID, sir."

"No, you had a body to investigate. Is that correct?"

Tom nodded.

"Anything we need to be concerned about, Tom?" Cole asked.

"Undoubtedly a murder case, sir, but it's early days."

The senior officer's brow furrowed deeply.

"Not a great start to my tenure," he said, glancing sideways at Tamara. "We could have done with a period of grace for the handover. Get things underway."

Tom was unsure of what he was missing, but Tamara and Eric were acting oddly since his arrival and perhaps something was going on he was as yet unaware of. He met Tamara's eye but her unspoken dismissal by way of an almost imperceptible tilt of the head made him not ask the question.

"Crime waits for no man," Tamara said, smiling grimly.

Cole arched one eyebrow, disapprovingly it appeared to Tom. Tamara's smile faded.

"Indeed," Cole said.

There was something about this man that Tom didn't like. Ever since their former Detective Chief Superintendent, Watts, had taken early retirement, a decision widely perceived as forced on him in the wake of a corruption scandal, they had been under the watchful eye of a temporary senior officer while a permanent successor was vetted. The process seemed to take a great deal of time with rumours swirling around a reorganisation of the structure, itself only recently imposed. Tom didn't join in with the speculation. It made little difference to him. He did his job regardless of who he answered to or where the power shift went. Criminals didn't care who investigated them either. Besides, there was little he could do to influence matters and so why waste the time and the energy contemplating it?

Tamara's phone rang and she took it out, glancing at the screen.

Cole smiled. "Duty calls, DCI Greave."

"Always, sir," she said smiling.

"Don't let me hold you up. A busy team is a happy team," he said. "Good to meet you, Tom. I hope we get time to work together."

Tom smiled, shaking his hand once again before the detective chief superintendent took his leave and departed CID. Tamara watched him go, the mobile still ringing. She clutched it tightly. Tom indicated it with a nod.

"Are you going to answer that?"

Tamara rejected the call with a purposeful tap of a pointed finger. "I don't need her right now."

Tom looked at her quizzically.

"My mother."

He grinned. "I see. I thought things were better now they'd moved out?"

Tamara's parents had been living with her up until recently since their move from Bristol; a temporary situation which had rolled into a semi permanent one, much to Tamara's chagrin. That had changed when they'd finally completed on a house purchase and moved out a month prior.

"I see more of Mum now than I did when they were living with me."

Tom cocked his head, frowning theatrically.

"Okay, not quite… but it feels like it!" Tamara said, shaking her head.

"What was all that about?" Tom asked, looking at the space Cole had just occupied. "All that about innovation and doing more with less?"

"That's all you took from what he said?"

"There was more?"

Tamara laughed. "What about the I hope I get to work with you?"

"Oh, yes. What was that about?"

Tamara arched her eyebrows. "A new broom and all that."

"Really? He wants to make sweeping changes?"

"I fear so."

"Why? Our clean-up rate is well above average."

Tamara nodded. "That doesn't make up for the fact we exposed his predecessor's mistakes."

Tom scoffed. "Mistakes? They were failings he made in a murder investigation… deliberate ones in order to conceal the potential involvement of his relative."

Tamara held up a hand to placate him. "I know. Everybody knows… and Cole's likely just flexing his muscles to let us know who's the boss."

"Completely unnecessary," Tom said, shaking his head.

"I agree, but let's let him settle in. Maybe once he has his feet under the table it will all calm down and we can get on with the job."

"Maybe," Tom agreed.

"What do you have out at Fring?" Tamara asked, concerned, switching the conversation.

"A male, stabbed or strangled to death and dumped in the boot of an old car." Tom's brow creased. "He's been there a day, maybe a day and a half, but not much longer according to Fiona."

"Any ID?"

Tom shook his head. "We found a wallet at the scene that we think likely belonged to the victim. It's been stripped clean, but there's a business card inside for a bar in Sheringham. If we don't have the victim's prints on file, then maybe we'll get a break there. Speaking of which," he turned to Eric, "are we aware of any missing persons reported in the last two days? Male, thirties, black hair?"

"Nothing flagged that I'm aware of," Eric said, "but I'll take a look."

The telephone on Eric's desk rang and he answered, apologising silently to the two senior officers.

"Cassie is squaring off the scene," Tom said, turning to Tamara as they both stepped away from Eric. "It's an old compound, a breaker's yard or similar. It doesn't look like it's been occupied in years. I didn't even know it was there."

"Don't tell me there is an end to your local knowledge?" she asked, smiling.

"I would say it hasn't been a working business since I was in short trousers, if not before that."

"Now there's an image," Tamara said. "Tom Janssen in short trousers. I'll bet you were in adult sizes before you started primary school."

He laughed. "There is that."

"Not again?" Eric said aloud, exasperated. "I mean... we do have a murder investigation underway—" He sank back in his chair. "All right. One of us will take a look."

Eric hung up, spinning his chair to face the room.

"What is it?" Tom asked.

"Katy Roper's gone walkabout," Eric said glumly.

"Again?" Tom asked, reacting much the same as Eric did. Tamara looked at him quizzically. He sighed. "A local tearaway, prone to a moonlit flit from her foster home."

Eric nodded. "Happens at least once a month."

"Why is it coming to us?" Tamara asked.

"Because this time it's different," Eric said, before adding, "apparently. The foster parents are adamant."

"Uniform have looked into it already?' Tom asked.

"Yep... tried all the usual haunts and she's nowhere to be found," he said, shrugging. "She usually turns up after a day or two. I mean, I could palm it back off on to uniform—"

"No, no," Tamara said, "don't do that. If they think we need to look into it, then that's what we should do."

"I'll nip over to the house and have a word with the foster parents," Eric said, standing up and taking his jacket off the back of his chair and putting it on. "They're decent people, if a little quick to worry."

Tamara's mobile rang again, and she checked the screen as Eric left them. She answered the call.

"Hi, Mum. I'm working. Whatever this is, can it wait?" She looked at Tom, covering the mouth-piece, "Can I borrow your office?" Before he could answer, she was distracted. "Yes, it is… but…" she sighed, rolling her eyes. "No, Mum, I won't put him on speaker! Why? Because I'm at work—" Taking a deep breath, she looked skyward before closing her eyes momentarily and relenting. Pursing her lips, she put the call on speaker.

"Honestly, Tammy, I really don't understand why you have to be so obtuse. It's not a major issue, surely—"

"You're on speaker, Mum."

Francesca Greave's tone changed, noticeably lightening. "Hello, Tom! How are you?'

"I'm very well, Fran, thank you for asking."

"And Alice… and little Saffy?"

"Very well," Tom added stifling a laugh as he saw Tamara tensing.

"Mum, you said this was important?"

"Yes, well I'm in your place now and… honestly, Tamara… how do you live like this?"

"Mum, I like to live how I live… wait a second,"

Tamara said, her eyes narrowing. "Did you say you're in my house?"

"Yes."

"What are you doing in—"

"Just stopping by to see if you needed help with anything."

"Mum! I let you keep your key for emergencies."

"Well… I was passing… and looking at the state of the place, I think this qualifies as an emergency."

"Mum, I like living the way I live."

"And what about David?"

Tamara frowned.

"What about him?"

"Does he like living the way you live?"

Tom bit his lower lip, screwing his nose up, knowing full well how this intervention was likely to play out in Tamara's mind. She replied through evidently gritted teeth but trying to convey a sense of calmness.

"David does not live with me, though, does he, Mother."

"And he's unlikely to… living like this," Francesca said defensively. "How on earth do you expect to keep a man if—"

"If he doesn't like it, then he's not the man for me, is he?" Tamara said with an edge to her voice.

"Well… you might not have many options, Tammy."

Tamara sighed. "And exactly what is that supposed to mean?"

"Well, you're not getting any younger—"

"You said help, Mum," Tamara said, moving the discourse on.

"Yes, I called in to see if I can help... but I'm afraid all of this is beyond me."

"Well, maybe you could help," Tamara said.

"Name it, dear."

"Perhaps you could look into cleaners... find someone local who would be willing to drop in once a week and—"

"I think it'd need more than once a week," Francesca muttered.

"Fine! Twice a week," Tamara said. "See if there's a local cleaner who would be willing to come in and tackle the basics a couple of times a week, kitchen, bathroom... that type of thing. Could you do that?"

"Yes, of course. I'd be happy to help."

Francesca seemed genuinely delighted to be of use.

"Thanks, Mum. That'd be very helpful."

"Lovely!" Francesca said. "Now, when should we get the gang together?"

"Excuse me?" Tamara asked.

"All of your lovely colleagues, Tom and Alice... Cassie and her special friend..."

"You can call Lauren her girlfriend, Mum. They are partners."

"I know, it's all very exotic, isn't it? Especially for Norfolk. Oh, and young Eric and… oh, is he still separated from Rebecca?"

"Yes, Mum. He is."

"Oh… such a shame. They make such a pleasant couple—"

"Okay, thanks, Mum. Bye for now," Tamara said, hanging up and taking a deep breath.

Tom grinned. "Your mum is quite, quite lovely."

"She's a nosy old bat… who is currently mooching her way around my house."

"She lived there for months. What's the difference now?"

Tamara jabbed the mobile phone in his direction. "It's different… because it's different! Understand?"

"I understand completely."

"Good. And we'll say no more about it. All right?"

He nodded. "One thing though?"

"What's that?" she asked.

"Just how bad is it in your house?"

Tamara mock grimaced and raised a hand as if to slap him. He held up both his hands in supplication.

"Mum exaggerates. You know that," she said and he nodded. She looked at the clock on the wall.

"With that said, it is pretty bad at the moment. David said he doesn't want to come around until he's had his booster vaccinations."

Tom laughed, inclining his head. "Okay, that's pretty bad."

Tamara conceded with a curt bob of the head. "A cleaner, do you think?"

"The new boy is taking the witness who discovered the body home, and then Cassie should be back." He checked his watch. "Briefing at noon."

"Good. I'll be here. What do you make of Danny?"

Tom shrugged. "Too early to say. He's keen, I'll say that."

"He comes highly recommended."

"Yes, but was that said to help us or to help them get rid of him?"

Tamara pursed her lips. "You're a cynical man, Tom Janssen. A cynical, cynical man."

CHAPTER SIX

ERIC PARKED his car on the road, turning his attention to the bungalow, one in a long line of similar properties measurably different in their exterior presentation only. It was a nice street in the Redgate area of Hunstanton; sixties-built brick properties on a gentle incline up from the holiday caravan parks on the seafront. The water of The Wash was visible in the distance now that the coastal fog bank had drifted inland on a developing stiff breeze and the sun had managed to burn off the remainder.

The front garden was delineated by a knee-high picket fence stained a reddish brown with well-kept flower borders around the perimeter. Only the plants and bushes that maintained leaf through the winter were thriving, but the beds had been painstakingly prepared for the season with only fallen leaves lying across the turned soil.

Eric had barely rung the bell before the front door opened, a concerned but kindly faced lady greeted him. She was older than he remembered, for Eric had been to the address before but, thinking back, she'd seemed elderly to him then too. Perhaps it was her dress sense, fastidious and austere much like he recalled his grandmother presenting herself, or the way she moved, putting her weight slightly to one side indicative of a hip or leg problem.

"Mrs Moulton?"

"Yes," she said, looking past him and to either side, half expecting him to be accompanied by someone else. "Have you found her?"

"Katy?"

"Yes," she said again. "You're with the police, aren't you?"

"I am. Detective Constable Collet," he said, producing his warrant card. She half inspected it, clearly disappointed to find him alone. "We've met before, actually."

She eyed him, surprised.

"On a previous occasion when one of your charges stayed out late," he said, smiling. "Although, I was in uniform back then."

"You don't look old enough to be a detective."

"I've heard that before, Mrs Moulton."

Eric's smile broadened. The woman sighed, easing herself to one side with a grimace and encouraging him to step inside.

"Please, call me Grace," she said, closing the door behind him and pointing along the narrow hall towards a door on the right. "My husband is just through there in the sitting room."

Eric nodded and led the way, noting Grace shuffling behind him. He was right about her hip problem. The door was open and as he entered a short man, stocky but not muscular, rose from an armchair in front of the bay window overlooking the front garden. He was a barrel-chested man, wearing tan trousers, a white shirt that closely matched the colour of his receding hair, beneath a dark knitted cardigan. He took Eric's hand in a firm grip with a stern expression on his face.

"Cliff Moulton," he said gruffly.

"DC Collet," Eric said as Cliff released his grip and offered Eric a seat on a floral print sofa.

"Have you found her?" Cliff asked.

Eric shook his head. "Not yet, but I assure you we are looking."

He glanced between them, Cliff sitting back in his chair, but Grace chose to remain standing, arms folded across her chest which surprised him as he figured she'd want to sit down if she had a joint condition. Grace appeared very concerned whereas her husband was far harder to read.

"There can't be many places for a teenager to be, surely?" Grace asked.

"We have uniformed officers visiting the usual haunts, Mrs Moulton," Eric said.

"Grace, please."

Eric smiled, nodding.

"Do you think something has happened to her?" Cliff asked.

Eric was surprised. "Not necessarily, no. Why do you ask?"

"Never had CID come around before, that's all. Have you not got enough proper crime to deal with?"

Grace shot her husband a dark look and he seemed embarrassed.

"I'm sorry. I didn't mean it like that… it's just… you know? Katy does this a lot," he rolled his eyes, flicking his hand in a flippant gesture.

"Clifford!" Grace said, chastising him.

"Well, you know what I mean. The child does this! What is this four… five times since she's been with us?"

Grace shook her head but pointedly failed to address the question.

"How long has Katy been with you?" Eric asked, before adding, "And we've no reason to believe anything untoward has happened to her."

"Seven weeks now," Grace said, glancing at her husband who nodded.

"We're supposed to be emergency care, not permanent foster parents," Cliff said begrudgingly, drawing another disparaging look from his wife. On this occasion, he remained unapologetic, turning to Eric. "Please don't get me wrong, Detective Collet, I… we… are committed to fostering, but at our age… taking on children for a prolonged period is quite a challenge and it's not getting any easier."

"Forgive me, but what is the difference between emergency fostering and…?"

"We are able to take on children at very short notice, Detective Collet," Grace said.

"Eric," he said, smiling.

"You see, Eric, because we are older, and very experienced, we are able to provide shelter to a vulnerable child; one at risk of violence, parental bereavement, if the family are evicted from their accommodation—"

"Or if the police are involved at home!" Cliff added.

Grace pursed her lips, averting her eyes from Eric's and nodding. "Yes, if the police are involved."

"I see," Eric said, pen poised over his notebook, "and how did Katy come to be in your care? Was it an emergency?"

"Very much so," Cliff said. "Are you aware of her history? Her familial complications?"

"I'm afraid not. I've not been able to speak with her social worker yet."

Grace smiled, panting as she spoke. "Karen… a lovely woman. Overworked and I daresay underpaid, but she's doing her best."

Eric smiled. "Perhaps you could fill me in in the meantime?"

"Of course," Grace said. "What we know anyway. Obviously, we're not given all the information, only what we need to know."

"And we need to know far more than we've been given," Cliff said. Grace gently slapped the back of his hand, resting on the arm of the chair. "Well, it's true!"

Grace came over to sit beside Eric on the sofa and he turned in his seat to make it easier for eye contact.

"Katy came to us late one night. Her mother had an episode… or should I say, another episode. She's unwell, you see."

"Schizophrenic," Cliff added glumly. "One who apparently chooses not to take her medication."

"That's true," Grace said. "She also has a history of drug use which complicates things. Anyway, social services needed somewhere for Katy to go while her mum received treatment. And so, she came to us."

"By treatment, you mean…?"

"I believe she was sectioned under the Mental Health Act."

"Is she still?" Eric asked.

Grace shook her head, clasping her hands firmly together in her lap, perched on the edge of the sofa as she was. "She was only in for a couple of days until she could be stabilised. She's been home since."

"But Katy has stayed with the two of you?"

"Yes. Karen, Katy's caseworker, doesn't think it appropriate for her to return home."

Eric nodded, taking notes. "And how does Katy feel about that?"

Grace took a deep breath, glancing at her husband who winced. It was Cliff who answered.

"That's tough to answer. She misses her mum… or her home. Whatever challenges she faces there, it is her home, the space where she feels… safe."

"Safe!" Grace said, shaking her head. "How can she be safe there… with all the comings and goings."

"Comings and goings?" Eric asked.

Grace cleared her throat, looking awkward.

"It's not clear, and so we can't say for certain," Cliff said quietly, "but there is the suggestion that Sarah, Katy's mother, might be entertaining regularly."

Grace pursed her lips as Eric glanced between them.

"And by regularly, you mean…?" Eric asked.

"Men," Grace said. "Katy has implied it with some of the things she's said. Karen is looking into it."

"You think her mother might be engaging in prostitution?"

"What with that and the drug use…" Grace shook her head, "it's not considered to be in Katy's best interests to return home."

Eric considered this, looking between them. "Does Katy agree?"

Grace inclined her head. "Not exactly."

"So, she wants to go home?" Eric asked.

Cliff grimaced. "I don't think it's as simple as that. You see, Katy is fifteen going on thirty! I reckon she feels a responsibility to her mum… or at least wants to take care of her."

"After all," Grace said. "She is her mum. We all want to do what's right by our family, don't we?"

"So, she's concerned for her mother's wellbeing?" Eric asked.

"I believe so, yes," Cliff replied, shaking his head. "That's too much weight to place on the shoulders of such a young girl."

"I think she feels guilty," Grace said. Eric looked at her inquiringly. "That she is here, safe and well, while her mum is going through what she's going through. Katy can't stop her mum from living the life that she does, but she wants to keep her safe. Katy worries that something awful will happen to her mum if she's not there to help."

"Do you think she might have gone home?"

"Maybe," Grace said. Cliff sighed, shaking his head.

"You will have looked there first, right?" Cliff asked.

"I'm sorry, I'm not fully up to speed," Eric said. "I was passed this case…" he frowned, annoyed with his choice of language, "Katy… this morning."

"That's okay, dear," Grace said, patting his knee. "I'm sure you'll do your best."

Eric suddenly felt like he was a child and wondered if she'd have said or done the same if it were Tom sitting there in his place. He pushed the thought aside.

"I'll follow it up. Don't worry. Does Katy have any friends she is close with or someone special to her?"

"She's quite insular," Grace said, frowning. "I mean, she doesn't appear to have many friends. At least, not any that she's mentioned. What do you think, Cliff?"

He shook his head. "She has a mobile phone though… and she's always tapping away on it, so she must be chatting to someone."

"Foster children are allowed mobile phones?" Eric asked.

Grace narrowed her gaze, indignant. "This isn't a penal colony, Eric."

He smiled, feeling his face redden. "I'm sorry. That's not what I meant. It was more the financial aspect... a teenager with a mobile costs money..."

"I see. Well, she gets an allowance from social services. It's not much—"

"But far more than she gets from home," Cliff added, "but you're right; she had the phone before she came to us and we've no idea how she pays for it. It doesn't seem to be a problem, mind you."

"True," Grace added. "She's never complained about running out of credit. Maybe it's a contract phone her mum pays for."

"Does her mother work?" Eric asked. "In a... conventional sense?"

Both foster parents shrugged. They didn't know. Eric made a note.

"So, she has a friend, or friends," Eric said. "What about boyfriends?"

"Wouldn't know," Cliff said. Grace agreed with a nod. "She walks to school from here... and I've not seen her with anyone." Again, Grace nodded. "But I guess it's possible. She hasn't mentioned anyone. Not that I'd expect her to."

"No?" Eric asked.

Cliff shook his head. "Ninety percent of the children who come to us are troubled in some ways. They are very unlikely to open up to strangers, even good-natured ones like ourselves," he said with a smile. "We are here to provide them with safe refuge, usually until they can go back to their family home. Often that is a matter of a day or two at most. We don't really get into what is happening beneath the surface of their lives. We don't get the time."

"But Katy is not in that ninety percent, is she?" Eric asked, glancing between them. "She's been with you for a… what did you say? Seven weeks?"

Cliff nodded, looking away.

Grace smiled weakly. "Katy… is a difficult case. Underneath what is a rather tough suit of armour, I'm sure we will find a caring, compassionate and very intelligent young woman. But…"

"But?" Eric asked.

Cliff exhaled heavily. "But, despite our experience, we are ill equipped to deal with in the longer term. She is a real challenge."

"As you can see with the number of times she's absconded from here," Grace said, her voice cracking as she said the words.

"But she always comes back?" Eric said.

"Usually in the back of one of your cars," Cliff said, dispirited. "I hate to say it… and I've said it to Karen, so I'm very open about it… we're just not equipped for this any more."

Eric appreciated the resignation in his tone. Grace appeared disheartened as well.

"We're not getting any younger, Eric," Grace said. "We try. Honestly, we do, but it is difficult chasing after a teenager."

"I can imagine," Eric said. "How long have you been fostering, if you don't mind me asking?"

"Twenty-five years now," Grace said.

"And we wouldn't change a thing, would we, love?" Cliff asked. Grace nodded, smiling at her husband. "We thought about jacking it all in a few years ago," he said, casually pointing at Grace's leg, "particularly when your hip started playing up, but we kept on. Didn't we, love? Kept going."

"Why?" Eric asked, genuinely curious.

"Do you have children, Eric?" Grace asked suddenly, catching him off guard. "No, I guess you're too young—"

"Actually, I do," Eric said. "I have a son. George."

"Lovely," Grace said, smiling warmly. "Then you'll know what it's like to want to protect him from the world. To keep him safe and let him know he's loved."

"I do… yes," Eric said, feeling a stab of pain in his chest. It was a door to his soul he'd kept tightly closed of late. He hadn't seen George in weeks. Becca was still avoiding him. Not that he could blame her.

"Imagine when your little George… I assume he's little?" Grace asked. Eric nodded. "Well, imagine when he is fully grown and is building his own life, but you still have those same feelings. The desire to ease a child's suffering—"

"And having both the ability and the emotional resources to do so," Cliff added. "Which is why we still do it, Eric."

"For how much longer," Grace said, resignedly. "I don't know. But while we can, we will help."

Eric was warmed by their devotion. He wasn't sure he would have the strength to take on another's pain in that way, even if only to provide shelter and support.

"One thing," Eric said, a thought occurring. "You are both temporary foster carers—"

"Emergency," Grace corrected him.

"Right, yes. In that case, why has Katy been with you for seven weeks?"

"Because there are so few of us around," Grace said, "and the need seems to keep on growing."

"You said that Katy has taken off a few times since she's been with you," Eric said. "May I ask why you think this time is different to those other occasions?"

"Her attitude," Grace said. "Since she has been with us, Katy has been… distant, which is to be expected. In the last week or so, she's been very guarded, keeping herself to herself and only ever saying the bare minimum she thinks she can get away with. It has been noticeable. Hasn't it, Cliff?"

"Yes, it has. I spoke with Karen, Katy's social worker, and she has tried to speak with her too, only to come up against the same barriers. Karen suggested we give her space and that she would likely find her feet… which is good advice, but… this time."

"When you reported her missing, you were adamant to my colleagues that this time is very different."

"Yes, it is," Grace said.

"Can you explain how? She has only been gone for just over a day. Has she ever been gone for this length of time before?"

"Longer," Grace said.

"Then why is this time different?"

Grace glanced nervously at her husband, and he gave her an almost imperceptible nod of approval. She got up, gesturing for Eric to come with her. He followed at a respectful distance; Grace appeared to find moving after sitting still for a period quite difficult. She led him down the hall to a closed door past the entrance to the kitchen at the rear of the property.

"This is Katy's room," Grace said, opening it. Gesturing for Eric to enter, she allowed him to pass before following him in. The room was clean, tidy and of a modest size. There was a single bed against one wall, a single window overlooking the rear patio with a desk and chair beneath it. An abstract picture was framed on the wall, an array of colours in contrast to the standard magnolia-painted walls, white gloss of the woodwork and pale carpet. "We don't come in here," she explained. "Not unless we have good cause to."

"I'm sorry, what am I looking for?"

She indicated the wardrobe and Eric opened the door. There was very little inside. School uniform hung on hangers or was folded on the shelves along with some casual clothing.

"We had a phone call from the school last week to say Katy had been seen with a man at the school gate. They are well aware of her situation and take their safeguarding responsibilities very seriously. We are their first port of call."

"Who was this man? A boyfriend? Her father?"

Grace shook her head. "As far as we know, her father isn't on the scene in any capacity. I did ask her about the man, but she clammed up, refused to speak of it which is worrying. If it was nothing to be concerned about then why be defensive and deflect? Whoever he was, the school were concerned enough to call."

"Did they give you any further details?"

She shook her head. "Just a man, far too old to be speaking to a child at the school gates. I mean, you hear horrible stories about such things, don't you?"

"Not usually in Hunstanton," Eric said.

"True, but the wider world does come to our doors too, and we should always expect that."

"So, what happened?"

"That night… after I spoke to Katy, I was talking to Karen and Cliff heard something odd outside. He went to look and found Katy sneaking out through the side gate. He stopped her, not physically you understand, but he wouldn't be doing right by her to let her wander off after ten o'clock at night."

"Was she running away?"

"We don't think so. When Cliff confronted her – confronted is probably too strong a word – spoke to her, she became abusive, shouting. By the time I came outside curtains were moving. It was probably the most dramatic event on the street in years! I saw a car drive away. Afterwards, I had the thought that the driver had been watching the altercation. The car had its engine running the whole time. I'm quite sure of it. When it moved off, it did so with no lights on."

"Did you get a look at the driver?"

"Not really. A man, for sure. I can't say how old he was, but he was alone."

"You're sure?"

"Reasonably so, yes. Katy stopped yelling at one point and glanced at him. It might be my imagination…"

"What might be?"

"I thought she recognised him, perhaps she even knew him."

"That's quite significant if true."

She shrugged. "I've learned to trust my instinct over the years. After the car left, Katy gave up the ghost and came back inside, shutting herself away in here." Grace looked around the room.

"You weren't worried she'd climb out of the window again?"

She smiled. "It's not a penal colony," she said, repeating the assertion again. "She didn't though. She stayed."

Eric glanced around the room. "What am I looking for?" he asked again.

"She had a bag, and she had a few more clothes that we got her after she arrived," Grace said, pointing into the wardrobe at the spartan contents. "The bag, and most of the clothes, have gone. Katy's not staying at a friend's house or anything." She shook her head. "She's not planning on coming back."

Eric saw the resignation in her expression. She was certain.

"The car. What can you tell me about it?"

Grace's brow furrowed. "A hatchback. Quite large. It wasn't very new. Sorry," she said, frustrated. "I'm not great with cars."

"Colour?"

"Silver. It had four doors."

"Okay," Eric said, smiling in an attempt to reassure her. "I'll look into it. Do you have her mobile number?"

"Yes, I have it saved on my phone."

"And I'll need the name of your contact at Katy's school as well."

Grace nodded. "Thank you, Eric. I can give you an up-to-date photo as well, if you like? The school have just taken their individual pictures. We ordered them… well, just in case her mum wanted a copy."

"Do you know if Katy's mum wants her to come back to live with her?"

"Karen says she does, yes, but where they are with that isn't really a conversation I'm a part of. Katy is welcome to stay with us as long as she needs to."

"I'll speak to her caseworker," Eric said.

Grace took a moment, holding Eric's eye. "Please don't take this the wrong way, but the other officers… the ones who came before you. I'm sure they didn't mean to seem callous, but they didn't take any of this seriously. At least, it didn't appear so to us."

Eric didn't want to do his uniformed colleagues a disservice, but he could understand where they were coming from. Teenage runaways were common and they almost always came home within a couple of days having spent a weekend away with friends or a boyfriend. Someone like Katy, with a track record of absconding only to reappear a day later was unlikely to garner a great deal of interest. Right or wrong, the police, even in sleepy Hunstanton, were hard pressed with their resources and without evidence that she was in serious danger, were unlikely to generate more than a cursory investigation until she'd been missing for two days or more. Of course, in many cases, by then it could be too late if she was hell bent on skipping town for the bright lights of somewhere like London.

"I'll do my best to find her, Grace. I promise."

CHAPTER SEVEN

"Where are we with the deceased, Cassie?" Tom asked, scanning the information boards that were slowly being populated with information.

"Waiting on pathology," Cassie said, looking up from her desk. "They didn't think obtaining usable fingerprints would be an issue and they were scanning them in for me and sending them over. Should come through any minute."

"Great," Tom said exhaling. Turning to face the room, he saw DC Danny Wilson, arms folded, standing alongside Kerry Palmer, whispering something into her ear. She smiled, her face reddening. "Danny, in Eric's absence, what have we got regarding missing persons reports?"

"Drew a blank, sir. The last MisPer locally was six months ago and there's no reason to believe anything untoward happened there. An unhappy marriage, by all accounts. There have been no incidents reported regarding anyone remotely similar to matching our victim's description."

"That's a shame," Tom said, thinking aloud. "It would have been nice to have a simple case for once."

"Then they wouldn't need the likes of us," Tamara said, entering ops at the back of the room. "What about the location where the body was found?"

"I've been doing some digging on that," Cassie said, leafing through her notes. "The site used to be a breaker's yard by the name of Westfield's, owned presumably by the person holding the title deed, one Arthur Westfield. Sadly, now deceased. Natural causes. He died in 1976—"

"And it looks like the site hasn't been touched since," Danny said, frowning.

Tom glanced in his direction. "Well, someone fitted a new padlock on the gate more recently than that. Who did the site pass ownership to, Cass?"

"Um… the title transferred to Sally Westfield, Arthur's wife – also deceased – and then to Terence Westfield. The latter looks like their son."

"Is he still alive?"

Cassie shrugged. "No record of him in the death registry, but he isn't registered on the electoral roll anywhere in Norfolk currently and has no council tax record post 1999 either… but I'll keep digging."

"Well, someone owns and is responsible for the site," Tom said. "What happened to the business, the breaker's yard?"

"Digital records at Companies House don't go back that far, so I'll have to contact them and have someone go into the archive. But, as Danny says, it doesn't look like it's been in operation for a long, long time. It's just a dump for old wrecks now, hence why Bowles was trying to get it cleared up."

"Do-gooder," Danny said. "Annoying, aren't they?"

Kerry smiled.

"Speaking of which," Tom said. "What do we know about Mr Bowles? Awfully convenient that he stumbled across a dead body in such a remote place. Let's have a look at him, if only to rule him out."

"I can do that," Danny said, making a note.

"At what point do we lose the timeline with Terence Westfield?" Tom asked.

"Around the same time his council tax lapsed."

"You have an address for him up until that point?"

She nodded, looking at her notes. "It's an address in Old Hunstanton. Maybe he moved on? If he left the county, that'd explain it. Also, local authority councils barely talk to one another."

"We'll have to drop by and see if anyone there knows where he moved to."

"Bit weird though," Cassie said, "dropping out like that. Unusual if you don't die."

"As you said, Cassie. He could have moved abroad," Tamara said.

"Yes," Tom agreed. "Danny, put a request into the Border Force and see if they have any record of him leaving the country."

Eric hustled into ops, taking off his coat and hurriedly trying to hang it up. He missed the peg and caught his foot on a nearby desk, the coat falling to the floor as he muttered a curse.

"That's one way to make an entrance," Danny said, smiling.

Kerry grinned and Eric flushed.

"Sorry I'm late," Eric said, hanging up his coat and crossing to his desk. "It took longer than I thought it would."

"How did you get on?" Tom asked him, keen to hear about the missing girl.

Eric frowned. "On the face of it, it seems like uniform figured; a troubled teen playing up… but I think there's more to it." A look of consternation crossed his face. It was fleeting as he appeared to catch sight of Kerry leaning into Danny, the two of them sharing yet another in-joke between them. "As I said… I-I… think there's more to it than that." He turned his attention to Tom. "I really think we need to look into it further. Maybe uniform are right and it's nothing and she'll come back of her own accord, but…"

"Okay, it's your call, Eric." Tom glanced at the information boards. "Take the rest of the day and see where it gets you, but if there's nothing concrete forthcoming, then I'll need you back with us on this tomorrow."

"I'm on it," Eric said, pulling out the chair at his desk and sitting down. He glanced fleetingly at Kerry and Danny.

Cassie's mobile phone rang and she excitedly answered, pointing at the screen as she did so. "Pathology."

Danny Wilson came to stand behind Eric.

"That girl's in care, isn't she?"

Eric looked over his shoulder, nodding. "Temporary foster care, yes."

"Right. Do you think something has happened to her?"

"Maybe," Eric said. "I don't really know until I can have a proper look. Something's suss, though."

"Have you considered the foster parents? Sometimes the best answers can be those right in front of you."

Eric turned his chair to face him, Kerry Palmer coming to stand alongside Danny.

"Yes," she said. "It's often the closest to the victim who did it."

Eric exhaled heavily. "Great. The two of you haven't spoken to anyone involved and you're already solving the case." He applauded slowly, drawing Tamara's attention and she glanced over. Eric stopped clapping and shook his head. "Honestly, the girl has gone AWOL and I just need to find her and bring her home."

"To the foster home," Danny said, tilting his head to one side.

"That's right."

"Well, while you're doing that, Kerry and I will be cracking on with the murder investigation." He seemed quite satisfied that that was the case. "I didn't expect to catch such a big investigation in my first month up here."

"Have you ever worked a murder inquiry before?" Kerry asked.

Danny nodded. "Yeah… caught one in Lowestoft a while back. You remember that lorry driver who got done for killing a prostitute?"

Kerry nodded. Danny tapped his chest.

"Wow, that's pretty cool, Danny," Kerry said.

Eric coughed. "Well, if you'll excuse me, I have work to do."

"Of course, Eric," Danny said. "Sorry to keep you."

Kerry smiled at Danny and looked across at Tamara. "I have to get out of uniform and into civvies."

Eric cocked his head. "Are you coming into CID again?"

"Yes," she said, smiling at Danny who returned it with one of his own. "The DCI wants some extra bodies on board. It'll be fun… aside from someone being dead and all."

"Great to have you on board, Kerry," Danny said, the smile broadening. "I'm looking forward to working with you."

Kerry took her leave, glancing down at Eric as she made to leave. He remained straight-faced and Kerry's smile faded. "Right, I'll see you boys in a bit."

Danny watched her go, Kerry glancing back at them as she left the room. Danny tapped Eric on the shoulder to get his attention, flicking his hand in the direction of where Kerry was last seen.

"What's the story with her then?"

"What story?'

"Well, you know? Is she single, married… taken… what's the story?"

Eric sniffed, glancing around to make sure no one else was within earshot. He lowered his voice to a conspiratorial tone. "Sorry, mate. I'm pretty sure she's gay."

"Really?"

Eric nodded. "Apparently so."

"Damn. I thought I was in there as well."

Eric shrugged. "Appearances can be deceptive. And you call yourself a detective," he said, smiling.

Danny looked over at Cassie. "What is it they put in the water around here?"

"So, did you have a hand in catching the killer?"

"What's that?"

"The case you were working in Lowestoft… did you catch the guy?"

"Yeah."

"No, I mean, did *you* catch the guy?"

Danny cleared his throat. "I was on the team."

Eric smiled. "A decent team effort then!"

"Yeah… yeah, exactly that."

Danny stepped away without another word. Eric sat quietly, smiling to himself.

"And the database has a match!" Cassie said triumphantly. Everyone gathered around her desk as she speed-read the results. "Our victim is Simon Shears… thirty-two-years old and… wow… not a stranger to us." She frowned. "His highlights include arrests for ABH, GBH… assault… what a charmer this guy is."

"What is the most recent?" Tom asked, trying to read over her shoulder. Tamara glanced at him and he cocked his head. "If he moves in the wrong circles and was stabbed, strangled and unceremoniously dumped in an old breaker's yard… it's perhaps suggestive of retaliation?"

"Good shout," Tamara said.

"He was questioned last month over an assault that took place outside a pub in Sheringham."

"Drunken brawl?" Tom asked.

"No, not from the report logged by the first responders," Cassie said, her brow creasing as she read. "Shears was working security… and got into a fight—"

"How does a guy with that kind of history get a licence to work the door?" Danny Wilson asked.

Cassie shook her head. "It shouldn't happen."

"There are ways around it," Tom said. "Was he charged?"

"No," Cassie said. "The complainant didn't wish to press charges. Shears was warned as to his future conduct and the file closed."

"Do you have the name of the complainant?" Tom asked.

"We do. Tim Rayner. He was taken to hospital following the incident where he gave a statement to police, but subsequently withdrew the complaint." Cassie glanced up at Tom. "He lives in Sheringham… on Priory Road. Do you know it?"

Tom nodded. "Aside from this record, what else do we know about our victim; next of kin, acquaintances?"

"Unmarried… no children listed on the database," Cassie said. "We have a brother… Tony Shears. He also lives at an address in Sheringham, on Heath Road."

"Right." Tom glanced at Tamara. "Once we're done here, I'll head over there and break the bad news, if you've no objections?"

Tamara shook her head. "Not at all. If they're close, then he may have an insight into who may have wished his brother harm." She turned and surveyed the information boards slowly populating with details. They were still scant at this time. She pointed at a photograph of the shelter they found at the breaker's yard. "Someone has been staying there. Any suggestion that person might be involved?"

Tom thought on it. The idea had occurred to him, but it was far too early to make the link.

"Whoever it is could well have something pertinent to add to the investigation but, as of right now, we've no reason to think either way." He also looked at the photographs. "The shelter looks like it's been there for some time. Certainly prior to our victim being killed there—"

"Are we sure this is the murder site?" Tamara asked.

He nodded. "Blood pooling… disturbance of the ground indicative of a prolonged fight. Yes, I'm confident Shears was killed there."

"Then whoever is staying in that shelter will be aware of something; witness or assailant."

"That means," Cassie said, "if they're a witness, they'll likely be in danger too. They could not only be our witness but our *only witness*. That's problematic."

"For them," Danny added. "Problematic for them."

Tom was pensive. Cassie had a good point.

"Well, whoever it is, is not likely to come back there whilst we're crawling all over the site," he said. "And that shelter might look makeshift to us but some attention to detail has gone into its construction."

"How do you mean?" Tamara asked.

"Were you never in the Guides?" he asked. She smiled. "Two layers of roof covering, like with a tent where you have a fly sheet; an air gap between the materials used to minimise condensation and damp ingress. It's the same with the walls and flooring. The walls are padded out with cardboard and the floor is raised off the ground. It's quite rudimentary, but effective. Whoever has been staying there has made the most of it."

"Presumably you were a Boy Scout?"

"I got most of my badges," he said with a smile. He looked at the pictures again. "If they're not coming back there, then they'll need somewhere else to sleep."

"It's cold at night now," Tamara said. "They can't sleep exposed to the elements."

Cassie interjected. "Why don't we stop by the shelter in Hunstanton? They might head there."

Tom nodded. "Do it. Even if they're not there, the community might have an idea of who we're looking for."

Cassie agreed. "Quite a few of them don't appreciate police attention though."

"You'll have to disarm them with your north-east charm, Cass," Tom said.

"Aye, that'll do it," she said, grinning. "I'll see what I can find out."

"I don't suppose pathology were able to give us any further information from the postmortem?" Tamara asked.

Cassie shook her head. "Dr Death will work on him today and has promised the preliminary report first thing tomorrow morning."

"Well, we have enough to be getting along with for now," Tom said. He turned and surveyed those waiting for tasks to be handed out. "When Kerry comes back have her go through everything she can find on file relating to Simon Shears. Seeing as he is known to us, I want a breakdown of his work life, past and present, friends, associates, social media… anything and everything that's out there."

"What do you want me to do, Guv?" Danny Wilson asked, clearly keen to get involved.

"I want you to go with Cassie. See what the two of you can find out about who in the area is living on the streets; where they hang out, how they get by. We might get lucky." He pointed to a transparent evidence bag containing the cigarette tin and the old photographs. "Take copies of those with you. Someone might react to seeing them, even if they don't admit to owning them. We've got a killer among us, and I don't want them on the street any longer than absolutely necessary. Stay focussed, talk to one another and let's catch this guy."

The team separated, gathering their things and preparing for their assignments. Tom joined Tamara at the information boards, sticking a photograph of Simon Shears up in the middle.

"We need this investigation to run smoothly, Tom," Tamara said in a hushed tone.

"The new boss?"

She nodded. "It's just a gut feeling but... I think some of the stink is still attached to this department."

"Watts is gone. None of us were present in the original investigation."

Tamara met his eye. "That's true, but we're here now and whether we like it or not, fellow officers don't like it when we take down one or two of our own. You know that."

Tom arched his eyebrows. "I don't fancy a transfer."

"Neither do I, Tom. Neither do I. How is Alice?"

Tom looked at his watch. "Damn!"

"What is it?"

He winced. "I said I'd call in at the hospice this afternoon. I'll cancel."

"Is it bad?"

"It'll not be long now, I don't think."

Tom and Alice brought their wedding forward due to the prognosis of Alice's mother's terminal condition. Although determined to outlast even the most optimistic time frame she'd been given, the reality had become unavoidable and, reluctantly, Alice's mother had called time on treatment several weeks ago. She was now receiving palliative care and each day was one more than any of them necessarily expected her to have.

Tamara reached out and gripped Tom's forearm, squeezing it supportively. "You should stop by."

"But—"

"Visit the next of kin… and call in to see them on your way back." Tamara smiled at him. "Shears will still be dead when you get back." She looked around ops at the team busily getting on with the preliminaries of the investigation. "Make the time, Tom… or you'll never forgive yourself."

"I will. Thanks."

CHAPTER EIGHT

TOM PULLED off the main road, bypassing the queue onto the petrol station forecourt and making for the open ground to the side and rear. A line of cars was waiting at various stages of the cleaning process as a team of workers guided vehicles forward from one stage to the next. The car cleaning business was doing a roaring trade thanks to the mixture of inclement weather, the multitude of agricultural vehicles moving between the local fields and the fact the local council were routinely gritting the highways nightly as winter began to bite.

Pulling his car to a stop, one member of the team, holding a pressure washer, began frantically gesturing for him to stop at the rear of the line of cars waiting to be seen. Tom waved him away and got out of the car. The man hesitated as Tom brandished his warrant card. He was short but muscular, his English heavily accented. Many sites like these had sprung up across the county in recent years staffed predominantly by European migrant workers.

"I'm looking for Tony Shears," Tom said. "Is he around?"

The man pointed to a shipping container, the second of three on the site, before striding back to the vehicle he was cleaning. The hose started up, but he kept a watchful eye on Tom as he crossed the short distance to the cabin.

The site was illuminated by floodlights above, the sounds of multiple pressure washers could be heard, there was a portable drying gantry to blow the water off the cars and a covered area to one side; presumably this was for hand waxing and interior cleaning. The nervousness, if that was the accurate term, appeared to be catching as more watchful eyes drifted in Tom's direction as he entered what was a makeshift office.

Behind a desk at the far end was a heavyset individual, phone clamped to his ear, laughing as he shared a joke with someone at the other end of the line. He saw Tom, acknowledged him with a curt nod but continued on with the conversation, albeit toning down the joviality. Tom looked around. The seating was made up of mismatching plastic patio furniture with a small standalone unit in one corner housing a kettle and a microwave. A panel heater offered the only form of heating, woefully inadequate, in the container and the man behind the desk had a large gilet over a knitted jumper and woollen beanie. He was older than Simon, and in fact they shared very few similarities in appearance that one might expect with siblings.

Saying his goodbyes, the man slammed the phone down on the desk and looked at Tom.

"What can I do for you, fella?"

Tom smiled, approaching and taking out his warrant card. "Mr Shears?"

He nodded, squinting to read Tom's identification, frowning as he did so. "Detective Inspector? What can I do for you?"

The phone on his desk rang again and he held up a hand to stop Tom from answering his question, rising from behind his desk. He hurried to a side door, a uPVC addition cut into the shipping container, and leaned out, calling into the darkness. "Karen! Can you take the phones please?"

A woman with scraggly brown hair and a thin face appeared from somewhere and hurried past Shears, dropping into the chair behind the desk to answer the phone.

"It's that time of day," he said, tapping the dome of the Rolex chronograph on his wrist before gesturing for Tom to join him outside.

"People booking valeting?" Tom asked, raising

his voice to be heard above the sound of the pressure washers and verbal interchanges between the staff in a language he couldn't understand.

"Nah… private hire. That's my other business," he said. "People never seem to learn that you can't get a taxi around here between two and four in the afternoon. It's just not possible."

Tom looked at him quizzically. Shears smiled. "I guess you've never needed a ride around school pick-up time either?"

Tom shook his head. "Contracts?"

"Exactly. We're booked solid every day." He sighed. "It doesn't stop people asking though. We'll get to them, but they'll just have to wait." Once clear of the general hubbub, Shears fixed Tom with a stern look. "So, what can I do for you?"

There appeared to be a tinge of trepidation in his voice, fear of what Tom wanted, yes, but something else as well; almost as if he was preparing himself. As if Tom's visit wasn't wholly unexpected.

"I'm afraid I have come with bad news. It's about your brother, Simon."

"Ah… I should have bloody known." He shook his head. "What's he gone and done now?"

"I'm sorry to inform you that your brother's body was found this morning, deceased."

Tony Shears stopped walking, turning to face Tom with a look of astonishment. "I'm sorry. Can you say that again? Are you telling me that Simon… that he's dead?"

Tom nodded. "Yes, I'm sorry."

"Bloody hell," Tony said, crestfallen. "That's… that's quite a shock."

"We haven't been able to carry out a formal identification. You are the next of kin as far as we know."

"Yes, that's right. Mum and Dad died years ago… and Simon isn't married or anything… are you sure? I mean, sure it's my brother?"

"Your brother's fingerprints are on file, so we are certain that it is him, yes. I'm sorry."

Tony stared into Tom's eyes.

"What happened?"

"We are still processing the scene—"

"Processing? That's copper speak for something bad going down! What the hell happened to my brother?"

His stance switched swiftly from amiable to aggressive, his expression hardening with equal speed. That unnerved Tom, regardless of the consideration of the news he'd just delivered. He figured he'd need to go carefully.

"We're still trying to work out exactly what happened. Perhaps you could help us, Mr Shears?"

Tony held Tom's eye; his expression remained dark.

"What is it you want to know?"

"How well did you know your brother, Simon? Were you close?"

"He was my brother. Of course I knew him well."

"Has he fallen out with anyone recently? Anyone who would wish to do him harm?"

Tony reached out, gripping Tom's forearm. "Did someone do him in? Is that what happened?"

Tom glanced at the hold Tony had on him and it was immediately released. "It does appear as if Simon was involved in an altercation with person or persons unknown. I appreciate this is difficult—"

"Difficult, my arse, you do," Tony said, his jaw moving as if he was chewing something. "You want to know if he deserved it, don't you?"

Tom shook his head.

"Yeah, you do," Tony said. "He's got a record and you want to know if he got what he deserved. Nice and simple for you, if that's the case, isn't it?"

"I'm looking for the person responsible for your brother's death. Nothing more. We need to establish a possible motive and that is likely to come from his life, work or his circle of friends and acquaintances."

Tony held Tom's gaze, seemingly taking his measure. Presumably satisfied, he nodded slowly. "All right. I'll take you at your word."

"So, has he fallen out with anyone as far as you know?"

"No, can't say he has… as far as I know."

Tom nodded. "What about the fight he got into a few weeks ago, over in Sheringham? What was that about?"

Tony sniffed hard, looking away. "I wouldn't know about that."

"Your brother didn't mention it?"

"Nope."

His response was too blasé for Tom's liking.

"Really? He was arrested for assault. I'd have thought he'd have mentioned it to you."

Tony shrugged. "No, can't say he did. Wasn't charged, was he?"

"No, the complainant withdrew."

"Well, there you go," Tony said, cocking his head. "Nothing in it. Probably a few too many beers were had. Happens all the time."

"I never said it was in a pub," Tom said.

"Ah… yeah, well… isn't it always down to drink?"

"Often," Tom said. "Simon was working though. Does he usually drink when he's working security?"

"Couldn't say."

"How long has he been working the security job?"

Tony shrugged again. "A while. Don't really know."

"It must get him into all kinds of trouble with people… I remember what it used to be like policing the town late at night. Particularly at the weekends."

"Yeah, well. If your lot did their jobs right then bars and pubs wouldn't need to employ third parties, would they?"

Tom ignored the barbed comment. You could fill a town centre with dozens of police officers but there would still be trouble; and if there wasn't, people would complain about the overbearing police presence threatening business and enjoyment alike. They couldn't win.

"Did Simon ever speak of a situation beyond what he might normally expect when working the door?"

Tony shook his head. "Simon knew what he was doing." He sniffed again. "We can both take care of ourselves. Have done from a very young age."

"Why's that?"

"The old man… was a bit heavy-handed and enjoyed a drink or ten, if you know what I mean? Mum used to get it most of the time, until I got a bit older and realised I could step in. Simon, too, when he hit his mid-teens. Then things really changed at home."

"Simon was more than capable of taking care of himself then?"

"Obviously not well enough," Tony said flatly. "He can't have seen it coming. He'd never walk into something unprepared."

"But you said he didn't have any enemies?"

Tony's upper lip curled as he sneered. "All men have enemies, Detective Inspector. I said I was unaware of Simon's. And that's different."

"What about his friends?"

"What about them?"

"Who were they? Where did they hang out?"

Tony shook his head. "Can't help you there. Sorry."

Tom didn't believe him.

"Did he have friends?"

"Probably. He'd lived in these parts all his life, and everyone knows everyone, don't they?"

"But you don't know who your brother associated with? Did he have a girlfriend, boyfriend maybe?"

Tony scoffed. "He wasn't some limp-wristed bloke, you know? He was a tough guy, decent."

The reaction betrayed his bigotry, but that did little to help Tom establish much about the deceased. He tried again.

"Girlfriend?"

"Nothing regular that he talked about. He was

pretty big on the dating apps though. Easy pick-ups, you know?"

"I'll take your word for it."

"Maybe one of them was married and her husband found out," Tony said.

"We'll look into it. Did your brother do any other work besides the security work?"

Tony chuckled. "Yeah, he was a bit of a wheeler dealer, my brother. Bit like me," he said, looking around at the people cleaning cars. Tom saw the sign for the mini cab hire firm above the containers that he hadn't noticed before as well. "He could turn his hand to most things if he saw an opportunity."

"Right," Tom said, making a note. "And when did you last see your brother?"

Tony's forehead creased as he thought hard. Exhaling, he maintained the frown. "Last week. Saturday, I think. I spoke to him on the phone two nights ago, though."

"How did he seem?"

"How do you mean?"

"Was he happy, sad… worrying about something?"

Tony scratched the back of his head. "I can't say anything springs to mind, but we don't live in each other's pockets."

"Would he come to you if he was in trouble?"

Tony screwed up his face, shaking his head. "I

doubt it. Not unless he was *really* in trouble, then he might but, like I said, he seemed perfectly fine."

Tony Shears' answers were incredibly vague, so vague that they offered Tom very little help. If he knew what his brother was involved in, he had absolutely no desire to share it with the police. That was quite telling in itself.

"We will need someone to carry out an official identification of your brother," Tom said, confident he'd got as much information out of Tony as he was likely to get. "If I arrange it for tomorrow, do you think you could come in?"

"Yes, of course. Why can't I come in now?"

Tom took a breath. "In cases like this, we need to understand how he died as quickly as possible. We were able to identify your brother quickly because—"

"You want the autopsy done fast, right?"

Tom nodded. "Someone killed your brother, and we need to get that person off the streets as fast as possible."

"Well, I hope you find him before I do."

Tom met Tony's eye. "It wouldn't be wise for you to take matters into your own hands, Mr Shears."

"Then you'd better do your job well, Detective Inspector. Otherwise, bad things might happen to bad people."

"The courts take a dim view of vigilante justice,

Tony," Tom said.

"Only if it makes it to court," he countered flatly.

Tom pursed his lips, considering his next comment. Tony held their eye contact.

"But you don't know what he was involved in, do you, Tony?"

He shook his head. "No, Detective Inspector. I can't say I do."

Tom broke the eye contact. "Can I have the best contact number to reach you on? I'll be in touch first thing in the morning regarding attending the formal identification."

Tony gave him a business card. Tom gave it a cursory inspection; it was faded and tatty.

"Thanks," Tom said, briefly holding the card up before putting it in his pocket. "Tell me, did your brother live alone?"

"He did."

"There were no keys found with him. Do you have a spare set for his house? We'd like to take a look around."

"Don't you need a warrant for that?"

"Why would we need a warrant? It's not like he's guilty of anything, is it? He's a victim of a crime."

"Still think you need a warrant."

"You don't trust the police, do you, Tony?"

"Any reason why I should?"

Tom watched him intensely, but Tony didn't appear likely to budge.

"I'll get a warrant then."

"You do that. Work hard, Inspector Janssen," Tony said as Tom turned to leave.

Tom didn't reply, registering the implied threat and malice contained in the short statement, confident their paths were very likely to cross beyond the next day's identification process. He had a strong feeling that Tony Shears was no stranger to the law, and it'd be worth pulling the file relating to him. Tom figured it was more than likely such a file existed. Checking his watch as he walked back to his car, he turned his thoughts to Alice and visiting his mother-in-law at the hospice, knowing he'd have to be back at the station pretty soon.

CHAPTER NINE

"Do you think we'll have time to grab something to eat after this?"

Cassie looked at Danny Wilson quizzically. "Say again?"

"Examining the crime scene and taking that Bowles guy back to his house, along with that mutt of his, the interior of the car will need a damn good clean by the way. Filthy creature."

"I thought I only had to deal with one DC in the office who goes around the houses when he has something to say."

Danny frowned, thrusting his hands into his pockets and stamping his feet to get some warmth into them. "What's that?"

"Your point, Danny," Cassie said, impatient. "What's your point?"

He shrugged. "The point of me in general… or right now?"

Cassie rolled her eyes.

"I missed lunch," he said, apologetically. "I'm hungry. Finding dead people always makes me hungry."

"Are you serious?"

"Oh yeah, absolutely. Weird, isn't it?"

"Damn right it's weird." Cassie looked at the building they were heading for. "Look, I reckon I can speak to the people who run this place by myself. I was told over the phone none of the residents will be there yet, so it'll just be staff we get to speak to." She pointed towards the high street. "There are several cafes round the corner to choose from. Just text me which one you're in and I'll meet you afterwards."

Danny's face lit up. "Really? I mean… you don't mind?"

"You're hungry."

"I am."

"You're weird," Cassie said, "and hungry. Probably for the best if I go in alone anyway."

"Nice one, Cass."

"DS Knight or sarge," she said. "Don't get overly familiar until I say so."

Danny smiled, winking. "No problem, Boss, Sarge… Detective Sergeant Knight." He saluted and Cassie gave him the finger. His smile broadened into a grin.

"I'll see you in a bit," Cassie said, turning and resuming the short walk to the homeless shelter.

Cassie rang the bell beside a nondescript door in an unassuming building tucked down a side alley near the high street. Waiting patiently, she took in the building's appearance. The paint on the door was peeling badly, particularly at the base, showing several previous coats of varying colours beneath the fading red of the topcoat. The glass pane had wire mesh running through it in a grid pattern, common in schools and council buildings put up in the sixties and seventies before toughened glass became the norm. A shadow appeared on the other side and a bolt slid open before the door moved.

A slight, round-faced lady offered her a welcoming smile.

"DS Knight?" she asked.

Cassie returned her smile, showing her identification. "Yes, Michelle, is it?" The woman nodded, opening the door fully. "We spoke on the telephone."

Michelle Weaver was in her fifties, shorter than Cassie, standing at roughly five foot five, with a warm demeanour. It was likely that helped her in her present role.

"Please, do come in," Michelle said, beckoning Cassie to enter.

"Thank you for seeing me on such short notice," Cassie said, closing the door behind her. Following Michelle along a narrow corridor, they passed through an inner door into a hall. The floor was wooden, polished, and laid out in a herringbone pattern. At one end was a hatch where Cassie could see several people busying themselves in a kitchen. The smell of a beef stew or similar carried in the air.

"We're prepping the evening meal," Michelle said.

Cassie looked around. At the other end of the room were roughly a dozen camp beds set out a metre or so apart from one another. Aside from a sheet, a pillow and a rolled-up blanket were the only adornments. Michelle noticed her looking.

"This is where the men will sleep. We have a separate room for the women."

"It sounds like you have a fair few residents."

Michelle smiled weakly. "We do. It fluctuates, but the numbers are growing, especially at this time of the year."

Cassie inclined her head quizzically.

"When the temperature drops, many who wouldn't normally come to us do so out of sheer necessity."

"A free meal and a dry place to get your head

down," Cassie said. "Why wouldn't they come all year round?"

Michelle laughed. Cassie suddenly felt naive around issues relating to homelessness.

"I'm sorry, I shouldn't laugh," Michelle said, briefly touching Cassie's forearm by way of an apology. "As much as we try to offer sanctuary for everyone, it isn't ideal for everyone."

Cassie was confused. "I'm sorry. I don't understand."

"People find themselves homeless for all manner of different reasons, DS Knight. With some it's the end of an unfortunate set of events that pull the rug out from under you: unexpected redundancy, illness, threat of domestic violence or some other traumatic event that sees them unable to meet their commitments and, ultimately, they lose their home. For others, you get the stories that feed the rabid tabloids; drug or alcohol abuse that culminates in losing everything or foreign nationals who come here in expectation of a new life and find they're largely being exploited. For the most part however, they are people who, for one reason or another, are struggling with their mental health which crosses all of those previous reasons and then some. We also have strict rules that everyone must adhere to for their safety as well as for that of the staff. Substances are not tolerated, and the fact violence isn't goes without saying."

Cassie nodded along. "What if they turn up half cut?"

"Then they are turned away. Many of our guests have their battles with their demons and it is a sad fact that many have to numb themselves to the world in order to get by. They'll often do that with whatever they can get a hold of. I'm not judging, there but for the grace of God go I, but we can't allow that to come through the door. In the main, our residents understand and adhere to that."

"What sort of people do you get through your doors?"

"All sorts. Like I said, we get women fleeing from their partners, some with children in tow. We've had military veterans who struggle to sleep, let alone sleep inside a building. Old, young… from all walks of life."

"Do you usually have the same faces?"

"Yes, quite often. We have our regulars. When the funding runs out, we often find some don't return when we are able to open up again."

"So this isn't a permanent shelter?"

Michelle shook her head. "No, we're purely funded through donations. Many local businesses are very generous, especially this year what with a downturn in the economy and the increase in the cost of living. We were concerned it would go the other way, but the people in Hunstanton are very charitable."

Cassie looked around. "How long do you think you'll be here?"

"We're confident we'll be okay until the end of January. Hopefully a little longer. There are no shortages of bodies willing to help," Michelle said, waving a hand towards the kitchen.

"What time do people start arriving?"

"We open the doors at six, and quite often they'll be in shortly afterwards. We are full and word spreads quickly. They can't book. It is first come, first served."

Cassie looked at the beds again, surprised. "I didn't think the town had such a problem with homelessness."

"There aren't many shelters along the north coast, DS Knight. They travel here from all over. It's not necessarily a Hunstanton problem."

"No," Cassie said. "It's a societal one."

"You'll get no argument from me." Michelle checked her watch. "Forgive me, DS Knight, but you were quite vague over the telephone as to what you needed."

"Sorry, you're quite busy."

"No, no, it's not that… necessarily. It's more that our guests can be spooked by a police presence, even one not in uniform," she said, eyeing Cassie.

"Ah… of course. I understand. I'm looking for someone who we believe is homeless but may have been staying out of town. To cut a long story short, they may well be looking for somewhere safe to bed down on short notice. We thought it would make sense they might come here."

"And this person… has done something wrong?" Michelle asked, nervously.

Cassie smiled, trying to allay her fears. "Not as far as we know. We are looking for them as a witness rather than a suspect."

"I see. Who is it you're looking for? I'm afraid, we don't ask for ID when people come in here, but if you have a name?"

Cassie winced. "I'm sorry. I don't have a name or a description, other than a man was seen early this morning. He was tall, but it was dark… foggy."

"A tall man?" Michelle asked, frowning. "Oh dear… is that all you have?"

Cassie cocked her head. "I know. Perhaps, is there anyone who has come to you in the last week or so who you haven't seen for a while? Anyone who has been behaving oddly?"

Michelle smiled. "Honestly, DS Knight, that could be any of them!"

"I appreciate it is difficult, but does anyone come to mind?"

She shook her head. "I can ask around, if you like?" Cassie smiled gratefully. "Although, most people tend to keep to themselves, the odd one can appreciate a chat if they are so minded."

"I'd appreciate it," Cassie said, passing her a contact card.

Michelle read the card, holding it in front of her with thumb and forefinger of both hands.

"I'll get out of your hair," Cassie said. "Don't worry, I'll see myself out."

Outside, the sun was already setting as it was approaching mid-afternoon. The blue skies that helped the sun to burn away the morning fog were long passed, replaced by a thick bank of ominous cloud moving westward from the North Sea. Cassie pulled her coat tightly about her, shivering as she contemplated what it must be like to be sleeping rough at this time of the year.

Off to her left, at the end of the high street she clocked a man sitting on the steps outside the opticians. He had to be waiting for the shelter to open, for the bag at his feet along with the rolled-up sleeping bag and multiple layers of heavy clothing couldn't mean anything else. Crossing the street in his direction, he glanced up as she approached, smiling. He returned the smile, his olive skin cracking around his eyes denoting his age, although it was hard to tell under the layer of facial hair he sported.

"Afternoon," Cassie said. Pointing towards the nearby coffee shop, she said," Do you need anything? I'm just popping in for a coffee."

He glanced at the shop, smiled and shook his head. "No, thank you. I've just had a coffee. I have enough trouble sleeping as it is and one more will keep me up all night."

"A cake or something?"

Again, he shook his head. "No, but a conversation with a friendly face goes further than a cup of coffee any day."

Cassie came over, sitting herself down on the step alongside him.

"Rough time to be… well, you know?"

"Sleeping rough?"

"Yes."

He shrugged. "It's not so bad."

She looked sideways at him to see if he was merely making light of his situation, but he seemed sincere.

"Really?"

He laughed.

"Yes, really." Stretching out his legs, he exhaled and grimaced. "The scenery changes… I'm not beholden to one place." He looked at her, his smile broadening. "And the rent is pretty good value."

"The life expectancy isn't, though!" she said, immediately regretting it. Contritely, she smiled. "Sorry. I didn't mean to be flippant."

"Why be serious all the time? It's the stress that kills you young. That's what my old mum used to say."

"She sounds wise," Cassie said. "Do you still see her? Is she local?"

"Nah… I don't know where she is now."

"You're not in touch?"

He shook his head. "I burned that bridge a long time ago."

"Sorry to hear that."

"Ah… my fault."

"Tell me?"

"Long story," he said, shaking his head.

"I've got time."

"One I *really* don't want to tell."

Cassie laughed. "Fair enough." She swept the hair away from her face, tucking it behind her ear. The breeze caught it immediately and blew it back again. "It's going to be a cold one tonight."

"It is every night."

"Are you going to the shelter tonight?"

He nodded. "If they'll have me."

"Meeting friends?"

He looked at her, his gaze narrowing. "You're asking a lot of questions for a random stranger. You're either the law or a proper nosy cow."

"I'm both," Cassie said, producing her warrant card. He eyed it suspiciously, slowly nodding. "And I'm only asking."

"Coppers are never *only asking* anything."

"You don't like the police?"

He smiled but it was fleeting as he turned away,

looking at a non specific point along the high street. "I kinda liked you," he said. Cassie smiled. He tilted his head. "For a moment anyway."

She laughed. "I'm looking for someone, it's true, but they might be in trouble."

"They? Are you looking for more than one or are you very politically correct and going all woke with pronouns?"

"I can assure you," Cassie said, grinning, "that I am certainly not politically correct."

He nodded. "Do you think all homeless people are drug addicts or deserving of where we are?"

"Not at all," she said. "Well, not all of you."

"An honest copper. Never thought I'd meet one of those."

Cassie took his measure. He seemed remarkably capable of holding his own in an adversarial conversation. "Look, the person, or possibly persons I'm trying to find could be in trouble."

"We're all in trouble, Constable."

"Detective Sergeant," she said, raising a pointed finger.

"Apologies, Detective Sergeant, but it still stands. We're all in trouble in one way or another."

"They might be in real danger," she said. "I'll help if I can."

He held her gaze, assessing her sincerity.

"Who is it you think you're looking for?"

"Someone who's been living rough for some time. Maybe they have their own place, after a fashion," she said, shrugging, "away from it all. Maybe out past Fring?"

"Fring?" he asked, his brow burrowing in thought. Cassie nodded. He shook his head. "I can't say I know anyone who is out that way."

"Okay, how about someone who has been having trouble with the locals? Maybe someone who has been targeted or said something in passing, threats to their lives… safety. Anything like that?"

He laughed. It was a bitter sound, and he shook his head, looking down at his feet.

"What's so funny?"

"You know… there was one time, this time of year I think, or maybe a bit later, the Christmas decorations were up all around, sales in shops, the festive backing tracks are on everywhere you go. I was kipping in the park… don't remember where exactly, but I'd grabbed a corner where two walls met, behind some bushes to give me a bit of a windbreak… and privacy." He looked pointedly at Cassie. "No one likes being gawped at. It's not quite as bad as being ignored, mind you, but only a little better. Anyway, I'm bedding down for the night… it's cold, damn cold. At some point I hear people passing… they're pissed, probably on a work night out or something," he shrugged, "I don't know. But I realise they've stopped and there's some muffled talking. I try and stay asleep or, at least, pretend to be asleep. They'll pass me by, move on like, you know?"

"They didn't?"

"Nah," he said, shaking his head. "I knew something was up. I figured they were going to pee on me… or my sleeping bag. That's what's happened a few times in the past. It's a laugh, isn't it?"

"Did they?"

He shook his head. "No, not that time. They figured it would be funnier to set fire to my sleeping bag."

"With you in it?" Cassie asked, stunned.

"Yeah. With me in it."

His expression was such that she didn't doubt him for a second.

"Watch the scummer dance, someone shouted as I scrambled out of the bag," he said, arching his eyebrows as he recalled the memory.

"That's awful!"

"Yes," he said. "Yes, it was. The worst experience of my life…" he tilted his head, "and there have been a few beauties to compete with.

"What happened?"

He shrugged. "I got out as fast as I could. I remember terror… absolute terror. I was screaming… at them, at myself."

"What did they do, the ones who did it?"

He splayed his hands wide, Cassie noting a swallow in flight tattoo on his left hand in the area of skin between thumb and forefinger. "They thought it was hilarious. There were at least a half dozen of them, maybe more. What was I to do? I was cornered… alone."

"What happened?"

"They had their fun… and they left."

"And you?"

He sniffed, a vacant look crossing his face. "That was a cold night, I can tell you."

"Did you report it?"

He laughed. "Who to? The police?"

She nodded.

"Don't be daft," he said, shaking his head. "Who cares about people like me?" He met Cassie's eye and she saw pain in his. "They'd probably charge me with arson, if I had." He picked at his sleeve, as if he'd found a bit of lint to remove, rolling it between thumb and forefinger and throwing it aside absently. "No, you just get on with it."

"Why are you telling me this?"

He took a deep breath, holding her gaze. "Because we are all in trouble and we are all in danger. Every single day, in one way or another."

"Can I ask your name?"

He thought on it for a moment, shaking his head.

"Are we going to be friends now?"

"If you like?" she said. "It'd be nice to know who I'm talking to, on a personal level, not a professional one."

"Mark."

"I'm Cassie."

"Nice to meet you," he said, offering to shake her hand. She took his. Unsurprisingly, his felt cold to the touch.

"Well, Mark. This person I'm looking for is likely a witness to a murder. And the victim died violently," she said, conveying the seriousness of the comment with an intense stare. "In my experience, once someone has killed like this, whoever did it is unlikely to care about doing so again."

"And certainly not about a homeless guy."

"Exactly right. People like…" she hesitated, but it was true. "People like you don't trust people like me. I get that, I really do, but I'm trying to do right here. If they are a witness, even if they don't think they know anything significant, we still need to speak to them. And preferably before someone else finds them."

Mark held her eye, thinking.

"What if the guy you're looking for did it?"

Cassie couldn't lie. "That's always a possibility, but I don't think so."

"How can you be sure?"

"I can't. But what I can say is that the shelter was still intact, bedding present… and personal effects are still there too. If you'd just brutally murdered someone, statistically speaking, the perpetrator flees to put as much distance between them and the victim as quickly as possible. They'd take their things with them."

Mark inhaled through his nose, pursing his lips.

"What if they did witness something? Wouldn't that also make them run?"

Cassie inclined her head. "Possibly. The shelter doesn't seem random though. Whoever is staying there has ties to the area. Something is keeping them here."

Mark scoffed but didn't explain why.

"I need your help," Cassie said. "People won't speak freely with me. Will you help us… help me?"

Mark looked skyward. Lowering his eyes to meet Cassie's, he slowly nodded.

"Thank you."

He laughed ruefully. "Don't thank me just yet. I'll ask. Nothing more."

"I'd appreciate it."

"Seriously, though. I'll not be doing any secret agent stuff. I'll ask around."

"Perfect," Cassie said. "Now, do you want that coffee or not?"

"Nah, I'm all right," he said. "Thanks anyway."

"I guess it's no use giving you my mobile number?"

Mark chuckled. "No, not really."

"How will I find you?"

"I'll be around," Mark said. "It's not like I have a particularly pressing social calendar at the moment."

CHAPTER TEN

TOM PARKED his car outside the house, a large semi-detached property on the outer edge of Hunstanton, a short walk from Cliff Parade and the lighthouse. Casting an eye over the address, he saw the house was in darkness and with no garage in view, he also noted there was no vehicle in the drive. There were no roadworthy cars found near the crime scene on the outskirts of Fring, which begged the question how did Simon Shears get out to where he was killed? If he was driven to a meeting, why was it held there? It seemed a peculiar location for the man like him to be in. He made a mental note to have someone contact the DVLA and see what was registered in his name.

Before getting out of the car, he quickly typed a

text to Alice letting her know he was running late but that he'd see her at the hospice as soon as he could. This end of the town was elevated and the wind was picking up coming in off the water and he shivered, pulling his coat about him as he locked the car and made his way up the drive to the house. It was nondescript, blending into the surrounding properties around a substantial green; a mix of traditional bay-fronted 1930s-built semis and sixties bungalows, many of which were extended in both width and height.

The gravel-lined driveway crunched underfoot as Tom approached the front door. A security camera was mounted directly above the door in a recessed porch, pointing straight at him. Tom took a step back and looked up to the left and right seeing two similar cameras covering the driveway and the access to the rear along the side.

The front window, a large, curved bay, was fitted with shutters. These were closed, hiding the interior from view. He wasn't expecting anyone to be inside, but he rang the bell, thrusting his hands into his pockets as the chill of the afternoon cut through his coat. His mobile beeped. It was Alice, the message simply read, *I love you*. Putting the mobile in his pocket, he banged a fist on the door. Satisfied he'd made the required effort, he made his way down the side of the house. A six-foot-high fence and a locked gate barred access to the rear. It wouldn't take much to get over it, but he looked around for something to make it easier. The wheeled bins were in a store to his left. He pulled one over to the gate.

Clambering up, he easily climbed over the gate and dropped to the other side, spying another camera pointing at the gate along with a set of floodlights that burst into life as soon as he touched down. The garden, overlooked only by two properties, one to each side with the attached having direct line of sight, was overgrown and in dire need of attention. Gardening clearly wasn't a pastime that Simon Shears enjoyed. Mature trees shrouded the rear of the house from the second neighbouring property. Tom found the kitchen door locked, unsurprisingly, as were the patio doors into a rear sitting room. At least he could peer into the darkness, using the torch on his mobile to illuminate the interior. There was nothing to see of any note.

Forcing entry was entirely justified. He would need to get a locksmith out to gain access. Smashing a window would be far easier though but leaving the property secure was still a consideration.

"Can I help you?"

Tom looked to his left to see a man peering over the fence from the neighbouring property. He didn't look particularly friendly, his expression set in a scowl. Tom walked over to him, taking out his identification and holding it up.

"DI Janssen," he said. The man was taken aback.

"Oh, sorry. I didn't realise you were the police. I thought you were Simon at first… and was thinking about giving him a piece of my mind."

Tom's curiosity was piqued. "Is there a problem? Between you and Mr Shears?"

"Well… not so much a problem… nothing specific, I mean. He's just not an easy neighbour to have, if you know what I mean?"

"Not really," Tom said. "But I'd like to hear it. Can you come around for a word."

"Erm… yes, I guess so."

Tom heard him getting down off whatever it was he was using to see over the fence and the footsteps as he walked away. Tom headed back to the front of the house, sliding the bolt securing the gate back rather than climbing back over. He met the neighbour in the driveway. He was a short man, overweight and red-faced, his shirt, tucked in at the waist, was bursting at the buttons.

"Is Simon in?" he asked.

Tom shook his head. "Nobody's home, no."

"I must admit, I'm not surprised the police are here," he said, leaning in towards Tom and lowering his voice even though no one else was within ear shot. "Although, a detective is a surprise."

"Can I ask your name?"

"Yes, yes of course. I'm Malcolm. Malcolm Deaver." He pointed at the adjoining semi. "I've lived here with my wife for the last…" he thought hard "twenty-two years."

"How well do you know Mr Shears?"

"Fairly… at least, we've been neighbours that entire time."

Tom cocked his head.

"Oh, this place used to belong to Simon's parents. Well, his mother." His forehead creased. "I don't remember the father being around. Not sure what happened there."

"You said you were not surprised to see the police here. Why? Do you suspect Mr Shears of involvement in something criminal."

Malcolm looked around, then nodded. "He must be up to something. Comings and goings all the time. Different people, parties… women. And I say women, but some of them are almost young enough to be his daughter." He shook his head. "Shouldn't be allowed."

"What shouldn't?"

"Parties and the like. Decent people live around here," he bemoaned. "I remember his old mum was all right. She was quiet. Kept a tidy garden. They'd have the odd gathering in the garden of a summer's evening but nothing like what her son gets up to." He shook his head. "Music until all hours. That stupid car of his with the exhaust."

"The exhaust?"

"Yes, yes… one of those aftermarket add-ons that make all the noise." He sighed. "Waste of money and a nuisance too. I've half a mind to call the council and have him served with a noise abatement order."

"That bad?" Tom asked, feigning interest.

"You don't know the half of it. This has always been such a pleasant place to live. As I said, he's a nuisance. It's not just me, you know?" He waved his arms around gesticulating to the neighbouring houses. "Everyone thinks he's a menace."

Tom pointed to the cameras. "He seems very security conscious."

Malcolm looked up, following Tom's hand and nodded. "Yes, filming all the comings and goings I should expect. I told him he should have a sign up letting us all know he's filming us on a public highway." He jabbed a finger in the air. "That's data protection, isn't it? That's illegal otherwise, you can't have the cameras up I mean."

"You could be right."

"You should know!"

Tom smiled. "That's more of a civil matter rather than a criminal one."

"Ah right… of course."

"When did the cameras go up, do you know?" Tom asked. "They look fairly new."

Malcolm shrugged. "Within the last year or so, I think. It could be longer. I don't know why he bothered. It's not like he has anything of any value."

"Mr Shears was the victim of an assault recently. I wondered if the home security was a reflection of that?"

Malcolm shrugged. "I can't say I'm aware of that, but I'm not surprised. He's the sort of chap you'd like to give a bunch of fives to, if you know what I mean?"

Tom smiled. "Have you and he ever come to blows?"

He shook his head. "No... figuratively speaking, I meant."

"Of course. When did you last see him at home?"

"Yesterday evening, I think."

Tom's eyes narrowed. "Yesterday? Are you sure?"

"Well, I didn't see him, but I knew he was home. I heard him... and the lights were on indoors when I took the dog for a walk after dinner."

"But Mr Shears himself, did you see him?"

Malcolm frowned. "No, I suppose I didn't see him... but he lives alone, so he must have been home."

"Not one of his recent visitors? A different car parked out front perhaps?"

"Oh… I don't remember seeing any car out front. That's unusual, right enough."

"Is it?"

"Well, yes," he said, laughing. "Simon wasn't one to walk anywhere. He'd always take that silly, lowered German thing of his. I know he spent time in the gym, but he was a lazy so and so besides lifting iron or whatever they do."

"Pumping iron," Tom said.

"Yes, that's it. He did all that. He was always going on about strength. That was his motivation."

"So, you did speak to each other."

"That was in the early days after his mother passed. He seemed all right then. Little did we know what was coming." He shook his head again. "It shouldn't be allowed."

"Could it have been someone else at the house last night then?"

"I suppose so, thinking about it. But I've never seen people coming or going without him. I don't think he was the trusting sort."

"Why would you say that?"

Malcolm shrugged. "We've known him for years, me and the wife, and his mum for longer. We used to pop in and water the plants for her if the need was there. We offered to do the same for Simon, but he was quite dismissive, took the spare key back immediately after I made the offer. He seemed quite upset that we had one. Odd fellow. I should have known what was coming."

"The parties... noisy car and all of that?"

"Exactly. I should have known. What with that brother of his too."

"Tony?"

"Yes, Tony. Reprobate."

"How often do you see him here?"

"Not very often here at the house."

That implied he'd come across Tony Shears elsewhere.

"Then where?"

"Oh... the family have a holiday home; well, a caravan down on the seafront," Malcolm said. "I don't know why when they live a stone's throw from the beach as we are here. But maybe they rent it out."

"You see them there?"

"Oh yes. I manage the park. I say manage," he said, shaking his head from side to side. "I look after the facilities, make sure the laundry machines work and are stocked with detergent, that the showers are clean and all of that. There's not a great deal for me to do at this time of the year, but I make up for it during the season. So yes, I see the brothers coming and going from time to time."

"Do you know which caravan it is?"

"Oh yes, number thirty-two on the Perry Family Park. Do you know it?"

Tom nodded. There were multiple caravan parks in the town. Several of them were owned by large companies with multiple sites along the coast. The Perry Family Park had been in the town for years and was one of, if not the smallest in the area. Ownership had passed on recently after the death of Matthew Perry Senior, his children preferring to sell the site on rather than run it themselves. He was unsure who owned it now.

"You must get to know who uses the caravans as their own holiday home and who rents them out during the season," Tom said.

Malcolm nodded. "I do, yes. The Shears' one doesn't seem occupied much during the season. They don't pay for the on site cleaners to come in or anything. Not as far as I'm aware anyway."

"Okay, thanks. You've been very helpful," Tom said.

"You never said why you were here. Is Simon in some kind of trouble?"

He seemed hopeful rather than concerned. Tom smiled.

"There is an investigation underway, but I'm afraid I can't say anything more than that at this time."

Malcolm shot him a knowing look, tapping the

end of his nose with his forefinger. "I understand. Say no more."

Tom excused himself, glancing at his watch while walking back to his car. The holiday park would be his next port of call, after he'd called in to see Alice at the hospice anyway. Something about it didn't seem right, but it was an instinctive reaction that he couldn't justify if he were to be pressed on it.

CHAPTER ELEVEN

Eric parked his car in the street and made his way down the driveway of the stone-built Victorian semi-detached property. The drive had long since abandoned any hope of holding back the vegetation and was now overgrown with bushes from the side, grass growing where cars may once have stood but now all that was present was an old Transit van parked at the side. Once red, it'd faded to a dull pink with algae spreading across the paintwork and moss growing at the base of each window. The tyres were flat. It hadn't been on the road in years.

The house must have been quite grand at one time. Barely a stone's throw from the seafront and four storeys tall with steps climbing to the front door, covered by an intricately carved stone arch;

Eric could tell it had seen its best days. The basement windows were barred and the bay window to his left had thick curtains drawn, hiding the interior from prying eyes and no doubt ensuring no daylight, as much as there was at this time, could penetrate.

The building wasn't alone. There were many such properties in Hunstanton standing side by side with those already rejuvenated. As a Victorian seaside town its heyday was over a century ago when people sought to escape the choking smog of the cities and gather some fresh air and sunshine on the coast. Wealth was in abundance back then but, with the advent of foreign travel, the attraction of places like this declined. Many towns were shadows of their former grandeur whereas others had seen something of a resurgence in recent times. Hunstanton was such a town. People were returning to the coast not only to live but for recreational activity. Investment in both housing infrastructure and business had fuelled a mini boom in the local economy. Eric couldn't help but wonder what would happen to the locals priced out as their earnings couldn't keep pace with the rising interest in the area. It was a situation not uncommon in other destinations, befalling those living in hotspots where a second home or a holiday let proved popular.

Eric cast an eye up at the floors above as he rang

the bell to the ground-floor apartment. This place was a relic of the past. One day it might get the love and attention it needed to restore it to the beauty of old but, right now, the house had been converted into apartments and rented out. By the state of the upkeep of the place, they were likely to be low-value rents. Thirty paces to his left were estate agents' offices advertising properties upwards of seven hundred-thousand pounds whereas a similar walk to his right were hotels costing hundreds of pounds a night. Sandwiched in between were people who couldn't dream of residing in any of those on offer.

Snapped from his reverie by the crackling of the intercom, Eric leaned in as a disembodied voice spoke to him.

"Yeah?"

"I'm looking for Sarah," Eric said. "Sarah Roper."

"Who's asking?"

"Police. Detective Constable Collet. Could I speak with you regarding your daughter, Katy?"

The intercom switched off, surprising him and he waited. A moment passed and he thought about pressing the button again, but a buzzer sounded and he pushed on the main door that begrudgingly gave way. He entered an inner hallway. It was dark and felt cold. The original tiled flooring was cracked in places and the odd tile had lifted or disappeared entirely. The interior decay matched the exterior.

A door to his left, at the foot of the stairs, cracked open and the face of a slight woman peered out at him. He angled his head to see her, smiling warmly. Taking out his warrant card, he held it up towards her. She eyed him suspiciously.

"Eric Collet," he said, moving his ID closer so she could see it.

"You're here about Katy? I spoke to someone about her last night. I'll tell you what I told them; I've not seen her."

"Well, she hasn't come home yet."

"This is her home," Sarah said, a clear edge to her tone.

"She hasn't returned to her foster home."

"She will. When she's ready… and not before."

"May I come in?"

She hesitated, then closed the door. He heard the chain slide out and the door opened again. Sarah Roper averted her eyes from his, moving aside and allowing him to pass.

"Thank you," Eric said, waiting as she closed the door behind him. He assessed her. He knew she was in her forties but could easily pass for someone a decade or so older. The harshness of her expression magnified the lines in her face; the result of an adult life spent battling addiction. Barely five-foot-four tall without an ounce of fat on her, Sarah

Roper looked skeletal. Dressed in joggers, that were too large for her, beneath a vest top, that looked like it was once white but now a pale grey, she looked like a strong breeze would knock her over.

Pulling her hair back and away from her forehead, she tied it in a ponytail with the aid of a hair band she'd kept ready between her teeth. All the while he had the feeling she was assessing him just as he was her.

"You've not heard from Katy either?"

She finished fixing her hair and folded her arms across her chest. It was a defensive, defiant stance.

"No. I told you lot that yesterday."

Eric smiled. "But that was yesterday."

She shrugged.

"That was a whole other day," Eric said, arching his eyebrows.

Sarah shot him a look of disdain. "If I'd seen her, I'd say. And I'd tell her to go home."

"To the foster parents?"

She nodded. "Of course. But I haven't seen her."

"I asked if you'd had contact with her."

Sarah stared at him for a moment before sighing. "No."

"Forgive me," Eric said, glancing around them. The hall was narrow with coats and shoes scattered around behind the door. There was a smell of damp. Whether that was the age of the building or dirty footwear and clothing, he couldn't tell. "You don't seem particularly worried."

"Why should I be?"

Eric was surprised. "Because your daughter is missing."

She snorted with derision. "Staying out with a boyfriend is not going missing, is it?"

"You think she's with her boyfriend? I'm unaware of her relationship. Who would that be?" He took out his pocketbook and a pen.

"Don't know," Sarah said, leaning against the radiator on the wall. Cursing, she looked down at the thermostat. "Bloody heating's not on again. This sodding boiler."

"Your heating is broken?"

"Yeah," she said, deflated. "Almost every week now. And it's getting colder."

"Have you called your landlord? They have a duty to fix it."

She laughed. It was a dry and bitter sound.

"It's been a while since you rented, hasn't it?"

Eric cleared his throat. The truth was he'd never rented, not really. He moved from his mother's house into a place with Becca just before they were married. Shifting the conversation back to Katy, he stood with his pen poised.

"So, you don't know who she's been seeing?"

Sarah shook her head. "We're not close. Not any more, anyway. The social don't like it."

"The social workers?"

"Yeah. Nosy sods, always sticking their oar in. If they get their way, my Katy will never be coming home."

Eric glanced to his left and into the front-facing sitting room. Despite it being shrouded in darkness, he could see it was in something of a state and he could smell stale smoke, probably clinging to furniture and carpets.

"If you could get yourself straight, then I'm sure they'd let her come back."

"Get myself straight!" She shook her head, gritting her teeth. "Like they know anything about my life or what it would take to *get myself straight*. I've got no sodding chance of getting my daughter back, but one day, not too far from now, she'll be an adult and…"

Sarah sniffed, wiping the end of her nose with the back of her hand and looking away.

"And?"

"Nothing."

"When was the last time you had contact with Katy?"

She thought on it. "Last week, I think. Tuesday or Wednesday but I'm not sure."

"Right. And how was she at the time?"

"All right, I guess."

Eric fixed her with a stern look and Sarah relented.

"She was okay… not overly happy but not particularly sad either. She was… Katy."

"Anything bothering her? School, friends… boyfriends?"

Sarah shook her head and then stopped as if she'd remembered something. "She did say she wasn't getting on with the bloke she lives with, the old boy fostering her."

"Cliff Moulton?"

"Yeah, that guy. She said he's been a proper pain in the arse."

"In what way?"

She shrugged. "In the way they always do, these types of people."

"And what type is that?"

"You know, God-bothering judgemental types. Controlling."

"Is Cliff such a person?"

Sarah laughed. "Yeah! They've got to have themselves on a pedestal, otherwise they can't look down in judgement on the rest of us mere mortals who are struggling to get by."

"These people are carefully vetted and they're offering your daughter a safe place to stay."

"Safe. You reckon, do you?"

"Are you saying something different?"

She sneered at him. "Would it matter if I did? Who's going to take the word of a schizophrenic junkie? Recovering addict or not, my word isn't worth shit, is it?"

Eric frowned. "I'll listen."

"Hah!"

She pushed past him and walked into the kitchen. Eric followed, scanning the room as he entered. It was a mess with unwashed plates and utensils piled in the sink and on the surrounding worktops.

"Do you want a cup of tea?" She picked up the kettle and held it up to him. "I'm having one anyway."

"No, thank you."

"Afraid you'll catch something?" she asked over her shoulder, running the tap.

"No," he said, shaking his head. He didn't keep the dismissive tone from his voice, and she turned on him.

"You think you're better than me, don't you?"

Eric was surprised by the ferocity of her tone. Before he could reply, she snarled at him.

"I'm just the same as anyone else!"

"And yet that chip on your shoulder is weighing you down," Eric said, surprising himself with his candour. She stopped what she was doing and fixed her eye on him. He felt immediately awkward, which was a feeling he was familiar with. "I just mean..."

"Yeah, I know what you mean," she said,

turning her back to him and putting the kettle on. "And you're right." She fell silent, Eric unwilling to speak again. Turning back to him, the kettle starting to hum behind her, Sarah folded her arms across her chest, only this time it was less a gesture of defiance and more in resignation. "To be expected, my therapist tells me."

"It is? Why's that?"

She looked glum, staring at the floor. Inhaling deeply, she lifted her head and forced a smile.

"Look, I don't know where Katy is. If I knew, I'd tell you. Okay?"

"You're not concerned?"

She shook her head. "She's a smart girl. I taught her well… at least, I taught her some things."

"Such as?" Eric asked with genuine interest. It must have sounded like it, too, because Sarah didn't stiffen as he might have expected if she felt defensive.

"Resilience," she said. "Living with an addict requires resilience. And the ability to compartmentalise."

"To switch off?"

"Yes. Exactly that. To detach from everything going on around you and put yourself someplace else."

"Literally or figuratively?"

She smiled. "When she was small, a toddler I expect, she couldn't walk away. She had to stay, to endure. The only way a child can cope is to switch off, detach from it all because they can't stop you doing the crazy shit you're doing, or tell you to pack it in..." her expression darkened and she took on a faraway look, "and they sure as hell can't make a run for it." She inhaled, smiling weakly. "But they can endure. Have you ever heard a parent say their baby is so great because it stopped crying and never causes a fuss?"

"Once or twice, yes."

"That's because they've already learned not to bother." Her tone was soft, and she spoke slowly. "No one is coming, so you might as well just *shut up*."

"Are you speaking about Katy's experience... or yours?"

She looked at Eric, smiling. The lines of pain and anguish fell away from her, and she looked more like a woman her own age.

"Both."

He nodded, returning her smile. "And that's where she learnt resilience?"

"Yes. A blessing as a child and, believe me, a curse as an adult."

"In what way?"

"Because you still compartmentalise your emotions as an adult... you switch off... run away." She shook her head. "It doesn't bode well for the people around you in your life and, eventually, they run away too."

"Do you think Katy has run away?"

She exhaled heavily, looking to the ceiling. "I've no idea, Detective. I really don't. Maybe."

"Where would she run to, if she did?"

Sarah grimaced. "Friends… someone she trusts."

"How about her father?"

"Karl?"

"Yes," Eric said, drawing a smirk from her. "Why not?"

"Because he'd be less useful than me."

"Is he not involved in her life?"

"He left when she was little," Sarah said. "Can't say I blame him. We were both total wasters back then. Me, with my self-medicating," she said, looking at Eric. "I hadn't been properly diagnosed by then, so I took matters into my own hands. Karl… well, he liked his chemicals."

"Drugs?"

She nodded. "He wanted to get clean. I wanted to get clean, too, but there was no way we could do it together."

"But he was happy to leave his daughter with you?"

"Like I said… useless," Sarah said, smiling. "She'd not go there. Not unless she was desperate."

"Is he still around? In the area, I mean?"

She nodded. "I believe so. What he's up to, I couldn't say, mind you."

"You're not in touch?"

"Nah. No point."

"What about you, Mrs Roper? Do you have a partner?"

Her eyes narrowed. "What's that got to do with anything?"

Eric shrugged. "Just background. We have to look at everyone who, potentially, has a relationship with Katy."

"A relationship?"

"A turn of phrase, that's all."

Sarah didn't seem happy with this line of questioning, but she let it drop.

"Is there anyone in your life presently?"

"On and off," she said, offering Eric a veiled look. "More off than on, if I'm honest."

"And his name would be?"

"Gerry. Gerry Clarke."

"Thank you. And what does Gerry do for a living?"

"He's a fitter," she said. "He fits out commercial units… shops and that."

"Busy?"

"Always," she said, meeting Eric's eye.

"And how does he get on with your daughter?"

She shrugged. "They're both pretty stubborn."

"That's not answering my question."

Sarah considered her response. There was clearly more to their relationship than Sarah was willing to let on.

"The best answer would be the truthful one, Sarah," Eric said firmly. "If you hold anything back, I will find out later and all you'll have done is slow down my investigation into finding your daughter and bringing her back safe and well."

Reticently, Sarah nodded. "They butt heads from time to time."

"Serious issues?"

"No… not really. Teenagers and step-parent stuff… It's normal."

"What would they fall out over?"

She laughed. "Anything and everything; where she was going, who with… what she was wearing."

"Katy didn't take it well?"

"No, would you?"

Eric inclined his head. "I'm not a child."

"When you were at home, did your parents always tell you what you could and couldn't do?"

Eric momentarily considered the question. He never felt the need to go against his mum's wishes, although, thinking about it, was that a sign of his weakness to assert his character or his mother's nature? He knew Becca would say it was the former. The thought of his estranged wife popping into his head unsettled him and he forced her from his mind.

"So, they argue a lot?"

"Sometimes," Sarah said. "But I swear it's nothing serious."

"When did they last have words?"

Sarah hesitated, evidently reluctant to say, and Eric had to prise it out of her with a stern look.

"Last week, when she called by here. She's not supposed to see me unsupervised, which is utterly ridiculous by the way, but she turned up at the door. What am I supposed to do?"

"Tell me about Gerry. What happened?"

Sarah waved the question away, but Eric insisted.

"The usual," she said. "He wasn't happy with what she was wearing. He told her she was still a schoolgirl and should stop…"

"Stop what?"

"Dressing like a tart."

"I see," Eric said. "What was Katy's response?"

"She told him where to go, that's what." Her expression cut a wry smile. "Another of those things I taught her, that I told you about; to stand up for herself. Particularly where men are concerned."

"Was your father overbearing?" Eric asked, the question coming to mind. It seemed prescient, seeing as Sarah had admitted she was in therapy or had been at some point.

"Why do you ask?"

"You appear to carry a lot of anger around male

figures. I was wondering who your role model was?"

"My role model?" Sarah repeated, smiling. "Thanks, but I've had my therapy session this week."

"My rates are affordable," Eric said, smiling.

She shook her head. "My father has been gone a very long time… and he wasn't much good to begin with."

"I'm sorry to hear that. I lost my father many years ago as well."

"Well then, you'll know you're better off without him."

Eric remembered his father fondly. He doubted she could say the same about hers.

"Speaking of parents," Eric said, "what about Katy's grandparents? Are they involved in her life? Would she go to them?"

"My mum died before Katy was born. Karl's parents aren't local. I can't see her turning to them. They wouldn't be able to pick their granddaughter out of a line up anyway."

"I see," Eric said, making notes. "What about Katy's friends? Does she have anyone she's close to and where might they hang out?"

"Where did we always hang out in Hunstanton as kids? The bandstand and the pier. Where else is there to go in this town?"

Eric smiled. It was true. The teenagers have always congregated there. Some things never changed. Thinking he'd achieved everything he could on this visit, Eric took out one of his contact cards and passed it to Sarah. She accepted it as if it was hot to the touch, granting it a cursory inspection.

"Should Katy get in touch or if anything comes to mind," Eric said, "please give me a call."

She nodded, putting the card down next to the kettle. He wondered whether it would go straight into the bin as soon as he left.

"You don't trust the police, do you Sarah?"

She met his eye. "I don't trust anyone, DC Collet."

He pursed his lips, unsure whether to respond.

"You can trust me," he said quietly.

Her gaze lingered on him to the extent he began to feel uncomfortable.

"I believe you," she said, and Eric smiled.

CHAPTER TWELVE

Eric found a space in front of the Town Hall, parking up and getting out. The breeze coming in off the water was fresh and that was putting it mildly. A group of teenagers were huddled together in the bandstand on the edge of the green laughing and joking. They'd likely be there for the next couple of hours. The tunes coming out of the Pier Amusement arcade carried on the wind, the accompanying flicker and flashes of gaudy neon lighting up the open space in front of it. Tourists were thin on the ground but the bowling alley above the games machine level kept business ticking over in the off season.

"Eric!"

He turned to see Cassie and DC Danny Wilson at the end of the high street, Cassie waving to get his attention. Spying a break in the traffic, he crossed to the other side and hastened up the hill to speak with them. Danny was sipping at a cup of coffee, greeting him with a tip of the cup in his direction.

"How are you getting on with finding Katy?" Cassie asked.

"No one seems particularly bothered, other than the foster mother. Even her own mum reckons she'll be back when she's ready."

"What did you make of her, the mother?"

Eric shrugged. "What I expected, more or less. She cares, I think."

"You think?" Danny asked.

"Yes, it's hard to say though. Sarah is a woman with problems, I'll say that, but I think she cares about her daughter. Even if she has an odd way of going about it."

"Why did she lose her kid?" Danny asked.

"Drink, drugs… neglect," Eric said. "It's a sad case."

"She's a sad case," Danny said, sipping at his coffee.

"Mental health issues," Eric said. "Went undiagnosed for a long time."

"Should still know right from wrong," he countered.

"True."

Cassie arched her eyebrows. "So, what are you

up to now? We were just heading back to the station for the evening debrief. I doubt there's a lot more we can do until the forensic reports come in tomorrow."

"Other than background," Danny said.

Cassie nodded. "Yeah, other than researching the links to various characters."

"I'm going to ask the local kids about Katy," Eric said, waving a hand towards the group hanging out at the bandstand. Maybe I'll try the pier as well."

Cassie looked down the hill. "There's a few of them. Do you want some help?"

"I wouldn't mind."

Danny rolled his eyes and, unluckily for him, Cassie saw him.

"You have a problem with investigating the disappearance of a teenage girl?"

"No, not at all," he said, smiling.

"Good."

"Yeah, between the three of us it won't take long," Danny said.

"Three?" Cassie said. "I'm heading back to the station, but you can help Eric with the interviews. Now you've got a full stomach and are warmed through, you'll be all right getting some fresh air for a bit."

"Yes, sarge."

She winked at Eric as she turned to leave, and

he stifled a grin. Danny watched her go and he took a deep breath.

"Typical. Hates men, doesn't she?"

Eric set off down the hill and Danny fell into step alongside him.

"She seems to like me."

Danny looked sideways at him. "Yeah, well. Maybe she doesn't see you as a threat."

"And you are?"

They crossed the road at the bottom of the hill, heading towards the bandstand overlooking the seafront.

"I'm in line for sergeant. I took the exams a couple of months ago."

"Oh," Eric said, "I didn't realise. You passed?"

"No… not quite."

"So, you failed then."

"I dropped a few points…"

"So, you failed then," Eric repeated, restraining a smile.

Danny looked embarrassed. He wasn't half as confident as he tried to make out.

"Yeah, I failed but I'll get it next time."

Eric grinned. "Then you might be a threat, but Cassie isn't easily intimidated."

"No, northerners aren't, are they?" Danny moved off and Eric matched his pace. "Can I ask you something, Eric?"

He nodded.

"What's going on at the station?"

Eric looked at him quizzically. "How do you mean?"

"In CID specifically? There's something in the air."

Eric shook his head. "No idea what you're talking about."

They were approaching the group who noticed their arrival. Voices lowered and several stopped the conversation immediately. They eyed the approaching officers suspiciously.

"Evening, boys and girls," Eric said, smiling. He showed his identification. "We're looking for someone you lot might know. Katy Roper?"

He looked around the assembled group, all of whom were paying attention although some averted their eyes from Eric's.

"Anyone?" Danny asked.

A couple of people shrugged; others shook their head but the remaining half dozen made no indication either way.

"This could take a really long time if no one says anything," Eric said, taking a photograph of the teen in school uniform that Grace Moulton had given him. He held it up. "Katy Roper? Do you know her? Look, you all go to Smithdon," Eric said, referencing the only high school in the town. "So, you know her, yes?"

Most of the group nodded.

"Right, we're getting somewhere. Anyone seen her?"

Several shook their heads and a couple of others murmured they hadn't seen her.

"She might be in trouble," Eric said. "We're just trying to make sure she's safe."

"She's trouble all right," one boy said. Eric focussed on him.

"And?"

The lad shrugged. "She's always playing up, bunking off school… that kinda thing."

"Yeah, she's a legend," a red-haired girl said, smiling.

"Legend, huh?" Eric said, also smiling. "You know where we can find her?"

The girl looked down at her feet, her hands deep in the pockets of her coat.

"Friend of yours?" Danny asked. The girl didn't reply but shook her head. "Nice. Does she have any friends?"

Several members of the group exchanged glances, but no one spoke.

"She could be in trouble," Eric said, disheartened by their unwillingness to help. "Real trouble. If it was one of you, you'd want help, wouldn't you?"

One boy looked at Eric, shaking his head. "Katy's not the sort to want help, let alone ask anyone else for it."

"What do you mean by that?"

He shrugged. "She's a loner, that's all. She likes it that way." He glanced around his friends. "And so do we."

There was a murmur of approval and a couple of laughs at the comment. Eric was disappointed with their attitude.

"So, no one has an idea of where she might be?"

Confidence was growing among them and the general response was dismissive.

"Right," Eric said, looking at Danny who inclined his head to suggest they gave up. Although he hated to admit it, Danny was right. "Thanks for your help."

He turned and walked away, Danny falling into step alongside him.

"With friends like that, who needs enemies, eh?" Danny said.

Eric was about to answer when he heard footsteps on the path behind them. Turning just as the redhead who'd spoken reached them, slightly out of breath having run to catch up. Eric looked past her to the bandstand, but no one was looking their way. If they cared about their friend coming after the police, they weren't showing it.

"Are you okay?" Eric asked as she caught her breath.

She wheezed, leaning forward and resting her hands on her thighs.

"Asthma," she said between breaths. "The sea air is supposed to be good for it."

Eric waited patiently for her to gather herself together. Standing upright, she drew breath and winced a little. The air was cold and sucking a lungful of it in certainly stung the chest.

"Take your time," Eric said. Danny shifted his weight from one foot to the other, clearly irritated. "What's your name?"

"Sally."

"Are you a friend of Katy's?"

She shook her head. "Not really. I mean, I speak to her sometimes." She glanced across to where her friends were pushing and shoving each other, getting back to the larking around that teenagers get up to when they have nothing productive to do. "Don't be too hard on my friends. They don't mean Katy any harm, it's just that she is what Jamie said back there; a bit of a loner."

"Is she unpopular?"

Sally shrugged. "Not really, but she makes it hard to like her, you know? She's got an edge to her."

An image of Cassie sprang to mind and Eric smiled, glancing at Danny. "Yeah, I know someone like that."

Danny must have thought Eric meant him because he frowned disapprovingly but didn't comment.

"People like that can be difficult to be around."

Sally nodded. "Especially at school. I'm not surprised though… what with everything she has going on at home."

"You know her background?"

"Yes, everyone does," Sally said. "Well, maybe not all of it but we know she's a care kid."

"Is that a problem?" Eric asked without judgement.

"No, not at all," Sally said, laughing. "Every other kid at school either has one parent or four… or brothers and sisters by different dads. Sometimes it's hard to keep up."

Eric grinned. "Sign of the times."

"Yeah, the collapse of modern day late-stage capitalism and the nuclear family."

"Excuse me?" Danny asked. "Say that again?"

Sally looked at him. "What? Which part?"

"The bit about… you know? Capitalism."

"We're living in the ruins of empire," she said matter-of-factly. "Most people just haven't realised it yet."

Danny, momentarily confused, glanced at Eric and raised his eyebrows briefly before shaking his head.

"Anyway," Eric said, changing the subject, "Katy Roper? Any idea where she might be?"

"Not really. Sorry."

"But you know something?" Eric asked.

"She might be with her boyfriend."

"We were unaware that she had a boyfriend. Do you have a name for us?"

Sally shook her head. "No, sorry. He's a bit older than us, so we don't hang around with him and his lot."

"His lot?" Eric asked.

"Yeah, they have their own cars, all pimped up and that. They drive them up and down the seafront. You know the type: lowered, big exhausts… chrome spinners."

Eric smiled. "Yeah, I know the sort. Katy is seeing one of these guys?"

"I couldn't say for sure," Sally said, "but she does hang around with them a fair bit. I've seen her picked up after school every now and again."

"Just her?"

Sally looked back at her friends. Some of them were watching their conversation now and the result was a perceptible shift in her demeanour.

"Look, I don't want to get anyone into trouble…"

"No one is going to get in trouble," Eric said.

"Unless they're a nonce," Danny muttered. Eric shot him a dark look and he glanced away, rolling his tongue along the inside of his cheek.

"It might be important, Sally," Eric said, doing his best to encourage her.

"She hangs out with these guys. They're older.

Some of the other girls who are with them used to go to the school as well. They've left now."

"Friends of yours?"

She shook her head, and she meant it. "But they're not the sort of people you want thinking you're a grass. You know what I mean? They're a bit rough."

"We understand," Eric said. "But you think Katy hangs with this group?"

"Yeah, she fits in better with them."

Eric was unsure what she meant.

"I mean, she's older than her years, you know? Some of the girls…" she looked back at her friends who were once again paying them little by way of attention, "are a bit more advanced than others."

She looked at Eric, imploring him to understand so she wouldn't need to spell it out. Danny obliged.

"They are equally active?"

Eric couldn't help but let out an exasperated sigh. Sally glanced at him and nodded.

Danny bobbed his head knowingly. "Young women are always attracted to the older guys with loud cars."

Sally looked at him scornfully. "Hardly."

"I thought that was a big draw for girls?" Danny asked, doubling down.

"If you're into losers, then yeah." She looked him up and down. "Personally, they're for saddos."

"Never thought of myself as a saddo," Danny

said with a quick smile and an accompanying wink.

"How about as a nonce?" she asked, dead pan.

His smile faded.

"Thanks, Sally," Eric said, grinning. "You've been very helpful."

"Can I go?" she asked.

Eric nodded and she turned tail, hurrying back down the hill to re-join her friends. He turned to Danny.

"Learn anything?"

Danny's forehead creased. "So, girls don't like jazzed-up cars?" He shrugged. "Every day is a school day, isn't it?"

"Especially if you need to learn about the collapse of late-stage capitalism."

"Yeah," Danny said, grimacing. "What's that about?"

"I think it's when your streaming services keep buffering," Eric said.

"Yeah, that's a bummer. Can we go back to the station now? I think we've wasted enough time on this."

"It's not a waste of time, Danny!"

"Oh, come on, Eric! You're not buying into there being something out of the ordinary going on here, are you? It's crystal clear what's gone on."

Eric smiled, folding his arms across his chest. "Enlighten me."

"Katy has a boyfriend, or several boyfriends. They're older, ponce around in boyed-up cars, showing off to impressionable young women. They may well be borderline paedos, but hell, there are plenty of blokes like that around."

"Assumptions like that are why loads of vulnerable girls in the seventies and eighties were abused—"

Danny held up a hand. "Seriously, you're not actually comparing a girl who, by the way, will be of age in less than a year, with the kids abused in care before you and I were even born? Please, do me a favour. Besides, if you think prisons are already overcrowded, imagine trawling the internet browser history of half the male population who like perving on teenagers. The walls would buckle under the pressure."

"You can't assume—"

"Eric," Danny said, laughing, "she's with her boyfriend. You said it yourself, even her mother isn't worried about her for crying out loud." He splayed his hands wide. "Tell you what, you crack on with this and I'll get back to the real policing with the rest of the team," he said, striding away. "I'll make my own way back to the station," he called over his shoulder, picking up the pace as he turned left onto Northgate.

"Danny, you're going…"

He didn't look round at Eric, dismissively gesticulating with a hand in the air to indicate he wasn't interested in hearing it.

"That's the wrong way," Eric said to himself. Danny was walking away from the station. "Oh well, you'll figure it out when you reach the lighthouse… or walk into the sea. Don't worry about stopping."

CHAPTER THIRTEEN

THE HOSPICE WAS RELATIVELY quiet when Tom entered the lobby. Evenings and weekends saw the greatest number of visitors but, such was the nature of a hospice like this, people rarely got to know the staff too well. Residents were only ever here towards the very end. Despite this, the staff were friendly and attentive, to relatives as much as to the patients. The receptionist on the front desk offered him a warm smile as he closed the door behind him.

"Hi, Tom."

"Hello, Sharon," he said. "How are things today?"

"Oh, Julia's had a good day today. One of her better ones recently. Alice is in her room."

He thanked her and made his way along the

corridor past the open door to the day room. The television was on, the sound of an afternoon quiz show entertaining those present. Julia's room was at the end of the corridor with a window overlooking the rear garden. Julia had always been a keen gardener, and sometimes the simpler pleasures, such as being able to see the trees, could offer the greatest comfort.

The door to the room was ajar and seeing Julia apparently asleep in the bed, he gently eased it open. Alice turned to see him entering, smiling weakly and getting up from the chair beside the bed. She looked like she'd been crying. Going to her, he opened his arms and she leaned into him, resting her head on his chest as he encircled her. Looking upon his mother-in-law, Julia herself looked peaceful, her breathing was shallow but unlaboured. In recent weeks her weight loss had been staggering to see. She looked so fragile.

"It's so hard, Tom," Alice whispered.

"I know," he said, kissing the top of her head and squeezing her supportively.

"They've upped her medication. I don't think she really knows what's going on any more."

There were no words he could think of to lessen her pain, but he felt like he should say something. He didn't. Instead, he just held her closely to him, only releasing her when she made the move to separate.

"It'll not be long," Alice said. "Days… if we're lucky." She looked at her mother. "I don't know if that's a blessing or a curse."

Tom exhaled. "Will she… I mean, are they going to keep her…?"

"Sedated?"

He nodded.

"No, they've given her control of her medication," Alice said, pointing to a small control unit on the bed within Julia's reach. "If things get too much, she can increase her dose."

"Right. At least that's something."

She smiled at him, nodding slowly. "How is it going at work?"

He shrugged. "The usual. Nothing I can't handle."

"I know that face, Tom Janssen. This case you've picked up, is it that body they found over Fring way?"

"I see news travels fast."

She chuckled. "It is Norfolk… and the off season. What else do we have to talk about? Is it bad?"

"It is for the chap whose body we found, yes."

"You can't stay long, I presume?"

The accusatory edge to the question he picked up wasn't premeditated and he pulled her to him again, looking down squarely into her eyes. "I can stay as long as you need me."

"Really?"

He nodded. "Some things are more important."

Alice smiled and was about to reply when there was a knock on the door.

"Hello," a jovial voice sounded.

Tom turned to see a man in the doorway. He peered in awkwardly, seemingly forcing a smile as Tom and Alice looked at him. He was in his sixties, Tom guessed, tall with greying hair, almost white in places, swept back from his forehead. His tan, if natural, was about three months late for a Norfolk summer and judging from the weather-beaten lines on his face, Tom figured it didn't come from the bottle.

"Sorry to interrupt," he said, entering. Tom and Alice separated and the man's eyes flitted between them, settling on Alice. "So, do you have one of those hugs for your old man?"

"Dad, you came," Alice said flatly.

Tom was surprised. He'd never met Alice's father. He was aware there had been talk of him coming to the wedding, or at least a discussion between Alice and Julia about the prospect of an invitation, but once the wedding came forward, the subject hadn't been broached again. Not as far as he was aware anyway.

"Yes, I managed to get a flight into Stansted this morning via Amsterdam."

Alice's expression remained fixed, but Tom knew there was a lot going on beneath the surface.

She spoke about her father infrequently. It was a source of incredible pain for her, he knew that much. She glanced at Tom and then back at her father.

"Tom, this is Ian."

Tom stepped forward and offered his hand. Ian shook it firmly, smiling warmly and then looked past Tom at his daughter.

"Too much to call me Dad, is it?"

"I already have."

He tilted his head. "Only because I caught you off guard. I see the walls around you are still intact."

The tension was thick, uncomfortable.

"Good drive up?" Tom asked.

Ian shook his head. "Nightmare. I see the roads around here haven't changed much."

"There are a lot of things that haven't changed much," Alice said, eyeing her father up and down. "Did you come by yourself?"

He nodded. "Yes, I did."

"It looks like Croatia has been treating you well?"

"I can't complain," he said, grinning. Looking at the sleeping form of his ex-wife, Ian's grin disappeared. He gestured towards Julia with a slight nod. "How is your mother?"

Alice shook her head. Ian shifted his weight between his feet. He was uncomfortable. Tom's mobile rang and he hastened to retrieve it to silence the call. It was Tamara. He put the mobile away.

"Do you need to go?" Alice asked.

He shook his head.

"You do, don't you?"

He nodded. "I'm sorry."

"It's okay. Can you call me later and let me know when you'll be home?"

"Of course," he said. "Um… what should we do about collecting Saffy from her after-school club?"

"How is my little granddaughter? Still tearing the place up?" Ian asked, smiling broadly. Alice ignored him, turning to Tom.

"I don't know," she said, looking at her mum. "I could…"

"Why don't I collect her?" Ian suggested. "It'd be a surprise."

"Yeah, it would," Alice countered. "Some strange old bloke turning up to collect her. The school will be calling the police."

Ian's enthusiasm dissipated. "The police will likely do nothing anyway. Too busy wearing rainbow-coloured helmets and dancing in street parades, so I hear."

"You keep up with events from Dubrovnik?" Alice asked. She looked at Tom. "I guess I could get her, but…" she glanced at her father, "I'm not sure when."

Tom put his hands in hers. "I'll speak to Jenny,"

he said, citing the mother of Saffy's best friend. Her current best friend, anyway. "I'm sure she could go there for her tea, and we can pick her up later."

Alice agreed.

"I'll give Jenny a call on my way to the station."

"Station?" Ian asked. "Fireman?"

"No, policeman."

Ian's face flushed. "Ah… sorry."

"That's okay," Tom said. Turning back to Alice, he kissed her cheek and she squeezed his hands before he withdrew them. He shook Ian's hand again. "Pleasure," he said. "It's a shame to meet under the circumstances."

"Caught a case?" Ian asked. "That's what you say, isn't it, that you caught a case?"

"No, I need to pick up my helmet. The paint should be dry by now."

Alice looked down, smiling. Ian smiled too, only awkwardly, Tom clapping him gently on the arm as he walked by him and left the room. He wondered what state of mind Alice would be in when he saw her next, hoping very much that father and daughter would be able to find some common ground under these circumstances, putting any animosity aside, at least for a while.

THE OPS ROOM was buzzing by the time he walked in. Tamara was deep in conversation with Cassie standing together in front of the information boards that Tom was pleased to see had been populated with more detail. DC Danny Wilson appeared red-faced and flustered whereas Eric was sitting at his desk with his phone pressed to his ear. He'd need to touch base with Eric and see what was going on with his search for the missing teenager, Katy Roper. If she didn't show up soon, then they'd need to be more proactive regardless of the resources required for the Shears murder case.

"Hi, Tom," Tamara said. "How is everything with Alice's mum?"

"Not great. I fear it won't be long now."

"How sad. And Alice? How is she?"

"I'll find out later. An unexpected visitor showed up at the hospice this afternoon."

"Intriguing. Who?"

"Alice's father."

Tamara exchanged a glance with Cassie who looked equally surprised.

"No, I wasn't aware she was in touch with him either," Tom said.

"Come to think of it I've never heard her mention her father," Tamara said.

Tom shook his head. "Hardly ever brings him up. I think they lost touch after her parents split and he left the country. But he's here, so that's that."

"Happy families?" Cassie asked.

"I'm not sure that will be achievable, at least not initially," Tom said, "but let's hope something good can come out of all of this."

"Will Saffy be keen to meet her grandpa?" Tamara asked.

"Damn! I forgot."

Tom hurried into his office, reaching for his mobile phone. Fortunately, Jenny picked up immediately and was only too pleased to help with collecting Saffy from school, seeing as she was already in the car park, and having her to theirs for her tea.

"Thanks, Jenny. Either Alice or I will be over to pick her up later. Is half-past six okay with you?"

"Great. We'll see you then."

He made his way back into ops and Tamara picked up on his relaxed poise.

"Sorted?"

He nodded. "Disaster averted. At least for now, anyway. Cassie, how did you and Danny get on at the homeless shelter?"

"Pretty well, I reckon. Although we haven't got anyone specific in mind to focus on, I did speak with a guy who stays at the shelter and he's willing to ask around for us." She shrugged. "It's better than nothing and these people are far more likely to speak to one another than they are to speak with us."

Tamara touched Tom's arm. "How about the next of kin?"

"I spoke to Simon's brother, Tony. He's coming in tomorrow to make the official identification. Interesting character."

"In what way is he interesting?"

Tom arched his eyebrows. "Cagey. Doesn't trust us, that's obvious."

"You think he knows something?"

"I'd say so. Perhaps not about the murder itself, but he wasn't parting with any information that he didn't have to. Everything was pretty generic when it came to discussing his brother. I went to his house, Simon's, and it was all locked up, maybe too secure."

Tamara's curiosity was piqued. "Too secure?"

"Yes. The place had more cameras than Fort Knox."

"Has he got a lot to keep safe?"

Cassie looked at Tamara. "His footwear and clothing were high end. Maybe he has a lot of valuable items in the house? Collects watches or runs a lot of tech?"

"Perhaps. We need to get in there and have a nose around," Tom said. "His brother claims not to have a key, but a neighbour says there have been a lot of comings and goings from the house since the mother died. If he is to be believed, then Simon was something of a party animal."

"Cassie, can you get onto a magistrate first thing tomorrow and arrange a warrant to get us inside?"

She nodded.

"And make sure it covers their holiday home as well," Tom said. "There's a caravan in one of the seafront parks here in Hunstanton."

"Will do," Cassie said.

"Next steps?" Tamara asked Tom.

"Identification tomorrow with Tony Shears. The pathology report on cause of death should also be available along with the preliminary reports from the crime scene. We need to keep looking for whoever has been living within that compound and chase up the ownership."

"Good," Tamara said. "They might be our only witness."

"And suspect," Cassie said.

"True. Although we also need to speak with the guy Simon Shears had an altercation with recently," Tom said. "There was enough needle there to make a complaint to the police."

"I understood the complaint was withdrawn though?" Tamara said.

"It was," Tom said, nodding, "but who knows if that was withdrawn due to coercion or a genuine desire not to proceed? If it's the former, then there is every possibility matters were taken into their own hands."

"Certainly worth looking into," Tamara said. She glanced at Cassie. "But Cassie is right; we are short of suspects."

"Early days," Tom said. "We'll start pulling on the threads of his life and see what unravels. There's more to Simon Shears and we've barely scratched the surface of his life so far."

"Right," Tamara said, checking her watch. "Let's call it a day. Start fresh tomorrow. We'll need to make some inroads though," she said, "or the new chief super will be all over us like a rash."

Cassie smiled, turned away and went to pack up her desk for the night, letting Danny know they were done for the day.

Tom caught Tamara's attention. "What do you make of the new super?"

She was pensive, reluctant to speak, which Tom found odd. There was very little that ever went unsaid between them these days, so her reticence was telling.

"I spoke to a colleague from his old station… and from what I could gather, our new chief was on good terms with his predecessor."

Tom sucked in a deep breath. "He was close to Watts? Well, that'll explain the professional but frosty beginning."

Tamara lowered her voice to ensure they

wouldn't be overheard. "I wouldn't be surprised if he's looking to make a statement upon arrival."

Tom pursed his lips. "Oh well. It's been a pleasure working with you, Tamara. I hope your next appointment will suit you," he said, breaking into a smile.

"Hey!" She slapped his chest with the back of her hand. "And anyway, who says it's me that will be moved on? Maybe you'll be the one with more time on his hands to work on his boat."

"Don't mention the boat," he said, shaking his head. "I think the motor's had it."

"You need to replace it?"

"Yes, that's a distinct possibility but I need to get the thing out of the water and strip it down," he said, picking up his coat from the nearby desk where he'd thrown it. "And I just don't have the time."

"Oh well, if Cole has his way, you might very soon."

"Cheery thought," he said, waving her goodbye and making for Eric on the other side of the room.

The detective constable was so deep in concentration that he didn't pick up on Tom's arrival beside him.

"How are you getting on?" he asked.

Eric looked up, frowning. "Mixed results to be fair."

Tom looked at him quizzically.

"Well, speaking to her friends, well, I say friends, they're more like her school peers but I don't think they have a lot in common with Katy, she's a bit more… developed, I'd say. That's how it comes across."

"Is Katy hanging out with older kids?"

"Older, yes, but I don't know if they could be classed as kids. She hangs around with these guys with their pimped-up rides, you know?"

"She's a schoolgirl," Tom said, surprised.

Eric cocked his head. "A schoolgirl who's been through more in her childhood than most people do before they hit their thirties."

"Are you worried about her?"

"I don't know," Eric said. "Her mother isn't but, then again, she's a schizophrenic… and a recovering drug and alcohol dependent too. I'm not sure I can put much stock in her judgement. Social services also decided to remove her and place her into a foster home, so…" He looked at Tom apologetically. "I'm sorry, I know we're stretched at the moment."

Tom waved away the apology. "What do you want to do next?"

"Speak to the father. Maybe even the stepfather… mother's boyfriend… whatever he is. Maybe Danny and Sarah, Katy's mum, are right and she is just with her boyfriend, and she'll turn up soon enough. If he's older, this boyfriend, then that's a concern and we'll need to look again once he's identified. I was just going to see if I can get the ad dress for the father so I could call by tonight on my way home."

Tom placed a hand on his shoulder. "I'd suggest putting Katy's photo out to the local media. Step things up a bit, but ensure you keep it low key. I don't want them putting two and two together and coming up with five and linking these two cases."

"They wouldn't, would they?"

Tom wasn't so sure. "It's all about clicks these days, and even the local press will jump on it if they can get some extra exposure for themselves."

"I read that some large media conglomerates are buying up regional press companies," Eric said, glumly. "Similar happened to the local radio stations and we just get the same old tracks across every station now."

"That's progress, Eric," Tom said. "Get Katy's photo and description out. We might get lucky."

"Yes, okay. I'll do that. Maybe someone has seen her out and about."

"And then go home, Eric."

He met Tom's eye, shaking his head. "I have so much to do."

"You are allowed to go home, Eric. You'll be no use to anyone if you can't think straight."

"Not much reason to though, is there?"

Tom felt for him. "No improvement with Becca?"

Eric's expression softened a little. "I'm trying to give her some space." He looked around and seeing they were alone, he continued, "We have been attending counselling appointments. She's nice and everything, but I don't feel we are getting anywhere. Becca seems to get something out of it though, but we just can't seem to get past… something, you know?"

"Is there a particular sticking point?"

"Yes."

Eric wasn't forthcoming with more details and Tom didn't press for them. If he wanted to share, then he would. If not, that was his business.

"Don't stay at it too late," Tom said, placing a hand on Eric's shoulder and gently squeezing it supportively. Eric nodded and carried on with what he was doing.

CHAPTER FOURTEEN

Tom stood in the anteroom watching through the window. Tony Shears knew he was there, but aside from a brief glance in his direction, he'd made no attempt at communication. Cassie stood alongside him, and Tom noticed her say something quietly and the man nodded. The morgue attendant slowly drew the sheet back away from Simon Shears' face, folding it gently at the neckline across his chest.

Paying close attention, Tom watched for the brother's reaction. There was no drama, no outpouring of emotion. Tony Shears stared hard at his brother's face and confirmed it was Simon with a slow nod in response to Cassie's question. The attendant moved to recover the dead man's face only for Tony to stop him and move closer. His expression remained fixed, hard. Tom saw the man's eyes narrow and then he met the attendant's eye, glanced at Cassie and made to leave.

"I can have someone run you home, if you like?" Cassie asked.

"No need," Tony said over his shoulder without looking back at her. Cassie signalled to the attendant that the process was over and he set about covering the body and preparing to take it back to the cold storage.

Behind Tom, the door opened and Dr Paxton entered, peering over the rim of his glasses perched on the end of his nose before smiling warmly.

"Good morning, Tom. It's a fine day to be up and about, isn't it?"

Tom, glancing through the window at Simon Shears' body beneath the sheet, being wheeled out of the room, cocked his head. "Not for everyone it isn't."

"No, I suppose not." Paxton said, following Tom's eye. "Damn sight brighter than it has been for several days though. Puts an extra spring in the step, wouldn't you say?"

"Or a bit of lead in your pencil," Cassie said, entering the anteroom.

Paxton removed his glasses, frowning at Cassie. "It's been some time since that's been necessary, DS Knight, I can tell you."

"I'd rather you didn't, Doc. Far too much information, particularly seeing as you spend so much time with the dead, I'd hate to think what you might get up to. People do that don't they? They're drawn to professions where they can fulfil their darkest fantasies?"

Tom was about to chastise her, but Dr Paxton chuckled. Despite the two of them having an almost pathological dislike of one another at times, they did seem to be on a similar wavelength often enough.

"Very true, Detective." He held up his glasses in her direction. "But for me, the passion has always been focussed on what happened to the human body to cause death rather than what one can do with them after death."

She inclined her head. "Thin line though."

Paxton laughed again before putting his glasses back on and opening the file he had until now kept tucked under his arm.

"Now… who wants to hear the gory details?" he asked, flicking through his notes. "You'll not be surprised to hear, although maybe you will…" he said, staring momentarily into space, "that the deceased died from severe blood loss," he met Tom's eye, "from no fewer than forty-three separate stab wounds. Primarily focussed on the abdomen, from," he held his left hand with the open folder at the base of his midriff and his right-hand level with his Adam's apple, "here to here. There were shallow cuts to the upper arms along with deeper wounds to the wrists and forearms as well."

"Defensive injuries?" Tom asked.

"Quite, yes. The wounds to the upper arms I suspect were down to whoever was wielding the knife was slashing wildly, throwing their arm in an arcing movement from the left and the right. No doubt the victim was struggling to free himself at the time too, which would have helped with the inaccuracy of the blows."

Tom considered the description, trying to picture the scene in his mind. "He was trying to free himself?"

"I believe so, yes."

"From what?"

"From whom is the better question, Tom."

"More than one assailant then?"

"I should say so, yes," Paxton said, scanning his notes. "The petechial haemorrhaging visible around the eyes, the little red dots that appear, are the result of strangulation. The abrasions that I noted around the throat and neck are indicative of… DS Knight, may I borrow you for a moment?"

Cassie eyed the pathologist warily as he made a hook with his right arm, clearly intending to re-enact the hold someone had over Simon Shears.

"Er… no, if it's all the same to you, I won't." She smiled artificially. "But thanks for the offer."

"Hmm… you're right. It's probably best not to lead me into temptation," Paxton said, grinning.

Cassie snorted.

"Anyway," the pathologist continued, "I think your victim was in a headlock… and was sure to be trying to free himself. There is substantial tissue damage from where he was trying to work himself free. Whoever had a hold of him was strong, mind you, and tall because Mr Shears was an athletic specimen, and he didn't break free before death. In fact, I would go so far as to say he may well have lost consciousness due to asphyxiation prior to his bleeding out."

"You're sure? Shears bled to death rather than being strangled and choked?"

Paxton rocked his head from side to side. "I dare say it was a close-run thing. The poor chap lost several pints of blood. Three strikes in particular caused lacerations to vital organs and, quite notably, nicked the pulmonary artery which carries blood to the lungs, as well as the aorta which I'm sure you're aware carries blood from the heart to the body." He made a glum face. "There was very little chance of him making it at that point without immediate medical intervention. However, he was still being choked. Whether that was intentional, I couldn't say."

"But whoever was holding him, or wrestling

with him, would have been well aware of the knife wielding attacker?" Tom asked.

"Oh yes, without a shadow of a doubt," Paxton said. "The number of strikes he received… there would have been blood spatter arcing out in every direction. Anyone in close proximity would have been given a spray, so to speak. A crimson after-shave, no less," he said smiling and looking between them. Neither Tom nor Cassie saw the humour and Paxton cleared his throat, mildly embarrassed. "Is there anything specific you wanted to ask me?"

"Is there anything notable about the strike patterns of the knife?" Tom asked.

Paxton raised his eyebrows thoughtfully.

"He was likely upright for the vast majority, moving… perhaps restricted movement because someone had him by the throat but I would argue he was shifting left and right which is commensurate with the nature of the wounds. He was, quite literally, in a fight for his life."

"We noticed offensive as well as defensive wounds," Tom said. "Can you confirm that?"

Paxton nodded. "Absolutely. Before his body gave out Mr Shears was no doubt holding his own. He has both cuts and abrasions to his knuckles which are indicative of him landing blows against an opponent or opponents. X-rays revealed a hair-line fracture in the proximal phalanx of his right forefinger. Clearly recent, I should imagine that was a result of landing a heavy blow on something with very little give in it."

"Such as?" Cassie asked.

Paxton turned to her slowly, his forehead creasing as he tilted his head towards her. "Such as an individual's frontal cranium, DS Knight."

"You can just say the skull, Doc," Cassie said, folding her arms across her chest. "No one's impressed by your medical degree here."

"Not even a little?"

Cassie shrugged. "Maybe a little," she said, holding thumb and forefinger together in the air and narrowing her eyes. "Tiny bit…"

"Praise at last," he said, smiling. Turning back to Tom, he looked pensive. "I did manage to recover some trace evidence from the victim's fingernails. I've sent it up to the lab for analysis. I hope it is useful."

Tom nodded. "Anything that can help narrow the search would be helpful."

"Tricky case?"

"As yet we have no idea what he was doing out there, let alone a motive for killing him."

"Has he made anyone angry recently?" Paxton asked.

"Well, he's dead," Cassie said, "so I reckon that's a safe bet."

Dr Paxton shook his head. "That is obvious,

Cassandra," Cassie rolled her eyes at the use of her full name, "but I'm talking about the method of killing." He pointed at the paperwork in the folder in his hands. "Don't underestimate these injuries. These are not the calculated strikes of an efficient killer. They are wild… one might suggest born out of fury."

"People get angry when they are fighting, Doctor," Tom said.

Paxton waved the comment away. "Yes, yes, of course they do. Tempers fray… the red mist descends, but this… in my opinion, this is something else. It borders on a visceral hatred the likes of which one witnesses in serial killers who have a pathological hatred of… women for example. A Ted Bundy if you will. Whoever inflicted these injuries was in a rage. I said many of the injuries were consistent with the victim being in an upright position, but not all," he said, wagging a finger in the air. "At least a dozen wounds were inflicted when he was on the ground, evident by the angle of entry." He made a downward stabbing motion in the air with his right hand, glancing at Cassie as he did so. She screwed her face up and Paxton smiled.

"After he'd been dragged to the ground?" Tom asked.

"Or after he'd lost consciousness," Paxton said. "Visceral hatred."

"Just making sure?" Cassie suggested.

"Quite possible, yes. But you asked for my opinion."

"Anything else?" Tom asked.

"The toxicology report was interesting," Paxton said, leafing through his paperwork, turning the folder so Tom could read it and passing it across. Tom looked at the results in front of him; a list of substances by their chemical nomenclature which meant nothing to him. He looked at the doctor for explanation. "Your victim had quite a fondness for modern chemistry, as well as a penchant for the traditional too."

"Drugs?"

"Illicit ones, yes." Paxton took the folder back, tracing the list with his index finger. "His blood analysis showed traces of cocaine, the traditional recreational drug of the rich and shameless—"

"You don't have to be rich these days," Cassie said.

"Quite right, Detective Sergeant," Paxton said. "However, traditionally, it always has been." Cassie inclined her head to acquiesce to his point. "Along with the Colombian marching powder we also found trace elements of amphetamines, ecstasy and good old-fashioned LSD. Not to be outdone with the stimulants, your victim also saw fit to partake of some prescription drugs in the form of benzodiazepines. Nothing I can see in his medical history is suggestive of this man suffering from any hyperactive disorder."

"Uppers and downers," Tom said quietly.

"Indeed, Tom. Perhaps you might care to trawl through your list of known dealers," Paxton said, smiling. "Not that I wish to direct the course of your investigation."

"Interesting," Tom said. "What levels were there in his system? Might he have been under the influence—"

"No, no, not that it would have had a major effect on him at the time of his death," Paxton said, waving away the question. "But it is evidence of him being a habitual drug user. There is clear damage to his liver and kidney function. He sustained quite a habit."

Tom looked at Cassie. "The neighbour did say he was a party goer."

"Life and soul," Paxton said, closing the folder and passing it to Tom who accepted it graciously. "I'll email you a digital copy later today."

"Thank you," Tom said, and the pathologist acknowledged both of them in turn before leaving them alone in the room. Tom glanced through the window into the empty room, Simon Shears' body having been wheeled out. "The good doctor is not wrong. Cross reference Shears with known local dealers and see if any association comes up. Things can get pretty fraught when addicts can't pay their bills."

"You think he may have owed someone money?" Cassie asked. "Dealers tend not to murder their best clients. It's bad for business."

"Yes, unless you need to set an example."

She nodded.

"He worked the doors, didn't he?" Tom asked.

"I believe so, yeah."

"The doormen always know who the dealers are. It's their job to keep them out."

"Or to let the right ones in," Cassie countered.
Tom agreed. "I'll get right on it. Where are you going next?"

"The warrant should come through for Simon Shears' home at some point this morning but, in the meantime, I'm going to speak with the guy who made the assault claim against him and see what he has to say."

Stepping away from her, he took out his mobile and called Alice. After he'd collected Saffy from her friend's house the previous evening and taken her home, he was surprised to find his wife hadn't returned home. She sent him a text around nine o'clock to say she was with her father, and they were trying to sort things out. He'd been asleep by the time she got home and had been reluctant to speak about it before he left for work that morning.

Alice didn't answer her phone. Tom hung up

without leaving a message, hopeful she would call him back at some point during the day. It stung a little that she wasn't able to confide in him, but there was a lot going on. She would when she was ready. At least, he very much hoped so.

CHAPTER FIFTEEN

Tom rang the doorbell, hearing an excited dog start barking, a sound that grew louder culminating in a thump as something hurled itself against the door to the flat. Tim Raynor's block of flats were situated at the end of The Esplanade on the western edge of Sheringham, overlooking the town and the sea. The entrance to Raynor's flat was at the rear of the building, accessed from two dozen lock-up garages owned by nearby apartment block residents. These were separated by a strip of grass and some residents' parking spaces.

The block's bin store was spilling out beside the concrete steps up to his door located on the side of the building. The building itself looked tired and uncared for. In the town's heyday, this location would have been very appealing, positioned at the western end of the promenade on a raised coastal section with great views over town and the water. However, the recent resurgence in the popularity of the town came off the back of decades of neglect. Many of these blocks of flats were put up in the sixties and early seventies. Gradually they were being modernised and improved, but this one was one of the last to be touched and it showed.

Only a stone's throw away one of the dilapidated art-deco hotels had been sold to developers, a controversial decision at the time, and extended, converting it into luxury apartments. The two ends of the same street offering glimpses of both past and present. The building next door was now up for sale and would likely see the same approach made. Gradually, modernity was making its way along the seafront.

The dog had ceased barking, but Tom could hear him snuffling at the base of the door. Of its owner, there was still no sign. Raynor could be out, but Tom checked his watch. It was still early in the day. Tony Shears had been willing to come in first thing and so it wasn't yet nine o'clock in the morning. Besides, Raynor had told the investigating officers that he wasn't working at the time of the assault.

Tom pressed the bell, following the action with a rap of his knuckles on the obscured glass window of the door. This set the dog off again. He saw movement behind the door and a figure approached, yelling at the dog to shut up. The creature didn't.

The door opened and a bleary-eyed man stared out at Tom, squinting in the daylight. He was dishevelled and evidently Tom had woken him. Drawing an oversized dressing gown around him to block out the cool breeze coming in off the water, he looked Tom up and down.

"Mr Raynor?" Tom asked.

The man sniffed, eyeing Tom warily and doing his best to stop a small wiry terrier from slipping past him at his feet. "Whatever you're selling, I'm not interested."

Tom took out his warrant card. "Police. Tim Raynor?"

Raynor focussed on Tom's identification and then looked up, meeting his eye.

"Yeah."

"Detective Inspector Janssen. I'd like a word."

Raynor cleared his throat, nodded and shifted his dog back from the door with his left foot, trying to dissuade it from going outside. As soon as the door opened further, it moved past his owner and repeatedly leapt up at Tom, barely getting higher than his knee.

"Sorry about him," Raynor said, doing his best to bring the dog to heel.

"Don't worry, I have one myself."

"Is he as thick as this one?" Raynor asked, bending down and scooping the dog up in his arms. He put him down in a compact kitchen to his left and closed the door before the dog could get out. The scrabbling sound of claws on lino could be heard and he began barking again. Raynor shook his head. "Rescue dog. My missus chose him. I should have known better."

Leading Tom into a sitting room, Raynor threw open the curtains, shielding his eyes from the daylight that streamed in. Blinking, he turned to Tom and offered him a seat before sinking into an armchair set before the window and stifling a yawn.

"Late night?" Tom asked.

"I'm not much of a morning person if the truth be told. More of a night owl," he said, smiling.

"I'd like to talk to you about Simon Shears."

Raynor's smile faded and he slowly nodded. "I guess I should have seen that coming."

"Excuse me?"

"Shears." Raynor nodded towards the television in the corner of the room. "I saw it on the news last night. Can't say as I'm surprised, I must say."

"Why would you think that?"

Raynor shrugged, wiping his nose with the back of his hand and sitting forward in his chair.

"If you knew him, you'd understand."

"So, you knew Simon? Before the assault?"

Raynor met Tom's eye, his expression pensive.

Was he gauging Tom's motive for being in his flat? Probably.

He nodded. "Yeah, I knew Simon…" he wrinkled his nose, "or of him, at least. It's not like we were mates or anything. He's been working the doors of the bars for years. Most of us know him."

Tom was intrigued. "How would you describe him to someone who didn't?"

Raynor was thoughtful, then he sniffed and shook his head. "An arsehole, primarily."

"The two of you didn't get on then?"

He laughed.

"Was there a history between the two of you prior to the alleged assault?"

"There's nothing alleged about it," Raynor said pointedly, jabbing a finger towards Tom.

"And yet you withdrew the complaint."

Raynor sat back, placing his hands flat on his knees, nodding. "Yep, I did."

"You seem annoyed."

Raynor tilted his head but didn't reply.

"Is that because you dropped the complaint or because you're still sore about Simon giving you a pasting?"

The comment didn't go down well and Raynor's expression hardened.

"Let's just say, I'm not too bothered about him being dead."

"That's quite a statement under the circumstances," Tom said. "Someone could take that the wrong way."

Raynor scoffed, shaking his head. "Whatever he got himself into it had nothing to do with me."

"Can you tell me about the night you and he had your coming together?"

"Don't you have a report or something you can read?"

Tom smiled. "Humour me."

Rubbing furiously at his face, Raynor passed his hands up and through his hair, sighing deeply.

"Okay… it was something and nothing." He shook his head. "I shouldn't have got involved. We were out on the town, letting off steam on the weekend, you know? Anyway, I was down near the old harbour grabbing something to eat at Fat Ted's, you know it?"

"Best halloumi fries on the north coast," Tom said, inclining his head.

"Yeah, nice," Raynor said. "Anyway, I was with a couple of the lads and word came down to us that Callum was in a spot of bother up the road, so we legged it up there to see if he needed any help."

"And Callum is?"

"A mate, that's all."

"What was the nature of the *bother* he'd found himself in?"

Raynor shrugged. "I don't know, but it had all

gone off. By the time I got there, Callum was on the floor and your man was putting the boot in."

"Simon Shears?"

"Yeah, Simon. And that wasn't on. I mean, once a guy is down you're supposed to back off aren't you?"

"So the rule book says."

"Yeah, well, Simon makes his own rules and he was piling in on Callum." Raynor shook his head. "Seriously, Callum had his arms around his head, trying to protect himself and Simon was going to town, so I did what any mate would do."

"You attacked Simon?"

"I tried to push him away… and he didn't take kindly to it and turned on me." He stared at Tom. "I thought there were rules about what bouncers are allowed to do? Legislation for their licences and stuff like that?"

"There are, yes. I'm not familiar with the details but they need to exercise restraint—"

"Restraint? Is that a joke?"

"Why what happened?"

"He dragged me into an alleyway and beat seven bells out of me. That's what happened! I was trying to help my mate and Shears put me in hospital for the night."

"His justification was that you assaulted him and he was defending himself."

Raynor shook his head and laughed, but without any genuine humour.

"Yeah, right. If you've already made up your mind, then why bother to ask?"

"Your friend, Callum is it?" Raynor nodded. "How did he end up fighting in the street with Simon Shears?"

Raynor exhaled, staring straight ahead. "An incident inside the pub with some drunken bird, I think, but you'd have to ask him yourself for the details."

Tom nodded. "Callum have a last name?"

Raynor looked over at Tom. "Wardby. Callum Wardby."

"Will he corroborate your version of events?"

"Damned if I know!" Raynor said, the smile returning. "He was half cut, so I've no idea what he'll tell you. All I can say is that's what happened, God's witness."

"Do you know where I can find Callum?"

He looked up, thinking hard. "Sorry, but he moved to a new gaff not too long ago and I can't recall the address."

Tom nodded. "One last question, where were you the day before last, during the day and into the night?"

Raynor bit his bottom lip, fixing Tom with a stare. "Now look here… I didn't have anything to do with what happened to Simon Shears."

"What did happen to him?"

"How the hell should I know?" Raynor said, throwing his hands in the air, his voice rising. "But it has nothing to do with me."

"You were angry about the assault—"

"Of course, I was!"

"Then why did you drop the complaint?"

Raynor's lips moved but no words emerged as he stumbled over his thoughts. "Because… I…" he looked away, clamping his eyes shut. "It wasn't me, okay!"

"Then why?"

"Because it wasn't worth the aggro!" Raynor said, pained. "It just… wasn't worth it."

"Did someone threaten you? Was it Simon?"

Raynor leapt out of his seat, pacing the room with his hands pressed against his temples.

"Was it Simon Shears?" Tom repeated.

"No… not directly."

Tom assessed his reaction. He was agitated, nervous. If Simon had threatened him, then that danger had passed. Did he feel the threat from someone else or had he resolved the situation himself and was now worried that his actions were catching up with him? Tom's instinct told him this man wasn't a killer. He didn't have the demeanour of someone capable of such a brutal murder… at least not alone.

"Who threatened you, Tim?"

He stopped pacing the room, looking down at Tom, his hands deep in the pockets of his dressing gown.

"No... no one... it was nothing."

"You're not telling me the whole story, are you Tim?"

"I... I... don't know what to say."

"I find the truth is always a good place to start," Tom said, standing up. They had never met before and despite his confidence in his ability to handle a man like Tim Raynor, he didn't feel comfortable doing so from a seated position. Raynor appeared to notice Tom's stance, backing away and raising his hands in a show of deference. "I'll remind you that this is a murder inquiry, Mr Raynor. If you have anything to say to me, now would be a very good time to say it."

He waited patiently, allowing the silence to grow. He could almost see the cogs turning as Tim Raynor considered his position. His eyes flitted between Tom and the window, perhaps searching for inspiration on the horizon.

"Tim?"

He snapped out of it, looking directly at Tom.

"Look... I know how this works. You can't protect me, can you?"

"Protect you from what?"

"From..."

"Who is threatening you?"

Raynor took a deep breath. When the answer came, it didn't surprise Tom at all.

"Tony. Simon's brother."

"Tony Shears threatened you?"

"Him and his mates… all the guys who work for him."

"Why would he do that?"

Raynor shrugged. "To protect his brother, I guess. I don't know. They fancy themselves as some kind of local mafia… and to be quite honest with you, Tony operates like one." He held Tom's gaze. "Do you know Tony?"

Tom shook his head. "I've never come across him before professionally, no. You talk as if I should have."

Raynor shook his head. "All those businesses he runs… all cash and migrant workers. I'm not surprised he's stayed under your radar. But… other people have noticed…"

"Who has noticed?"

The nervousness returned, Raynor swallowed hard, struggling to do so. He shook his head, sitting down forcefully.

"It doesn't matter," he muttered. "Forget I said anything."

Tom thought about pressing the issue but decided now wasn't the time.

"You didn't answer my initial question. Where were you the day before yesterday?"

He met Tom's eye with a steady gaze. "I was here."

"All day?"

"Yes."

"Can anyone corroborate that?"

"My missus can. Kayleigh. She was here. She'll tell you."

"The whole time?"

Raynor hesitated and then nodded.

"I'll need to speak to her."

"She's at work. She'll not be back until late this afternoon."

"Does she usually work until then?"

"Depends on her shift. She works reception at the golf club," he said, nodding towards his right as if they could see the golf course through the wall."

"Front desk or clubhouse?"

"Wherever. It varies," he said with a shrug.

"Must keep her out until different times, evenings and weekends."

"Yeah," Raynor said. She doesn't know what she's working from one week to the next."

"Her work schedule should be easy to verify then," Tom said.

Raynor looked away and then down at the floor. He nodded and then mumbled, "Yeah, easy enough."

"I'm going to ask you for a DNA sample, Tim.

Would you have any objection to providing me with onc?"

He looked fearful, eyes flitting around the room.

"It will help rule you out of our investigation."

"I… suppose that's fine."

"Good."

Once outside in the fresh air, Tom made his way back to the car, evidence bag with the DNA swab in one hand, his mobile in the other, Cassie answered his call.

"How did you get on with Tim Raynor?"

"Illuminating," he said.

"Really? I'm keen to hear all about it."

"Later," Tom said, reaching his car and putting the bag with the sample on the passenger seat. He shut the door and looked back at the flat he'd just left. He couldn't see any movement, but he doubted Raynor would be going back to sleep. The man was rattled. The question is, by what? "Do me a favour, would you, Cass? Look up Callum Wardby. Raynor says Simon Shears was giving his friend Callum a beating and he tried to intervene which is when Shears assaulted him. I'd like anything you can find on him, prior arrests, convictions, known associates…"

"Shoe size, favourite colour pants," Cassie said. "The usual."

"Exactly. Also, Tony Shears."

"Tony, Simon's brother?" Cassie asked. "I'll get on it right away?"

He could hear her tapping away on the keyboard as they spoke.

"It would appear it was Tony who put the frighteners on Tim Raynor to drop the complaint against his little brother. He did a good job, too."

"Ah… brotherly love is quite a thing. If you can't count on your brother to help you escape a charge for battery, then who can you count on?"

Tom laughed. "Yeah, something like that. Now Raynor is under the impression that Tony is someone to be reckoned with and I didn't get the impression it was idle gossip. Maybe he has his thumb in various different pies, so reach out to intel and see if he, or any of his businesses, is on anyone else's radar. It's possible he would be blagging it to intimidate a stoner like Raynor, but you never know. There could be something in it."

"You think his brother could have been killed for something Tony is involved in?"

Tom was unsure. It was a reach, but at this point they had very little of substance to go on.

"Let's just cast the net and see if we catch anything." A quiet beep in Tom's ear notified him of a text message arriving.

"Does Raynor have an alibi for when Shears was killed?"

"A piss-poor one, but yes. We'll need to check with his partner."

"Ah right, the old *my other half will vouch for me* routine."

"That's it. Keep me posted, Cassie. I'll be back in the office soon. Any sign of that warrant for Shears' house and holiday home?"

"No, not yet. I'll chase it up."

"Right, I'll speak to you—"

"Well now," Cassie said, "that's certainly interesting."

"What is?"

"Callum Wardby," Cassie said. "Hang on a second. You're going to want to hear this. Wardby has two convictions for possession with intent to supply… served eight months the year before last. His probation ended six months ago."

"That is interesting."

"What did Raynor say the fight with Wardby was about?"

"He was suitably vague. An altercation with a woman inside the pub is what he told me."

"I guess that's possible," Cassie said. "Although, you know who isn't popular with pub bouncers?"

"Yes, I know. Drug dealers."

"I've got an address for him from the probation service. Wardby lives here in Hunstanton."

"Makes sense; keeps him away from his dealing ground and most likely under our radar."

"Shall I pay him a visit?" Cassie asked.

"I'll pick you up on the way through. We can go together."

Hanging up on her, he tapped the text message notification. It was from Alice and simply read *I'm sorry about this morning. I love you. Speak later.*

CHAPTER SIXTEEN

CALLUM WARDBY'S address was a two-up, two-down terraced property overlooking an unused car park close to one of Hunstanton's largest supermarkets. The exterior of the house was blackened by traffic fumes sitting as it was so close to the main through road with nothing but a narrow pavement acting as a barrier. A boundary wall, barely shin high, ran across the front of the house acting as a perfect trap for litter, leaves and general detritus which piled up in one corner. There was no doorbell, so Tom rattled the letterbox and knocked on the glass of the door.

A couple of minutes passed before a figure loomed out of the interior darkness and came to the door.

"Who is it?" a muffled voice asked.

"Police!"

The figure stepped back from the door and for a moment Tom wondered if he was going to open it or not. By way of encouragement, Tom banged a closed fist on the door again. It worked. The door opened and Callum Wardby looked out at the two of them, suspiciously.

"Callum Wardby?" Tom asked. He nodded. Tom brandished his ID. "DI Janssen and DS Knight. May we come in?" he asked as a lorry rumbled past threatening to drown out his voice. Wardby glanced over his shoulder, back into the gloom behind him.

"Why?"

"Because it would be easier to speak inside," Tom said.

Wardby smacked his lips, sniffed and acquiesced, backing away to give them room to enter. Cassie closed the door behind them, immediately reducing but not eliminating the din caused by the passing vehicles. It was a cramped feeling standing in the narrow hallway of this small Victorian terrace. Their host relented, reading Tom's expression and led them into the front sitting room. This wasn't a great deal larger, perhaps three metres by three and dominated by a sofa far too large for the room. The air smelled stale and musty, Tom spotting black mould on the external front-facing wall in the far corner.

"What do you want?" Wardby said, sitting down and reaching for a pouch of tobacco and a packet of rolling papers. He set about building a cigarette with practised ease.

"We would like to ask you about your relationship with Simon Shears," Tom said.

Wardby paused, glancing up at Tom momentarily before running his tongue along the glue strip and sealing up his cigarette. Tapping the end on the coffee table in front of him to squeeze in the stragglers, he put the roll-up to his lips and sparked a disposable lighter, taking a steep draw and exhaling a thick cloud of pungent smoke into the small room directly at Tom and Cassie.

"Cheers," Cassie said flatly. Wardby offered her his pouch, but Cassie declined with a sarcastic smile.

"Simon Shears?" Tom asked.

"I don't have a relationship with him. I don't know the piece of shit." He blew out another plume of smoke but this time angling it away from them. "Not really. This about the other week?"

"Yes, in a way."

"In what way?" Wardby sat forward, fixing Tom with an intense stare. "Has he made an official complaint, because I shit you not, he was the one who was out of order, not me!"

"Simon Shears has been found dead."

Wardby's lips parted, his eyes narrowing and he cocked his head ever so slightly.

"Say that again?"

"Simon Shears has been murdered."

Wardby tapped the end of his cigarette, knocking ash into an overflowing tray on the table before him and sank back in his seat.

"Well, well, well… karma's a real bitch, isn't it?" he said, smiling and inhaling a steep draw on his cigarette.

"You don't seem particularly upset," Tom said.

Wardby splayed his hands wide. "Why should I care?"

"Because he gave you a kicking," Tom replied.

"And because it puts you squarely in the frame for his murder," Cassie added.

He scoffed. "You know where you can go with that idea," he said, smiling ruefully and shaking his head. "I'm a lot of things, but I ain't no killer."

"Grammar isn't your strong point either, is it?" Cassie said.

Wardby looked at her, confused.

"Double negative," she said, and he nodded, but his expression denoting that he clearly missed the point.

"I didn't have nothing to do with that."

Tom saw Cassie flinch at the comment, but she didn't say anything.

"What led to you and Mr Shears coming to blows?" Tom asked.

He shrugged. "He got a bit carried away, too heavy-handed. A lot of these meathead doormen do that. They have a bit of muscle, mostly between the ears, and start to think they are something special. Give most people a bit of power over others and it goes to their heads." His gaze moved between them, nodding in their direction. "Know what I mean?" he asked, smiling.

Cassie sighed. "You have a lot to say for a man facing a murder charge."

"Get stuffed!"

"Seriously," Cassie said. "You have a grudge against him… and with your record, I'd be nervous."

"Can you not read?" Wardby asked her.

"Excuse me?"

"I mean, you're really good with grammar and that, but can you read?" He stubbed out his cigarette, raising his hand and pointing at her. "I've done time, yes, but I sell recreational drugs."

"You sell?"

"I *used to sell* recreational drugs," Wardby said. "I'm clean now, and even if I wasn't, I'm not a killer."

"You and Shears were going at it pretty hard judging by the CCTV footage recorded in the pub."

"Doesn't mean I can't look after myself," he countered. "If I couldn't before I went away then trust me, eight months inside will make you a fast learner."

"So, you were involved in fights in prison?" Tom asked.

Wardby laughed, shaking his head. "You have no idea… the levels of violence you see in those places are like nothing you can comprehend."

"Then don't break the law," Cassie said.

He grinned. "And I don't. I'm a reformed character. Ask my probation officer. The system works."

Tom took the man's measure. He was pale and slim of face, perhaps even gaunt, with sunken eyes framed by dark patches of skin hanging beneath them. Far from the picture of health, he had the physicality of a drug user. They weren't difficult to spot once you knew what to look for.

Tom met Wardby's eye with a stern look. "I appreciate your confidence in your innocence, Callum," he said, taking a seat in the armchair beside the television in the corner of the room. Wardby watched him warily. "However, I don't think you fully appreciate your position."

"And what position is that?"

"You see, we believe you were dealing in the pub that night," Tom said. Wardby's expression clouded. "And Shears knew too, so he dealt with you the only way he knows how. To teach you a lesson. To encourage you to stay away."

Wardby shook his head, irritated.

"And you didn't like that," Cassie said, "did you, Callum? So you went looking for him later when no one was around."

"You have no idea!" he muttered. "You really don't."

Tom took up the mantle. "Juries don't much care for premeditated murders, Callum." He shook his head. "And judges detest repeat offenders, don't they, DS Knight?"

"Tend to give higher sentences, too," Cassie said flatly.

"Look here," Wardby said, wagging an accusing finger at them both. "I had nothing to do with what happened to Shears. Nothing at all. And you can't pin it on me just because you have no one better."

"There's where your bravado falls down," Tom said, shaking his head, "because that's exactly what we can do. Where were you two days ago? What were you up to?"

"I was here, at home, minding my own damn business."

"You live alone?"

Wardby scoffed, his lips curling into a snarl as he shook his head. "This isn't on… it just isn't on," he said almost inaudibly. "I'm not going down for this. I'm not."

"Then you should stop wasting our time and drop this little act you've got going on," Tom said.

"Start telling me something I want to hear, Callum, or I'll have you back in a cell faster than you can skin-up a joint."

Wardby glared at him, slowly shaking his head. "You just don't get it, do you?"

Tom sat forward, resting his elbows on his knees. "Then maybe you should explain it to me."

"I'm not some master criminal, you know?" Wardby said, resignation in his tone. "I sell a bit of weed and a few pills… just to fund my own supply. The way you're talking is like I'm running some cartel or something."

"Spare me the pity take, Callum."

Wardby spoke through gritted teeth. "Like I said, you don't get it. Shears didn't give me a kicking because he caught me dealing. He was taking out his competition."

"What?"

Wardby chuckled, his expression lightening. "You coppers really aren't very bright." He looked between them, beaming with self-congratulatory satisfaction as Tom and Cassie exchanged glances.

"Are you saying Shears was dealing?"

"Of course he was dealing! Where do you think all that designer gear he loves to wear comes from? They're not all knockoffs, you know? Bouncers aren't known for getting paid a lot of money."

"That's quite an allegation to level at a dead man."

Wardby threw his hands in the air and grinned. "Well, that's what I'm here for." Tom wasn't amused. "Look, you wanted to hear the truth and that's it right there, signed and sealed."

"You can back that up with some evidence, right?" Tom asked.

"You expect me to do your job for you as well, do you?" he said accusingly. "I've given you a reason for him dying. What more do you want from me?"

Tom leaned forward. "You've given yourself another motive for murdering him."

"What are you talking about?"

"Revenge is one," Tom said, "and taking out a rival is another."

Wardby laughed, rising from his seat. Holding his hands in the air, he presented himself to Tom and then turned to face Cassie.

"Now, I may well be a fine figure of a man," he said, smiling, "but do you honestly think I could take down a man like Simon Shears?"

"No," Cassie said.

He jabbed a finger in the air at her, celebrating. "Exactly right. No."

"Unless you had help," she added and Wardby's face dropped. He tilted his head to one side.

"Do I look like a guy who has friends?"

She shook her head. "You look like a guy who has customers."

He nodded glumly. "I'm the first number on many contacts lists, DS Knight. That's true, but no one is going to help me murder a man in exchange for twenty quid's worth of weed now, are they?"

"So, you're admitting to dealing?"

"I'm admitting nothing."

"If we turn this house upside down what are we likely to find?"

"Once you've got a warrant, you can do whatever you wish, DS Knight," Wardby said, "but until you have that warrant, you can get lost."

Cassie looked nonplussed. "Maybe I'll arrest you now on suspicion of murder and turn the house over immediately."

Wardby laughed.

"Something funny?" Cassie asked.

"Yeah, you," he said. "If you had anything on me, other than the fact I have a record and knew him, I'd already be in an interview room, so let's not waste each other's time."

Cassie's expression clouded, but Wardby was right. Aside from the ruckus in the pub in Sheringham, there was nothing to tie him to the murder. Not yet anyway.

"We have your DNA on the database, Callum," Tom said. "We'll run it against the samples found at the crime scene."

He shrugged, but his eyes betrayed the nonchalant attitude. He looked fearful. "You do what you have to do, Inspector."

Tom held his gaze for a few seconds, the two locked together with neither man wanting to break away. Tom stood up, gesturing to Cassie for them to leave. They reached the door before Wardby spoke.

"You know, there are rumours floating around."

Tom turned back. "Rumours? About what?"

"Simon Shears."

Tom stared at him. "Well? I'm waiting."

"He owed money. A lot of money."

"Who to?"

Wardby was pensive, focussed.

"People. Scary people," he said. "The kind of people you really don't want to be in debt to, you know?"

"Got a name?"

Wardby looked away, smiling.

"Thought not," Tom said, turning to leave.

"Do you think I'm stupid?"

Tom looked back. "No, I think you're calculating… and a man like you will say whatever he thinks is necessary to get out of a sticky situation."

"Is that right?"

The smile gone, Wardby was indignant.

"Yes, that's right," Tom said. "Expect to see us again, Callum. Maybe sooner than you think."

"Yeah, I'll look forward to it."

Tom left the room without a backward glance. "We'll see ourselves out, Callum. Have a nice day."

Once the door closed behind them, Tom exchanged a sideways glance at Cassie and they set off for the car.

"Are you buying that?" Cassie asked.

"Which part?"

"Any of it?"

Tom was thoughtful. "I think you can't take anything he says as credible. He's a lowlife, but..." he stopped and looked both ways before crossing the road between oncoming cars, "he's a petty criminal. He isn't on record supplying Class A drugs and his time inside was off the back of how much cannabis he had in his possession and totting up of previous offences. A more lenient magistrate could have given him a lighter sentence. He's a small-time dealer primarily selling to fund his own habit."

"True. He's not exactly Al Capone. So, what are you saying, rule him out?"

Tom shook his head. "No, not at all. I meant what I said back there. Callum Wardby would say, and I'm absolutely certain he'd do, whatever he had to do to get himself out of trouble."

"Even if that meant killing Simon Shears?"

Tom nodded. "Even if that meant killing Simon Shears, but until we have something concrete to tie him to it, we leave him be."

Cassie's mobile rang and she glanced at the screen. "Eric," she said, answering.

They reached the car and got in. Cassie thanked Eric and hung up. "The warrant has arrived. Eric has called out a locksmith to gain entry."

"Good."

"Shall we head over there?"

"I'll drop you off at the station," Tom said. "See if there's any substance behind what Wardby just said about Shears... any suggestion of dealing or his owing money." She met his eye, arching her eyebrows. "Worth checking," he said, shrugging. "And I'll go and see what Shears has left for us at his place."

CHAPTER SEVENTEEN

PC David Marshall was waiting for Tom to arrive in the driveway of Simon Shears' home. A locksmith was also present, sitting in his van, waiting for approval to gain entry to the property.

"Has anyone shown an interest in what you're doing here?" Tom asked.

The constable shook his head. "Not really. Some local kids were hanging out on the green over there, having a nosy and," he looked at the neighbouring property, "the chap next door popped his head over the hedge to say hello. Aside from that, only the usual curtain twitching you'd expect when a police car is parked outside."

"Right, let's get inside and have a look around then."

Tom beckoned for the locksmith to join them and, once he'd gathered his tools from the rear of his van, he joined them at the front door. Examining the lock, he tutted under his breath and stepped back.

"Problem?" Tom asked.

"No, not really," he said, flicking a hand casually towards the door. "Those locks are the only ones I've never been able to get past. Decent bit of kit, they are."

"Can you still bypass them?"

He nodded. "Yep. I'll just have to do it the old-fashioned way. Back in a tick."

Retrieving another bag from the van, he returned, kneeling down and taking out a power drill. He smiled at Tom as he stood up, testing the power in the battery with a quick turn of the drill bit.

"This'll not take long," he said, and he wasn't wrong. The drill bit made short work of the lock and seconds later, the door was open. The call-out fee was a waste of money, Tom thought. He could have done that himself. The locksmith must have read his mind, shrugging apologetically. "But can you fit a new lock to secure the house after you're done?"

Tom didn't reply as the locksmith sheepishly stepped aside and he pushed the door open, glancing up at the security camera above the door as he entered. A tiny green light was on at the base of the camera suggestive that it was recording or at least picking up their activity. The hall was nondescript, a tiled floor and marked walls showing how long it had been since it'd been decorated. The day was overcast, and the deeper Tom moved into the house, the darker it became. He flicked on the nearest light switch bathing the interior in artificial light.

The kitchen at the end of the hall looked much the same as it had done the previous evening when he'd peered in through the window. There were two reception rooms on the ground floor, one to the front and the other overlooking the rear garden. Tom clocked another camera in the hallway at the foot of the stairs but this one faced down the hall, pointed at him. He entered the front room, standing in the doorway as he looked around. Gaming machines lined the walls, the arcade style commonplace in the entertainment venues populating the seafront. He counted twelve machines lining the walls. A large television was mounted on the chimney stack above a boarded-over fireplace, on the floor were several bean bags and cushions. On a small table he could see a games console and a number of controllers.

Empty bottles of flavoured alcohol were everywhere along with packets of crisps and chocolate bar wrappers. Mounted high in the corner of the room was yet another camera angled down at the room. Tom felt his chest tighten, a deep sense of foreboding passing over him. Backing out of the room, he looked back to the front door where PC Marshall was standing with his back to him.

"Sheriff!"

Marshall turned. "Sir?"

"Call the station and have a forensic team sent out here, as quickly as they can."

The constable nodded, reaching for the radio mounted on his left shoulder. Tom looked at the closed door to the rear reception room. Easing it open, the hinges protested, squealing as he moved the door aside. Blackout curtains hung at the far end of the room blocking any penetration of daylight. Turning on the light, he didn't like what he saw. A double bed was set up to his left, almost as if this room had been adapted for someone who could no longer manage the stairs. However, another games console was set up in the corner, not something one might expect for an infirm resident, neither were the posters of famous footballers and pop artists stuck to the walls. Looking around, he couldn't see any CCTV cameras set up in this particular room.

Taking out his mobile, he called Tamara.

"Tom, how are you getting on?"

"I think we have a problem," he said flatly. Something in his tone must have struck her because her own changed.

"What is it? What have you found?"

Tom scanned the room, feeling nauseous.

"The set up here… I've seen places like this before during my time in London. The house is full of gaming machines… the flavoured alcohol… all of it…" he held his breath, "to entertain kids."

"What are you saying?"

"This is what they do. They make the house a fun place to be… free drinks, snacks… entertainment. The house is fully wired up with cameras and it's not just to see who is coming to the door. They're recording everything that's going on inside too. They watch… figure out which of the children are the vulnerable ones, who they can get close to…"

"Simon Shears was grooming children?"

"I'm pretty confident that is what was going on here, yes."

Tamara didn't speak for a moment. The silence grew.

"Is there any evidence besides your instinct?"

"No, nothing that I've found… yet. If you have a better explanation, then I'm all ears."

"I can't think of one."

"I've requested a CSI team to come out here.

Can you have some uniform go down to the caravan at the holiday park and seal it off? Whatever Shears was up to here, I'll bet it stretched down there too."

"I'll arrange it straight away."

"I'll leave PC Marshall here and head down that way myself now," Tom said, hanging up. Pleased to be outside, he sucked in a blast of fresh air. It was cold and stung his lungs.

"Are you okay, sir?" Marshall asked.

Tom nodded, stepping out and walking to the end of the driveway. The locksmith was leaning against the side of his van smoking a cigarette, watching him. Scanning the immediate area, Tom saw the kids PC Marshall had likely seen before. They were on the far side of the triangular patch of grass, some on bikes, others kicking a football between them. Katy Roper's face came to mind and he felt uneasy. Calling Eric's mobile, he hoped for good news.

"Eric, can you update me on your search for Katy Roper?"

"I'm no closer to finding her, but I've spoken to her social worker and she's given me an address for her father. He lives in Blakeney, so I was going to head over there in a little bit. Is that all right?"

"I want you to hold off on going if you can. I have to head down to the seafront and check something out. Then I'll be heading back into the office.

Gather everything you have and be ready to present it to me when I get back, okay?"

"Yes, of course," Eric said, sounding concerned. "Is this anything to do with the Shears murder?"

Tom took a deep breath. "I hope not, Eric. I really hope not." Turning, he caught Marshall's attention with a wave. "Nobody in or out until forensics arrive, got it?"

The constable gave him the thumbs-up and Tom got into his car to make the short drive across town to the holiday park where the Shears had their caravan.

THE HOLIDAY PARK WAS DESERTED. At this time of the year most of the units were secured for the winter with both owners and tourists unlikely to return until spring at the earliest. The light was fading rapidly as the sun set over the horizon, peeking out from beneath the cloud bank momentarily prior to sinking from view. Unfamiliar with the numbering system, Tom walked through the maze of densely packed static homes trying to locate the one belonging to the Shears.

Two men, working within a sectioned-off area, paid attention to him. He was ready to move off when one approached.

"Can I help you with something, mate?"

Tom took out his warrant card, showing it to him. The man faltered, his expression lightening.

"Sorry, I didn't realise," he said, wiping his hands on the front of his fleece. "We didn't recognise you, and you can't be too careful with unfamiliar faces in the off-season. A lot of break-ins happen this time of year what with no one around."

Tom nodded. "No problem. I'm looking for one particular caravan."

"Oh, I know them all. Worked here for years. Which one are you after?"

"The Shears' caravan."

"Oh, right," he said, his expression darkening. "Of course. That's bloody awful what's happened to Simon, isn't it? To think, they only lost their old mum a short while ago. Lovely woman, she was. A bit odd, mind, but lovely." He caught sight of Tom's stoic expression and smiled awkwardly. "We're all a bit odd sometimes, aren't we?"

"Yes," Tom said, holding his hand up and pointing off to their left. "That way, is it?"

"No, down there. Fourth on the right," he said, looking along the length of his arm, outstretched in front of him.

"Thanks."

Tom set off, but the man carried on talking, giving Tom pause.

"I saw Tony here this morning. He didn't stop

to chat. Understandable I guess, under the circumstances."

"Tony was here?"

He nodded, his brow furrowing in concentration. "Yeah, around nine-ish… give or take." He laughed. "Why he felt the need to deep clean the caravan, today of all days, I'll never know, but he was at it for most of the morning. Not seen him here at that time of day before. Not unless he stopped overnight anyway."

"Use the caravan a lot, does he?"

"Tony? Yeah, both boys are around and about a fair bit. I think they do quite a bit in the community, you know?"

"Do they?"

"Oh yes," he said, nodding furiously. "Getting teenagers off the streets and giving them stuff to do. Kinda like a youth club set up, at least that's what Tony told me once a while back. I think it'd be great if more people got involved with that sort of thing. Very generous family are the Shears."

"So I gather," Tom said. Pointing ahead now, he nodded. "That way?"

"Yeah, fourth—"

"On the right," Tom said, and the man nodded. Leaving him to get back to work, Tom hurried to the caravan. There was still no uniform presence and he cursed under his breath. Most of the caravans around him had curtains, blinds or a mix of both hanging over the windows. The Shears' caravan didn't. The windows were cracked open, security forgotten and when Tom came closer he caught a waft of strong bleach carrying from inside. "Deep cleaning," he said under his breath. "Damn it."

CHAPTER EIGHTEEN

Eric reached into the knapsack that he took with him into work each day, rooting through the contents to find the banana he had left over from lunch. The canteen was subsidised but with Becca living with her parents he was finding it tough to make ends meet. The new house they'd purchased when they got married was a stretch on two salaries even with Becca's maternity pay but without it, he was feeling the pinch. Finding it, he sat down at his desk to await the scheduled briefing.

Cassie came over and perched herself on the end of his desk.

"That's seen better days," she said, indicating the banana in his hand. It was slightly mashed at one end, the skin pitted with black spots. It was overripe, but he wasn't going to throw good food away.

"They're sweeter this way," he said, unzipping it. Danny Wilson came to his desk, the one next to Eric's, sniffing the air. Spotting Eric tucking into his fruit, he scowled.

"That's disgusting."

"What is?" Eric asked with his mouth full.

"And speaking with your mouth full is too. Bananas. I hate them."

Eric and Cassie exchanged a look. Cassie frowned.

"Who on earth hates bananas?" she asked. Eric shrugged, taking another bite.

"Refined people," Danny said. "Isn't there some rule about eating in the office? Like… no fish… bananas or… Yeah, no fish or bananas."

Eric held the banana up at him, jabbing it in his direction. "I'd certainly never eat bananas and fish together. That would be awful. No wonder you hate banana if that's what you south folk eat."

"No, I don't eat them together—"

"Right, can I have your attention please," Tom said, standing at the front of the room. Everyone settled and conversation died. Danny tutted at Eric one last time, wrinkled his nose and moved to sit somewhere else, close to Kerry Palmer, who smiled as he sat down.

"Touchy," Cassie whispered drawing a dirty look from Tamara. Cassie sat down next to Eric.

"As you all know we are working on the Simon Shears murder. However, information has come to light that puts a different slant on it and that may well bring in what Eric has been investigating." All eyes briefly turned to Eric, hastily folding his banana skin and putting it aside as he swallowed.

"Sorry," he said. There was a titter of chuckling which dissipated almost as soon as it began.

"Can you fill us all in on where you're up to, please Eric?"

He nodded and addressed the room. "Katy Roper has been missing for three days now since she left her foster carers' home. She hasn't had contact with or been seen by any of her friends, although she is not close to many people, since she left the house. Having spoken to her mother, who is not concerned at all about her daughter's whereabouts, I can say that she isn't close to her biological father and there appears to be a little tension between Katy and her mother's partner. I'm yet to get to the bottom of that."

"What about her digital trail?" Tamara asked.

He looked over at the DCI. "I've been in contact with the network provider and her mobile hasn't been logged within range of any mobile phone mast since her disappearance, so there's no GPS tracking data at all." Walking to the front of the room, Eric stuck a photo of Katy up on a fresh whiteboard placed next to those detailing the timeline leading up to the murder of Simon Shears. "Both the Moultons and one of Katy's school friends have told me that she was seeing, or hanging around with, an older guy or possibly guys."

"Are we officially linking the two?" Cassie asked. "If so, why?"

Tom held a hand up to signify to Eric he'd take over from here.

"I strongly believe that Simon Shears, possibly aided and abetted by his older brother, Tony, was organising or attempting to organise the grooming of young children." There was an audible gasp from all of those gathered in the room. Tom asked for silence. "Simon's home is like a mini theme park for children, free at the point of use, with liberal amounts of alcohol and food on offer to draw them in. That is suggestive to me that they weren't targeting very young children, teenagers most likely, but children nonetheless. Now, one forensic team is processing the house while another is doing the same at a caravan that Simon shared with his brother along the seafront. At this time, we do not know how far along they were in their activity nor do we know how many children have been affected."

"In a housing estate, boss?" Danny asked, frowning. "How would he get away with it?"

"It's not where you expect to find this type of set up, Danny," Tom said. "Believe me, the old saying rings true: the best place to hide something is in plain sight."

"Sheesh," Danny muttered, shaking his head.

"It takes time to gear up to all of this, so if we're lucky we have nipped it in the bud before they got going."

"Well, someone did," Cassie said, "in taking out Simon!"

"We don't know if his murder is related," Tom said. "And for that matter, we don't know if Katy's disappearance is even linked, so we will continue the progress in both investigations separately, but with an eye for anything that might see their paths cross. This could be coincidental and I don't want anyone to become side-tracked by a single train of thought. That's when mistakes happen. To that end," he looked at Cassie, "what does the forensic report have to say about Simon's death at the scene?"

"It confirms what we already thought. Simon was involved in a fight, a sustained encounter with at least one individual, probably more."

"They can't be clearer on that?" Tom asked.

She shook her head. "The ground was so damp that the fighting churned it up, steps upon steps, so it's impossible to take casts or anything. Modelling the stab patterns and likely method of asphyxiation, they concluded that Simon was held from behind while someone else delivered the blows with the blade."

"And the blade itself?" Tom asked.

"Four to five inches long, one to one and a half wide… smooth edged," Cassie said. "The lack of a serrated edge tends to rule out a hunting knife or one of those mental zombie knives that some people throw up all over digital media. It could be a kitchen knife purchased from a supermarket or taken from a knife drawer. Nothing special, which means it'll be hard to trace."

"Okay, do we have any good news?"

Cassie smiled. "A little. You thought that shelter was pretty well made and you were right. The CSI techs reckon someone has been living there for several weeks. Whoever has been living there has cleared up after themselves. There's a designated place for rubbish and another for… you know… number twos and everything."

"Any idea who it could be?"

She shook her head. "I'm still to go back to see Mark, the guy from the shelter who said he'd ask around. I'll try and catch him tomorrow morning before they are all kicked out for the day."

"Maybe wait until they're leaving. If our guy is staying there, we don't want to scare him away.

Perhaps call the shelter and see if you can meet – Mark, is it? – privately beforehand."

Cassie grimaced. "I don't think the shelter staff will be happy about doing that. I got the impression Michelle is keen to help but not to the detriment of the shelter's wider goals."

Tom inclined his head. He didn't want to make things harder for them, but this was a murder investigation. "Try it. She can only decline." Cassie nodded. "Anything else?"

"Tyre tracks," Cassie said, "but not from a car."

"Motorbike?" Eric asked.

"Bicycle."

Tom was surprised. Cassie smiled.

"I know, odd huh? But it's right. There were fresh tracks in the mud and evidence that it has been repeatedly used at the scene recently." Cassie shrugged. "Maybe our homeless guy has a bike? I mean, they'd need to get around and, let's face it, Fring isn't the easiest place to get to on foot." She frowned. "Mind you, he doesn't exactly have pressing engagements to get to, so he could walk, I guess."

"Type of bike?" Tom asked.

Cassie shrugged. "The tracks were narrow which rules out a BMX or a mountain bike. I think a racer would be unlikely, bearing in mind the terrain, so something in between."

Eric caught Cassie's eye, a thought coming to

mind but he couldn't quite tease it to the forefront and hc almost imperceptibly shook his head and she didn't say anything.

Tom looked at the information boards, taking a deep breath. "Okay, we're still pretty much at square one when it comes to the crime scene. Any thoughts or suggestions?" He turned to face the room. "Anyone?"

Tamara, deep in concentration, looked up. "Why there? Why was that place chosen for the meeting or as a place to kill Simon Shears, if that was the plan?"

"Remote," Eric said. "You won't be overseen or interrupted."

Cassie nodded. "However, if you are seen then you'll stand out like a pig in blanket at a vegan wedding reception." She leaned in towards Eric, lowering her voice. "Which I can attest to."

"Where?" he whispered.

"I'll tell you later."

Tom looked around the room. "Any other ideas?"

"Who owns the compound again?" Danny asked. "Any lead there?"

"Terence Westfield," Tom said. "But we have no trace of him in the area for years and, judging by the state of dereliction of the breaker's yard, no one has been using it for decades."

That was the nudge needed to jog Eric's memory.

"Did you say Terence?" he asked and Tom nodded. "I wonder… could that be old Tramp Terry?"

"Did you just make that up?" Cassie asked.

Eric ignored her. "Tramp Terry. He's been in and around these parts for years… and he rides a bike. This old thing… like one of those ones you see in Holland when you go over to the continent. The old World War II style ones, you know, like you see in the films?" Eric looked around at blank faces. "Maybe it's him, Tramp Terry?"

"What do you know about him?" Tom asked.

"Not a lot," Eric said. "I mean, he's been coming and going for years. We all knew of him back when we were kids. We'd… well, we all knew him," Eric said, recalling something that he chose not to share. "He was a bit of an oddball, but most homeless people are a bit strange. He was always riding this old bike with those, what do you call them, panniers?"

Cassie nodded, "Yep, that's them."

"Yeah, panniers. He was old school… spoke well and didn't take kindly… well, he was odd."

"Was he an angry guy, drunk or abusive?" Tamara asked.

Eric shook his head. "No, no, nothing like that. He was a gentleman, as I recall. I bumped into him a few times when I'd joined the service, back when

I was in uniform. He would always stop for a chat. Decent chap, I always thought."

"And he lived rough?" Tom asked.

Eric nodded. "Yeah… always had done as far as I know. Tramp Terry."

"Okay, Tramp Terry and Terence Westfield," Tom said. "Let's see if they are one and the same guy, and if we can find him. Now, Callum Wardby stated that Simon Shears was not only working security in the pubs in Sheringham, but alleges he was dealing."

"Was he now?" Tamara asked thoughtfully.

"If we are going to take the word of a dealer," Cassie said.

Tom pursed his lips. "It's not beyond the realms of possibility. We know Shears worked collaboratively with others to provide multiple venue cover for the doors which meant he was in and out of a lot of pubs in the town on a nightly basis. So, he had the opportunity, and if he was working security, then who is going to suspect, or indeed stop, him?"

"Callum also claims Simon was in debt to some big hitters," Cassie said. "He wouldn't say who… or why, so it's likely to be bollocks, but he did say it."

"You doubt him?" Danny Wilson asked.

"I doubt everyone, Danny," she said, winking at him. Kerry smiled.

"You'll learn that," Eric told him.

"Except you, Eric," she said, patting his arm affectionately. He smiled.

"We still need to check it out," Tom said. "Speak to anyone you know who may know and we'll go from there. The same goes for Simon's brother, Tony. He knew we would be turning over Simon's house sooner or later. We don't know if he went there but he definitely went to the caravan and cleaned house. CSI are going over it now, so let's hope if he has anything to hide that he got sloppy with the deep clean."

Tamara caught Tom's attention. "Dr Paxton found trace evidence under the fingernails, didn't he?"

"Yes," Tom nodded. "Skin particles, but there has been no DNA match in the database. If we find a suspect then we can rule them in or out." He shrugged. "Until then, it's of no use."

Tamara nodded. "What do we know about Terence Westfield?"

Cassie picked up the thread. "Aside from inheriting the yard when his father died, not a lot. We have him registered living at what I presume was his family home in Old Hunstanton. When the parents died, he remained living there, so I guess he inherited that as well."

"Did he marry or have a family of his own?"

Cassie checked her notes. "There's an Eloise

Westfield who is recorded there, but no idea on whether that's a spouse or family member. Their family tree seems a bit sketchy. I put a call into the council and spoke to the archive administrator and he reckons it's a problem with the switch over to digital records. A fair bit of data got lost or corrupted from back in the day."

"Right, let's focus on the tasks at hand," Tom said. "Eric, I want you and Danny to keep on looking for Katy. Both of you go and see the father. Find out if he's had contact from her. Likewise, establish if Katy's issues with the mother's boyfriend are relevant."

Eric glanced across the room and saw Danny roll his eyes, ensuring first that Tom didn't see him do it. He then leaned in and whispered something to Kerry which made her giggle. Eric felt a pang of jealousy. Kerry glanced over and saw him looking and he averted his eyes a second too late.

"Cassie," Tom continued, "chase up your contact at the shelter. Do what you can but I understand we don't want any hostility to or from the staff. Kerry, I want you working on background; breakdown of Tony Shears, updated bearing in mind what we think he and his brother might have been up to recently. Callum Wardby, speak to his probation officer, see what they make of him. And while you're digging around, Katy's family, the mother, her boyfriend and the biological father.

Anything and everything you can find." He looked around the team. "I know it seems like we are operating a scattergun here, but one or more of these people knows what has happened to Katy along with who killed Simon and why? If they're related, it will become clear and, if not, we'll find Katy and catch a killer." He took on a stern expression. "One more thing, none of this information leaves this room without either my or the DCI's express permission. Understood?"

The general murmur of agreement could be heard and everyone set about preparing their tasks.

Cassie hovered by Eric's desk until the others had moved off and then she leaned into him, so only they could hear one another.

"What is it about Tramp Terry?"

He looked at her blankly. "What do you mean? I told you what I know."

"Yes, I don't doubt that," she said. "But I want to know what it is you *didn't* say?"

He felt her stare boring into him, forcing him to break eye contact. He shrugged.

"Come on, Eric. It's just you and me," she said, glancing around. "You know I'll get it out of you eventually."

He took a breath, checking no one else was listening. Tom and Tamara were deep in conversation whereas everyone else was busy setting themselves up. He shook his head.

"It's nothing, really."

"Then tell me," Cassie pressed.

Sighing, he winced. "Look, when I was a kid… I wasn't so…"

"Boring?"

He shook his head, frowning.

"Short?" she asked; Eric, increasingly annoyed, sighed. "Irritating?"

He glared at her and she held her hands up by way of an apology.

"Go on, Eric," she said. "I'll be serious. What is it?"

"Me and the guys… some of the guys, back when we were at school… used to be a bit wild."

Cassie chuckled. "You shock me, Eric! I can't see you ever being wild."

Eric felt awkward, embarrassed. "Wild by my standards, anyway. It's just… Tramp Terry…"

"What about him?"

"We used to be quite mean to him."

"How?"

He shrugged. "We'd see him a fair bit when he was in the area. He used to come by the local convenience store to where we would hang out outside. Sometimes we would shout at him, make fun of him and stuff."

"You used to abuse a homeless guy!" Cassie said, grinning. "You? Shame on you, Eric Collet."

He waved his hands at her, urging her to be

quiet as Kerry looked over at them, suspicion in her expression. Eric lowered his voice.

"Look, I'm not proud of it. Later, when I was walking the streets, in uniform, I met him and found him to be a really lovely bloke."

"Did he recognise you?"

Eric shook his head. "No, he can't have done. I tried to make it up to him, buying him food and stuff, but he'd never take anything off me. He was a decent bloke. One day he insisted on buying me a coffee. Can you believe it? It only made me feel worse."

Cassie placed a hand on his shoulder and squeezed gently. "I'm sure if you meet him again, he'll think you're a decent bloke too, Eric."

CHAPTER NINETEEN

Just off Wodehouse Road in Old Hunstanton was an unadopted shingle track named Smuggler's Lane. Barely wide enough for a modern car to pass down it, it petered out into a pedestrian track, overgrown with vegetation, and was used by local people as a cut through to get to the golf course and the golden sands beyond. The lane was short and gave access to only a handful of houses, some of the oldest in the settlement. Had he not known what he was looking for, Tom could easily have missed the Westfield family home.

It was a substantial, detached Victorian villa and, although more recent developments had sprung up around it, this house lay in a secluded plot hemmed in by mature trees providing a thick canopy to conceal the property from prying eyes. A wooden five-bar gate lay across the shingle-lined driveway, now pitted with pools of muddy water and heavily overgrown by grass and weeds. The gate wouldn't budge and Tom could see it had dropped on its hinges, burying the unsupported end into the ground, and was pretty much immovable.

There were no streetlights along the track, unsurprisingly, seeing as the owners of the few properties here would need to pay for the installation. It was probably a safe bet they didn't desire it anyway, taking advantage of the rural feel to the location of their homes. The passing clouds revealed a near full moon, casting the house in an eerie glow. Tom could feel the mist hanging in the air. He heard the odd muted sound of a car drive past as someone came home from work. Aside from going to the golf club, there was no reason for anyone to pass down this way, with the A149 passing through the edge of the village and taking traffic along the coast.

Testing the gate could support his weight, Tom climbed over. The breeze passing through the trees overhead whistled. Many of the trees were varying species of pine, evergreen, despite the onset of winter. The house was semi-derelict. Several of the windows were boarded over, the single panes likely cracked or broken through a mixture of age or storms. The roof was intact and Tom saw the moonlight glinting off the moisture condensing on the clay roof tiles, an abundance of moss growing over them and down into the guttering.

No one had lived in this house for a very long time.

Moving around to the rear, the house had a double-storey dog-leg extension and an orangery off that at the far end. The glass of the orangery was largely missing with only a handful of roof panes still in place. The frame had buckled slightly as the brick base appeared to have shifted. Over time the glass had twisted and fallen in. In places towering weeds grew shoulder high inside but Tom could still make out the geometric pattern of the tiled floor, itself cracked and broken.

The house was a snapshot of the past; a forgotten time capsule left surrounded and unloved as modernity crept forward around it. Realising he had nothing to gain from exploring further, he made his way around to the front of the house. Car headlights illuminated part of the front garden; a car had pulled up behind Tom's. A figure passed through the beam, coming to stand at the gate.

"Can I help you with something?" Tom walked towards him, taking out his identification. "You've blocked access to my drive," he said, politely, but evidently irritated.

"Sorry about that," Tom said, reaching the gate and looking past his car. The angle of entry to the man's drive was tight due to Tom's parking. In the dark, he hadn't realised. "I'll get it moved."

"What are you doing in there?" the man asked. "Are you another developer or something?"

Tom smiled. "No," he said, showing him his warrant card. "Police."

"Crikey. Is everything all right?"

The man sounded concerned at his presence. Tom climbed back over the gate.

"Nothing to worry about. Is that your house?" he asked, pointing to the driveway he was partially blocking.

"Yes."

"Lived here long?"

"Oh..." his brow furrowed in concentration. "Since the 90s. I'm awful with dates. Forget my wedding anniversary every year."

Tom indicated the house behind him. "You don't happen to know the owners or what happened to them?"

His concentration deepened. "Um... yes, well... there was someone living there when we moved in. A woman, I think. Sally will know better," he said, turning to his car and beckoning his wife out. She opened the passenger door and leaned out. "Sally, love, who used to live here in Holly Cottage?"

His wife got out and came to join them, hugging her arms about her body having left the warmth of the car.

"There was a woman there at the time, wasn't there?"

She nodded. "Had a daughter as well, I think," Sally said, smiling a greeting at Tom, curious to know what this was about.

"It's the police, love," her husband said, and she nodded, surprised.

"She moved out soon after we got here though."

"Where did she go?" Tom asked.

They both exchanged a look and the man shrugged. "Never really knew them to be fair. Kept to themselves, didn't they love?"

"Yes. She was quite strange though, as I recall," Sally said. "The little girl was quite sweet."

"How old was she? The girl, I mean?" Tom asked.

"Hard to say," Sally said. "Children always look older than you think, don't they?"

"And we don't have kids of our own," he said, regretfully. "Hard to gauge. Probably a teen though, wouldn't you say?" He turned to his wife.

"Younger than that." Her husband rocked his head from side to side, suggesting she might be right. "Not into double figures."

"Do you remember either of their names?"

They both shook their heads. "Sorry," Sally said, sensing his disappointment, "but we never knew them and we had so much renovating to do with our house, it was a good year before we made any effort in getting to know people around us. And they'd gone by then." She looked at the house, an abandoned home in the darkness. "It seems such a shame with all these people sleeping rough." She shuddered. "Especially at this time of the year."

Tom was disappointed. Another dead end.

"Do you remember anything about them at all? Did they have any visitors or do anything that stood out?" It was a long shot, but he had to ask.

Sally looked perplexed, slowly shaking her head as she looked at her husband. His face lit up.

"Come to think about it," he touched Tom's forearm excitedly, "it's nothing to do with back then, but you're not the only person who's been nosing around the house recently."

Tom was interested. "Tell me."

"There was that man I told you about, love, do you remember? Last week."

"The week before," she said, correcting him before looking at Tom. "But I didn't see him."

"No… he was hanging around the front of the house when I came home from the golf club social." He looked concerned. "Strange fellow. He had no business being there that I could see."

"When was this?"

He thought hard. "Would have been around quarter to ten… a week ago Tuesday."

"Two weeks," Sally said, rolling her eyes.

"Two weeks ago, Tuesday," he said, nodding.

"What was he doing?" Tom asked.

He shrugged. "Nothing. Standing in the dark, staring at the house, right about where you are now. It was dark and he gave me the fright of my life, I can tell you."

Sally leaned in towards Tom. "He's not great in the dark, my husband."

He was indignant but agreed.

"Did you speak to him?"

"No," he said, shaking his head. "I hadn't reached the end of the path," he said, pointing to the cut through to his right, "before he got on his bike and pedalled away."

This really caught Tom's attention.

"He was riding a bike?"

"Yes, one of those old squeaky things with no gears."

"Can you describe him to me?"

Exhaling deeply, he thought about it. "Hard to say… it was very dark."

"Anything you can recall might be useful."

"Um… he was tall… white. He had a big overcoat on. Like one of those bridge coats they used to wear in the merchant navy, high collar and big lapels you can fold across to block out the cold. His trousers were tucked into his socks… big socks, thick."

"Facial features?"

"Bearded… I think, wispy, but as I say, it's hard

to tell. He had a cap on. One of those old Baker Boy ones like they wear on the telly… in that show we watch with what's his name in," he said, looking at his wife for support.

"Oh yes, I know the one you mean; the little Irish fella," she said, and her husband nodded. "What's his name?"

"I don't know love."

"That's great," Tom said. "I get the picture, don't worry. Did he leave because you saw him or was he going anyway?"

"He glanced my way, and he did look like he was in a hurry, so maybe he was up to something and I scared him off." His expression clouded. "Is he who you're looking for? What's he done?"

Tom smiled. "No, don't worry. I was here for background purposes, that's all. Absolutely nothing for you to be concerned with. It's probably unrelated."

"Oh, good," he said, cheerily. "For a second there I was a bit worried."

"Nothing to worry about. I assure you. Tell me, would you recognise him if you saw him again?"

He shrugged. "If he was on his bike, probably. Why do you ask?"

Tom smiled again, taking out a contact card. He passed it to him. "If he returns, please could you give me a call. Don't approach him, just call me."

The couple looked confused. Tom sought to reassure them. "He's a possible witness. I wouldn't want to scare him away."

"Oh… a witness. Right you are," he said, holding the card aloft and glancing at his wife beside him. "We'll keep an eye out, hey love?"

She smiled.

"I'll shift my car for you," Tom said, thanking them for their help. "And please do call me, whatever time of the day or night."

They promised him they would, but Tom doubted the individual would return again. Turning away, he had a thought.

"One more thing," he asked. "Before, when you asked me what I was doing, you asked if I was a developer."

"Yes," he said, nodding.

"You actually said *another developer*."

"Yes, there was a chap here yesterday doing a brief valuation survey. A big man, sporting a lot of… what do the kids say… bling, is it?"

"I don't suppose you caught his name?"

He shook his head. "Sorry, no. He was looking to modernise the house though."

"I hope they don't want to knock it down and build several houses on the site," Sally said. "The lane can't deal with more houses."

Her husband patted her on the arm. "Don't worry. He said he was looking to renovate rather than build again."

Sally nodded and then chuckled. "Odd though, isn't it. We've not seen hide nor hair of anyone around the house for years and now there's been three in a couple of weeks."

Tom smiled. "Coincidence can be surprising."

Sally shivered, feeling the cold. She elbowed her husband. "Give me the keys and I'll get inside."

Tom walked to his car and he couldn't help but wonder if the elusive Terence Westfield had revisited his family home. Was he arranging a sale after all this time? As far as they knew, the house still belonged to him, so why would he stand at the entrance but not go in? For that matter, why would he choose to live rough if he had a house like this to call home? They were missing something about this man and whatever went on in and around the people who used to live in this house, and he wanted to know what it was.

Cassie slipped into a parking space at the end of Hunstanton high street. The vast majority of shops had closed up for the day, even the cafes were now in darkness. In the summer, businesses tended to remain open as footfall was high but during the off-season everything was different. The town almost seemed to go into hibernation. She switched the engine off, released her seatbelt and relaxed into the seat for the wait.

The shelter would open its doors soon and she had decided to try and catch Mark on his way in. If she was lucky, maybe their target would be there as well and she could kill two birds with one stone. It was a quarter to six and Cassie saw a couple of people hovering around the alley which gave way to the homeless shelter at the rear. Both of them were female and Cassie was genuinely surprised at how young they looked. Even though sleeping rough tended to age people, in their cases they looked too young to be on the streets.

She took a breath and sighed. "There but for the grace of God, go I," she said quietly, contemplating what could happen to you to wind up living rough. As much as most people think it would never happen to them, in reality it would only take a series of events and perhaps an unexpected illness and many people could find themselves on their uppers.

Mark rounded the corner, carrier bags in hand and a backpack over his shoulders, a rolled-up sleeping bag strapped to the top. She got out and he spotted her immediately, slowing his pace. She waited for him and once he was within comfortable earshot his face split into a grin.

"Fancy meeting you here again," he said,

beaming as he came to stand in front of her. "Anyone would think you were on the streets too."

"How are you keeping, Mark?"

He shrugged. "Been better, been colder," he said, sniffing and glancing towards the alley. The two women were watching them talk but trying not to make it obvious. "Are you looking for me?"

"Indirectly. I was hoping you had some joy with what we talked about?"

He glanced nervously past her. "Yeah, well you could have picked a better moment, you know?"

Cassie looked over her shoulder. "What's up?"

Mark cocked his head. "You're kinda cramping my style."

"Oh, I see," she said, smiling. "Sorry. I'll get out of your way soon enough."

"Please do. If they think I'm really pally with you..."

"They might think we're together?" Cassie said, scoffing.

"Hey!" Mark was indignant. "You could do a lot worse than Mark Oatley."

"I don't doubt it," Cassie said. The two women moved off and Mark frowned.

"Ah... Michelle's opened up. Can we make this fast?"

"Sure. What have you got for me?"

He looked at her, pensive. "Not a lot, I'm afraid. I

asked around, but no one seems to have any problems." He hesitated, winced and nodded as if he was responding to his own internal monologue. "No problems beyond what we've all got going on anyway."

"I see," Cassie said. "You wouldn't happen to know Terence Westfield, would you?"

Mark was surprised. "Terence… I know old Terry, if that's who you mean?"

"Maybe. Tell me about him."

Mark exhaled through tight lips, shrugging. "All right kind of guy, I suppose. He keeps to himself a lot. I don't really have much in common with him. He's not like the rest of us, not really."

"How do you mean?"

"Well… he's not an addict for one thing. He doesn't touch a drop of alcohol… and don't make me laugh by mentioning anything to do with drugs."

"How long have you known him?"

"He's always been around, at least, from time to time. He cycles around on that old bike of his." Mark nodded towards the shelter. "Michelle let's him keep the bike in the yard out back, so it doesn't get nicked, 'cos it would if he left it outside. Some little scrote would throw it in the sea just for a laugh."

"Is he around at the moment?"

"Can't say I've seen him, not for the last couple

of weeks." Mark pursed his lips, his expression focussed. "Mind you..."

"Mind you... what?"

"He was around... and then he stopped coming. It struck me as odd at the time, because you can usually set your watch by him. Terry's methodical, you know, studious? A creature of routine... unlike most of us who go with the wind whenever and whichever way it's blowing."

"When did you last see him?"

Mark met her gaze, took a breath and then looked away.

"It's important, Mark." She angled her head to catch his eye. He seemed uncertain. "Honestly. He might be in trouble and I can help him. I promise I'm on the level."

Mark sighed, his shoulders sagging. "Look, I don't think I can help you even though I might want to. And I do... want to help, that is." He looked at her cynical expression and raised his hands defensively. "It was weeks ago, and he's not been about since. I've no idea where he is now."

Cassie shook her head. "Really?"

"Really, I don't!"

"Okay, when did you last see him and please be specific?"

He thought about it, shaking his head. "Probably... ten days ago."

"Probably is not specific, Mark."

He scoffed. "I don't exactly keep a bloody diary, do I? I'll check the CCTV in my office, shall I?"

Cassie took a deep breath. "Right, Terry, what was his state of mind? Compared to what you'd expect, was he different to usual?"

"Yes, he was… withdrawn. Worried, perhaps?" Mark said. "And old Terry is one of the brighter ones. You know, he's really optimistic as opposed to most of us who are, let's face it, miserable sods much of the time. Terry's also a true gent."

"What do you know about him? Where does he go when he leaves the shelter? I mean, you all have somewhere you go to during the day, right?"

"We go our separate ways."

Cassie was displeased with the answer.

"You can pout at me all you like, Columbo, but it's true! Most people don't say where they're going. We all have our own little hideaways to get us through the day… and often you don't have space to share. Know what I mean?"

"All right, but if you see him, I want to know about it," she said, thrusting her contact card into his hand. He took it and put it in his pocket before glancing towards the shelter.

"Can I go? I'm hungry and they'll be serving up in a minute."

She nodded and he picked up the bags at his feet.

"You'll get in touch if you see him, yes?" she

called after him. He turned to face her, walking backwards and winked, clicking his tongue against the roof of his mouth as he did so. "There's no chance you'll be picking up the phone is there, Mark?" she said under her breath, opening her car door and getting in. She took out her mobile to call Tom to give him an update.

"Hey, Cassie. How are you getting on?"

She looked towards the shelter. "No joy. Tramp Terry has been around but not in the last ten days or so…"

Tom must have picked up on her reticence, questioning it.

"What's up, Cassie?"

"I don't know… something. I think my contact was off, and I don't know why."

"Off?"

"Helpful but not, at the same time."

"Push him."

"You didn't want me to ruffle the feathers of the staff—"

"Maybe it's time to."

Cassie hung up, getting back out of the car. A gust of wind caught her and she smelled rain on the breeze. Picking up the pace, she hurried down the alley and into the shelter. Walking into the main hall, the residents there for the night were queuing at the service hatch. A couple of others were already at the tables eating in silence. There was no sign of Mark. Michelle spotted her and came over, wiping her palms on her apron.

"DS Knight," she said smiling. "Back again so soon?"

"Yes," Cassie said, scanning the line of people, wondering if Mark had gone to use the toilet or claim his bed. "I was hoping to have a word with Mark."

Michelle cocked her head, following Cassie's eye line. "Mark? I've not seen him yet today."

Cassie was shocked. "But I was only speaking to him a minute ago, outside."

"Oh…" Michelle said, looking around. "Sorry, he's not come in. Are you sure it was Mark?"

Cassie smiled. "Oh, maybe I was… mistaken," she said, thanking Michelle and turning to leave. She'd been played by Mark. The question was, why?

CHAPTER TWENTY

Eriç and Danny arrived to find the boat yard still open. There were many small to midsize boats dragged up and out of the water. A large boat shed was the only source of illumination, the hangar-style doors were open and the sound of machine tools could be heard. Danny nodded in that direction and the two of them made their way across the open ground from the small car park. Danny cursed as he put his foot in a puddle deeper than he'd anticipated.

"Oh, to hell with this," he muttered.

"Sensible shoes will be on your Christmas list this year then?"

Danny met his eye, shaking the muddy water off his foot as he walked, but didn't comment. Reaching the entrance to the boat shed, they could see one man working. A boat was raised, the man was sanding back the hull with a palm sander. Wearing goggles, a respirator and ear defenders, he hadn't seen or heard their arrival. They entered, Danny not wasting any time in moving to the power point and switching off the sander. The machine died and the man stopped, momentarily puzzled before turning to see them.

Putting the sander down, he unclipped the respirator and set it aside on a small trestle table next to him. He sniffed, took off the ear defenders followed quickly by the goggles. Despite the cool breeze, he was sweating and he wiped his brow with his forearm.

"You could have just waved or something," he said accusingly.

"Is that any way to greet a prospective client?" Danny asked. Eric glanced sideways at him but said nothing. "Are you Karl Roper?"

He nodded. "Aye, that's me," he said, looking them both up and down, "and you two aren't clients."

Danny smiled, then shook his head. "No, we're police."

Karl sighed. "I should have known."

"Why's that?" Eric asked.

"The cut of your suits," Karl said. Eric and Danny looked at their choice of clothing. "Off the rack. Cheap material." Eric arched his eyebrows.

Karl held up a hand by way of apology. "No offence meant."

Danny was clearly bothered though. "Are you a tailoring aficionado as well as a master boat builder?"

Karl shook his head, ignoring the sarcasm and reaching for a rag to wipe his hands with. "I'm neither. I had a Saturday job in River Island once though; picked up a few things."

"Saturday job?" Danny asked, smiling mockingly.

Karl nodded. "A long time ago."

"And now you work on boats?" Eric asked.

"Yep. Now I work on boats. Is there something I can do for you gentlemen?"

He seemed displeased by their presence. He was clearly used to seeing the police and had no love for them.

Eric took a step forward, smiling, whereas Danny stood with his hands in his pockets, eyeing Karl menacingly.

"We were wondering when you last saw your daughter?"

"Katy?"

Eric nodded and Karl blew out his cheeks, tossing the rag aside and resting his hands on his hips. He shook his head. "I've not seen Katy for… a long time. Months."

"Can you be more precise?" Eric asked. Danny

moved to stand on Karl's left side, staring at him hard. Eric found the aggressive stance unhelpful, but Danny had a different approach to his own. Karl's gaze followed Danny. He didn't seem intimidated.

"Probably some time back in the spring; end of April, early May, I'd guess. Why do you ask?"

"You've not seen her more recently?" Eric asked.

"No."

"You sure?" Danny asked. Karl frowned at him, shaking his head. "Sure, sure?"

Karl laughed. "What the hell is this about? Has Katy done something wrong?"

Eric took Karl Roper's measure. He was almost six foot tall, slim but athletic. Working on boats seemed to help keep him in shape as Eric could see good muscle definition in his arms and chest. The way he carried himself, his confidence, demonstrated to Eric that he could likely handle himself.

"We're looking for Katy," Eric said. "She's… absconded from her foster home."

Karl exhaled dismissively, shaking his head in frustration. "Well, I'm not surprised to hear that."

"Really?" Eric asked. "Why not?"

He leaned against the hull of the boat he was working on, folding his arms across his chest and glancing between them. He focussed on Danny, tilting his head in his direction but speaking to Eric.

"This good cop, bad cop routine is a little tired." He arched his eyebrows at Danny. "You need to get a slightly more modern vibe going, my friend, because you're not scaring anyone."

Danny's shoulders sagged and Eric wondered if the bubble of bravado had been burst.

"Karl, it's important we find your daughter."

"How long has she been gone?" he asked.

"A few days."

"And I'm only hearing about it now?"

Danny stepped forward. "You've got no legal claim to her guardianship. You gave that up because you preferred shooting up, so why should you be told?"

Eric saw a gleam in Danny's eyes. He'd enjoyed that. Karl, on the other hand, was annoyed. He pointed an accusatory finger at Danny.

"That was a long time ago, and I've moved on."

"It's a pity your ex and your daughter haven't been able to," Danny said,

Karl shook his head. "Look, Sarah and me… we were toxic for one another." He looked pained, remembering the past. "Every day was all about one thing, getting the next fix… getting the money to pay for the next fix."

"Out at all times of the day and night, burgling and robbing," Danny said.

"I'll bet your colleagues don't like you," Karl

said directly to Danny. Eric didn't comment. "Despite whatever they say to your face."

Danny sneered at him.

"And now?" Eric asked, keen to keep the focus on Katy. "You're clean, right?"

"Yeah, I'm clean. Three years, two months…" he looked up, doing a quick calculation in his head, "and twenty-two days. Give or take."

"Do you get a medal for that or is it a sew-on patch?" Danny asked. Eric glared at him this time and Danny noticed, licking his bottom lip and averting his eye from Eric's stern look.

"Have you not thought to get yourself back into Katy's life?" Eric asked, genuinely interested. Anyone who could break an extensive drug addiction and make a go of their life had always impressed him.

"I'll not lie and say I've thought about it," he said, "but there's been so much water under the bridge… and I barely know the girl. What a lousy father I've been. Why would she give me the time of day?"

"You might be surprised," Eric said. "I've not had a father around for most of my life… and I'd love it if I had the chance." He saw Danny shake his head in the corner of his eye but ignored him. "Maybe it'd go better than you think."

Danny cut in. "Heart-warming. Listen, Karl, you said you last saw her in spring?"

Karl nodded.

"What did she want?"

"Money, I think," he said, glancing at Eric. "A chip off the old block. Find someone with money and try to squeeze it out of them. Classic manipulation, pull on the heartstrings and use emotional blackmail."

"So, she was shaking you down?" Eric asked. He nodded glumly.

"Did you give it to her?"

"Of course. I'm a lousy father, but I still love her."

"Did she not come back?" Eric asked. Karl looked at him blankly. "If you find a successful mark, you always go back. Right?"

"Not this time… I-I told her not to come back."

"Why?"

"Does it matter?" Karl said, turning his back on them and picking at his equipment on the table next to him. They waited for an answer, one that Karl eventually offered. "Look, I'm not exactly fatherly material, you know? I walked out on her, leaving her with her junkie, schizo mum." He looked between them. "What kind of father does that?"

"A shit one," Danny said flatly.

Karl looked at him, but didn't argue, and merely nodded. "Yeah, a shit one," he said quietly. "And you know what's worse than that?" Eric gestured for him to continue. "What's worse is that I was worried that even if I got myself clean and brought Katy with me, she'd turn out just like her mother, and I couldn't live with that. Proper selfish. That's me."

"Turn out like her mother? In what way?"

"Bloody mental… in that way."

"Sarah is a schizophrenic," Eric said.

Karl nodded. "Yep… have you any idea what it's like living with someone who suffers with that?" Eric shook his head. "Well, let me tell you, it's a nightmare. If Sarah forgot to take her meds… or chose not to take them, then it was just awful. Even with the medication, she was something else. From what she used to tell me about her mother and what it was like for her growing up… it seems to run in the family." He shook his head, his lips curling into a sneering smile. "I couldn't stay with that… and like mother like daughter."

"Is Katy schizophrenic?" Eric asked. "I'm not aware of that—"

"As I said, like mother like daughter." He shrugged. "Who knows, but I wasn't sticking around to find out."

Danny scoffed. "Some hero you are."

By now, Karl was absently toying with a chisel, and glaring at Danny, who seemed to enjoy having got under his skin. He was meeting Karl's eye, almost silently goading him into making a threatening move. Karl's eyes flicked towards Eric who nodded at the chisel and he put it down.

"I'm no hero, and never claimed to be. I get by, day by day."

Eric felt relieved as the tension dissipated. "So, you told Katy not to come back?"

"Aye. Said she wasn't welcome and that I had nothing else for her." He looked around. "As you can see, I don't have a lot going for me." Glancing at Danny, he smiled, "It's not like I'm a master craftsman or anything. I'm an odd-job guy. One day I'm sanding," he indicated the boat he was working on, "and the next I'm unclogging the drains. But the pay is regular, and I get to spend time outside." He arched his eyebrows, looking at both of them in turn. "And I'm grateful for what I have."

"Well, I certainly would be," Danny said, smiling broadly and looking at Eric. "Heard enough?"

Eric ignored him. "Do you happen to know Simon Shears?"

If the name meant anything to him, then Karl didn't show it. He shrugged. "Can't say I do. Why?"

"Because he was murdered a couple of days ago, that's why," Danny said.

"Oh right… that guy over in Fring? Yeah, I heard about that. Weird one, yeah."

"Most murders are," Eric said, "in one way or another."

"Why do you ask?"

"He was a dealer," Eric said. "I thought you might know him."

Karl shook his head. "Like I said, it was a long time ago. The dealers I used to go to are likely in prison or dead by now."

"Why would you say that?" Eric asked.

Karl smiled. "Just a throwaway comment… but dealers come and go. If you know one then you likely know three or four. But I didn't know… what was his name again?"

"Simon Shears."

Karl looked momentarily skyward and shook his head again. "No, doesn't ring any bells."

"What about Sarah, do you ever see her?"

"Nah… we've not spoken in years, and I'd cross the street to avoid her if I did."

Eric nodded. "So, you don't know her boyfriend?"

He shrugged. "Can't say I do… or care."

"Okay," Eric said, meeting Danny's gaze. "Shall we go?"

"I thought you'd never say," Danny said. Looking at Karl, he pointed at him. "Keep your nose clean… no pun intended, or we'll be back."

Karl kept a straight face, reaching for his ear defenders, he slipped them on and turned his back on them. The sander fired up again before they'd made it out into the night.

"You know, that wasn't very helpful of you in there," Eric said.

Danny dismissed the comment with a wave of his hand. "Ah… guys like that need a bit of a slap – metaphorically speaking – otherwise they walk all over you."

Eric disagreed but it wasn't a conversation he felt like having.

CHAPTER TWENTY-ONE

THE SOUND of conversation came to him as Tom opened the front door, adult conversation punctuated with familiar giggles that could only be Saffy. Hanging his coat on the newel at the foot of the stairs, he made his way through into the kitchen. It took a moment for them to see him. Alice, her father and Saffy were sitting around the dining table playing a game of cards; one of Saffy's by the look of it.

Ian slammed his card down on the table, exclaiming "I win!"

"No, you don't!" Saffy told him, reaching across and jabbing her forefinger against his card. "Yours only has a health point score of one hundred and mine has two hundred plus one hundred and forty damage points!"

Ian looked perplexed. Tom thoroughly understood why. Saffy could easily make up the rules as she went along, and no sane adult would be any the wiser.

"So… what does that mean?"

"I have a Challizar," Saffy said, pointing to the mythical creature depicted on her card.

"I repeat," Ian said, looking at Alice for help, "what does that mean?"

"It means you lose, Pops," Saffy said gleefully.

They spotted Tom's arrival, turning to him, all smiles. It was great to see Alice and her father interacting positively. Children often facilitated that; shared pleasure in something they couldn't fight over.

"Tom," Ian said, holding his hands up in surrender, "save me from this monster you've created. She's an absolute demon at this game. If she carries these skills into the business world, she'll wipe the floor with her competition." Saffy beamed at the description, nodding furiously.

"It's true, I will."

Alice rose from the table and came over to say hello. He put his arm around her and she kissed him.

"I've got food for you in the fridge. I'll just heat it through. Are you staying or—?"

"No, sorry," Tom said, "I have to go back in. How's your mum?"

Alice put the covered plate into the microwave and set the timer, looking back at him as she pressed start. "Better today. With control over her own painkillers, she's not really with it, but she's comfortable at least."

"That's good."

Tom looked over at Ian and his granddaughter who appeared to be getting on famously. Alice went across and tapped Saffy on the shoulder.

"Time for bed, young lady."

Saffy pouted, much as she did most days. "But I'm playing with Pops."

Ian smiled, putting his cards down on the table. "I think I'm well beaten, my dear. I'm not sure how it happened because I have no idea what is going on, but well beaten, I have been."

"Another game?" Saffy asked.

"No chance, Sapphire Janssen!" Alice said firmly.

"Oh, Mum… you are such a killjoy."

Alice raised her eyebrows and Saffy feigned contrition.

"Where did you hear that phrase?" Alice asked, glancing at Tom.

"Not from me!" he said, smiling. "But I can hazard a guess."

"No need," Alice said. "I'll have words with your Aunty Cass later." Saffy grinned. "Now, up to bed. Clean your teeth and I'll be up to read with you once you're in your PJs."

Saffy hopped down from her seat, ran around the table and flung herself into her grandfather's arms. He was caught off guard and the exchange seemed awkward. After a moment, he encircled her and gently patted her back before she slipped out of his grasp and ran to Tom, doing the same.

"Goodnight, Munchkin," he said. Saffy smiled up at him and then took off at a run upstairs. Russell, their terrier, lifted his head from his bed in the corner, conscious of not wanting to miss anything, got up and trotted after her. They would find him asleep at the foot of the bed later no doubt.

"You've got a lovely little girl there, Alice," Ian said. "Precocious… and in need of discipline, but lovely nonetheless."

"That was always your answer to everything, wasn't it, Dad; discipline."

Ian looked offended. "I just think she would benefit from a stay in a boarding school, that one."

"Over my dead body!" Alice stated firmly, turning as the microwave pinged. Tom waved her towards the dining table.

"You sit down, I'll get it."

Alice did so, returning to the table and sitting in Saffy's chair opposite her father.

"We're raising Saffy to be a confident individual

who embraces new things and tries her hand at anything she takes a fancy to –"

"Flighty… that's what she'll be."

"Nonsense. She'll be able to stand on her own two feet and won't live on her knees."

Ian snorted, shaking his head. "New Age nonsense."

"And sending her away to a boarding school at primary age will knock the enthusiasm out of her," Alice said, undeterred. "I don't want a carbon cut-out of a daughter. She'll be her own person."

"Pah! That's your mother filling your head with nonsense, that's what that is."

Now Tom could see Alice's irritation growing.

"Yes, Saffy should conform to stereotypes and find herself a successful man to take care of her, right, Dad?"

"When you say it like that, it sounds wrong, but it's been that way for generations."

"Then it's about time for a change," Alice countered. Tom decided to eat at the breakfast bar, steering well clear of what he could see coming. Father and daughter were actually very similar in many ways, opinions on certain matters aside.

Ian shook his head, unaware of the offence his views fostered in his daughter. "You're just going to make her life harder than it need be."

Alice nodded. "Much better for her to marry someone, have children, wait twenty-five years and watch her husband bugger off with another woman half her age…"

Ian looked away, pursing his lips.

"How is Elena?"

"Ewelina," Ian corrected her. "And I suppose we couldn't dance around not mentioning her for much longer, could we?" Alice pressed her tongue into her cheek, arching her eyebrows momentarily. "She's well, thank you for asking."

"Still working in… fashion, isn't it?"

"Yes, she is."

"And presumably, she's still a couple of months younger than me?" Alice asked.

Ian avoided her gaze, glancing nervously up at Tom. He cocked his head, smiling, embarrassed. "Razor-sharp tongue, this one," he said, inclining his head towards Alice and clearing his throat.

"Oh, I know," Tom said between mouthfuls.

"I get it from my mother," Alice said. Ian didn't object. "How's the curry, Tom?"

"Hot, but I like it."

"Spice gives me heartburn," Ian said, bumping his closed fist gently against his chest.

"Oh… sorry, I forgot," Alice said, rising. "I'll get you some tablets from the bathroom. I'll bring them down after I've put Saffy to bed. It shouldn't be more than half an hour."

Passing Tom, she leaned in and kissed his cheek.

"I'll be gone by the time you're down," he told her. "I'll try not to be too late home."

"It's okay," she said, leaving a trailing hand on his forearm before she went upstairs.

Ian sat back his seat, folding his arms across his chest. "Fiery one, Alice. A lot like her mother."

Tom smiled but didn't comment on either woman. "How long are you staying?"

Ian shrugged. "I'm not sure. A few days, probably. I thought I should come…" he looked at the door, half expecting Alice to appear, "but I'm not sure now whether it was a good idea."

"It's always a good idea to see your daughter… and your granddaughter."

Ian's face lit up. "She's great, isn't she?"

"I think so."

"The two of you are doing a grand job with her. I never liked her father… sorry, I didn't mean to… There I go again, putting my foot in it."

"That's okay," Tom said. Although Saffy wasn't his biological child, she still felt like his own and she called him Dad, so who cared? "I know what you meant."

Ian was silent for a few minutes, giving Tom the opportunity to finish his meal. It seemed like he had something on his mind.

"Tom, could I ask you something?"

Tom nodded.

"Do you think Alice is happy?"

"I'd like to think so, yes. Things have been pretty tough this past year, but overall, I'd say yes. Why do you ask?"

He didn't answer, dismissing the question with a casual wave of his left hand.

"And do you think… do you think she'll ever forgive me?"

That was a tough question to answer, not least because Alice had never explained her feelings regarding her father to Tom in any great detail. He hesitated.

"Your silence speaks volumes."

He looked dejected.

"I think there's a great deal of unresolved anger there… and a lot of pain."

"Hmm… that's not good for the soul," Ian said. "These are the people who get cancer, you know?" He faltered as he said the words, flushing red. "That's terribly crass… I didn't mean to cast judgement on her mother."

Tom held up a hand and smiled. "Don't worry, but I wouldn't say that in front of Alice, if you value your own life."

Ian chuckled briefly, then nodded solemnly. "I just meant that it's not good to hold on to too much animosity. The past can interfere with the present if you do, and life is so damned short."

Tom couldn't argue with the sentiment there.

Glancing at the clock, he needed to head back to the station for a team briefing.

"I'm sorry, I have to go," he said, rising and putting his plate in the dishwasher. Closing the door, he looked at his father-in-law earnestly. "If you wish to have a relationship with your daughter, the best thing you can do is give it time."

"You think I should leave?"

Tom shook his head. "Quite the opposite. You need to invest time into the relationship…" he noticed Ian stiffen, "and if she needs to vent, then you'll have to take it."

Ian blew out his cheeks. "That doesn't sound like much fun."

"No one said life would be easy."

"You sound like me."

Tom was perturbed by that. He hoped it wouldn't turn out that Alice had married someone who subconsciously reminded her of her father. Casting an eye over the man sitting before him, he doubted that was the case.

"I'll see you later."

Ian glanced up at him, smiling awkwardly.

"Thanks, Tom," he said. "I appreciate your honesty."

Tom left. It would be great if Alice could resolve her issues with her father, but there would need to be movement on both sides and Ian was right, Alice was angry. With her mother's illness so advanced, would there be enough emotional space for them to reconcile? He didn't know. If they couldn't find common ground, Tom hoped Ian would depart sooner rather than later, if for no other reason than for his wife's mental health.

CHAPTER TWENTY-TWO

Tom was pleased to find almost everyone waiting in the ops room for the evening briefing. Only Cassie and Danny Wilson were missing but they still had five minutes before they were scheduled to start. Cassie hurried into the room, throwing her coat across her desk and crossing to where Eric was sitting. Leaning on Danny's desk, she waved to Tom and tapped Eric on the shoulder as he moved to join Tom.

"Everything all right?" he asked her.

"Yeah, yeah," she said. "We've had the forensic reports back from Simon Shears' house and caravan. We've got nothing useful to work with."

Tom was surprised. "Nothing?"

"There are no digital records at either. The cameras in the main house all fed back to a portable hard drive but that's long gone." She shrugged. "Either someone knew Simon was dead and got there before us or he keeps the hard drive somewhere else. There was nothing at the scene. Multiple sets of fingerprints… but the clear sets that were identified didn't flash up on our system, aside from the two brothers anyway. And, as you suspected, Tony cleaned out the caravan so well that he left us nothing workable. I suppose we could strip it down and analyse carpet fibres and so on, but hell, we don't even know if it's a crime scene. I mean, if we knew categorically that someone had been killed there, then…"

"I get it, don't worry," Tom said, failing to hide his frustration. "Maybe something we have will prove useful later if we turn something else up."

He called them together for the briefing, Tamara arrived just in time, but she hovered at the back of the room. Danny Wilson had also made his way into ops and was sitting at his desk, Kerry Palmer next to him. He looked bothered, his face set in a frown.

"Are you okay, Danny?" Tom asked.

"Yes, sir. All good," he said.

"Right, who wants to go first?" Tom asked. Kerry raised her hand and Tom indicated for her to continue.

"I've been running through the backgrounds of everyone like you asked," she said. "The most notable mention is Gerry Clarke, Sarah Roper's boyfriend. We know of tension between him and Katy, and he has form for violence."

"Do you know where he is?" Tom asked.

"Wandsworth Prison," she said. "He got into a fracas down in London, put a guy in the hospital apparently. He was arraigned and the magistrate refused bail due to the viciousness of the attack and his previous record. He can't have been involved directly with Katy's disappearance because he was locked up."

"One down," Danny said under his breath.

"Well, we won't have to waste any time looking for him," Tom said. "Next?"

"Terence Westfield, sir," Kerry said. "He's quite a surprise. We already knew he has the title deeds on the family home over in Old Hunstanton along with his father's yard near Fring, but we didn't know much about him, so I thought I'd try and figure him out a bit."

"Good idea, Kerry," Tamara said. "What did you find out?"

"He used to be a lecturer at the University of East Anglia," she said. "He specialised in geology and taught classes there for years. I called the Uni this afternoon but no one there could remember him. I suppose it was a long time ago. It struck me as odd though; how does a man like that end up living on the streets?"

Everyone exchanged glances. It certainly challenged their preconceptions of those who lived rough.

Tamara looked at Tom. "Maybe I should ask David."

"Would he know him?" Tom asked.

Tamara shook her head. "No, it'd be way before his time, but he could ask around. Academics are known to be less transient than most professions. Once they find a faculty to work in that lets them explore their passions, they tend not to move often. Maybe someone there will remember him."

"It's worth a look."

"And then I have this," Kerry said, picking up a file from her desk and taking out some photos that looked a lot like screen prints taken from camera footage. She passed several copies to Eric and Danny beside her with the two of them passing them on. "Eric put Katy's photo out to media and we've had some feedback from the public. The usual, sightings that were impossible to corroborate along with a few names who might be able to help. I'm working through those, but I had a call this afternoon from a woman who's a supervisor in the Spar in Blakeney, the convenience store on Westgate Street."

"I know it," Tom said.

"Anyway, she was lovely and said she saw someone matching Katy's description arguing with a man outside the shop. I was sceptical because I'd already looked at three similar claims today, but she was adamant. I said I'd take a look and she emailed me the shop's CCTV footage. It's from a security camera mounted on the wall to the side of the entrance."

Tom stared at the footage. It wasn't the greatest resolution, but he couldn't deny the girl in the images did resemble Katy Roper. Eric drew a sharp intake of breath, turning and reaching for Danny who was having the same reaction. They both spoke at the same time.

"That's Karl Roper!"

Eric turned the image to face Tom, tapping the man seemingly arguing with the girl. He appeared to have her by the arm and she'd adopted an aggressive stance.

"Her father?" Tom asked.

Both Danny and Eric nodded. Danny exclaimed, "I knew he was lying to us."

"He said he hadn't had contact with Katy since spring," Eric said. "Danny's right. He definitely lied to us."

Tom glanced at Tamara and she nodded. "As soon as we're through here, the two of you go back to the boat yard and pick him up." They both nodded and Tom smiled at Kerry. "Good work, Kerry. Who's next with an update?"

Eric frowned, glancing at Danny. "Well, I was

going to tell you about Karl Roper, but I guess we can't take anything he told us as credible after seeing these," he said, holding the pictures aloft before tossing them to his desk.

"Don't worry about it," Tom said. "That's why we investigate. You'll be better placed next time."

Cassie raised a pointed finger and Tom nodded towards her.

"I followed up on my contact at the shelter, Mark. He was reluctant to speak to me about something, and I couldn't tease it out of him. He said he'd seen Terry around but not recently, not in the last ten days or so. As I say, he was holding back. I went into the shelter to speak to him again and Mark was nowhere to be seen. I saw him walk into the alley, heading for the shelter but he didn't go inside." She shrugged. "He must have gone straight down the other end and gone elsewhere."

Tom was puzzled. "What did you say to him?"

"Nothing controversial. I asked about Terence Westfield, that's all. It was the only reference that was different to previous exchanges."

Tom thought about it. "If they're friends and he knows where he is, maybe he's gone to tip him off?"

"The thought occurred," Cassie said. "But, if we don't know where either of them are, then it doesn't really matter, does it?"

Tom put his hands together, forming a tent,

touching fingertips to his lips. "So, if we can't find Terry… how do we find Mark?"

Cassie's brow furrowed. "He was hitting on a couple of women also staying at the shelter; accused me of cramping his style. They were paying attention to us chatting, so he'd likely prepared some of the groundwork."

"Do homeless people… like… fancy each other?" Danny asked.

"Of course, you dufus!" Cassie said. "People are people!"

"I guess so," he said. "I just thought they'd have more on their plate to deal with."

Cassie turned back to Tom. "Maybe I should speak to the women." She shrugged. "If they know where Mark hangs out during the day, he might go there if he's not staying at the shelter?"

"Good idea," Tom said. "Anything else?"

Everyone exchanged glances with one another and no one spoke up, so he called time on the briefing. Tamara came to join him at the front of the room, as Tom heard Danny muttering in the background.

"Seriously, can anyone else smell bananas?" he said, looking around his desk and frowning at Eric who splayed his hands wide.

"Not guilty."

"It can't still be lingering from yesterday,"

Danny said, running a hand through his hair. "I hate bananas!"

Tamara had her mobile in her hand and she followed Tom into his office. Perching herself on the edge of Tom's desk, she dialled David's number, set it on speaker and laid it on the desk. He answered quickly.

"Hi, love!" David's cheery voice came through.

"David, hi," Tamara said, "I've got you on speaker. I'm at work and I'm here with Tom."

"Hello, Tom," David said, adopting a more serious tone.

"Hi, David, sorry to trouble you but we need your help."

"Profiling?"

Tamara shook her head. "No, not this time. Nothing so entertaining for you I'm afraid. We're looking into a former lecturer at the UEA, Terence Westfield, likely known as Terry."

"That's strong detective work, guys," David said. "No wonder the two of you are in charge."

"Enough of that or I'll make you pay later," Tamara admonished him. "Look, I know it was before your time but could you do us a favour and ask some of your colleagues if they remember him?"

"Is this to do with the Shears case you're working?"

"It is... but can you keep that between us for now?"

"Of course, no problem," David said. "I'll make some calls... how about I—" he coughed, "—drop by yours later?"

Tamara picked up the phone, switching the speaker off. "Yeah, sure. We can have something to eat if you like... what? No... you'd have to bring it."

Tom felt a little awkward as the two of them finished their conversation. Tamara was smiling. It was heart-warming to see her so happy. He just wished he wasn't there feeling like a giant gooseberry.

"Bye, love," Tamara said, hanging up. Her smile faded as she looked at Tom. "Sorry."

"No problem. One thing," he said. She glanced at him quizzically. "Didn't you say he'd refused to come to yours because it was a mess?"

"Ah... yes. Well, absence makes the heart grow fonder... or desperate..." she shrugged "or something like that. If there's anything to glean from the UEA about Terence Westfield, David will find it."

ERIC AND DANNY arrived at the boat yard in Blakeney to find the lights still on in the shed and the same couple of cars parked out front along with a nearly new Range Rover that hadn't been there earlier in the day.

"Keen little beggar, isn't he? Working late," Danny said as they got out. Sounds emanated from within the boat shed. Danny buttoned up his overcoat, tilting his head from side to side, stretching the muscles to free himself up.

"Are you expecting trouble?" Eric asked.

"If I think he's lying to us again, I'll give him a slap. Only this time, I mean literally."

They entered the boat shed but the first person they saw wasn't Karl Roper but an older man. He was a short, barrel-chested man with almost white hair swept back from his forehead and dressed in red corduroy trousers and knitted jumper. Both had seen better days. He was the picture of shabby chic.

Eric took out his warrant card as he approached him. "DC Collet. We're looking for Karl, is he about?"

"I'm looking for him too!" the man said. "I'm Colin Briggs. This is my yard."

"Karl's not here?" Danny asked.

"Damn well should be! One of our clients was supposed to be meeting him half an hour ago to run through the laying-up procedure for their boat. The client showed... but here..." he waved his hand around in a circular motion in front of him, "everything's all open but of Karl there's no bloody sign."

Eric and Danny exchanged glances.

"He was here earlier," Eric said. "We spoke to him. Have you called him?"

Briggs nodded. "Of course. The call goes straight to voicemail. I've no idea where he's got to. His bloody car is outside."

Eric looked over his shoulder.

"The silver VW out there is his." Briggs shook his head. "I don't get it. He's always so reliable."

"Can you do me a favour?" Eric asked, handing him a contact card. "When he shows up, or if you hear from him, please can you let me know? Doesn't matter what time of the day or night, I'll pick up."

Briggs took the card and nodded. "Yes, of course." He frowned, offering Eric a wary look. "Is Karl in some kind of trouble?"

Eric smiled. "Just routine, Mr Briggs. Nothing to be concerned about."

Danny caught his attention. "Don't mention that we asked after him though, okay? Just give us a call."

Briggs seemed concerned but he nodded again and both detectives turned to leave, walking in silence until they were comfortably out of earshot. Then Eric spoke.

"What's he up to, do you reckon?"

"Karl?" Danny clarified. Eric nodded. "I don't know, but if you and I have let a killer walk away from right under our noses, we are up to our neck in it, my friend."

"No one else thought it was him. Don't worry, it'll be all right."

They reached the car and Danny looked across the roof at Eric.

"Well, if it all goes wrong, I'm blaming you."

"Me? How is it my fault?"

"You're too soft, Eric. Way too soft for this line of work." He must have seen Eric's face drop. "I don't mean any offence, mate."

"And yet you manage to deliver it almost every time you open your mouth."

"What's that?"

"Nothing. How's that smell of banana going?"

Danny nodded. "Yeah, fresh air has helped clear it, thankfully."

He got in and Eric took a lung full of air himself. He still couldn't figure out if Danny Wilson was merely full of brash bravado or simply full of something else entirely.

CHAPTER TWENTY-THREE

HUNSTANTON WAS QUIET. In the centre of town, the shops, cafes and bistros were closed with the only activity going on closer to the seafront with the arcades and amusement parks illuminating the lower green and the promenade. Footfall might be low in the off-season, but locals still ventured out. Cassie parked at the entrance to the alley leading to the shelter, drawing her coat around her as she got out, feeling the wind rattling between the buildings bringing the cold off the water.

The evening meal was almost over as she entered, the staff taking the plates into the kitchen and the residents, those who wanted to, were chatting quietly in small groups whereas others sat alone. Cassie scanned the group looking for the two particular faces. Several people noticed her interest and looked uncomfortable. Here, everyone knew everyone and an outsider especially in official-looking clothing made her stand out.

Michelle approached her, wiping her hands on her apron, and smiling.

"Good evening, DS Knight," she said. "Did you call?" She glanced into the kitchen. "No one told me you were coming."

"I didn't know I was coming either until just now." Cassie looked past her. "I guess Mark hasn't turned up?"

"No… which is odd. It's cold out there tonight." Michelle seemed pained. "I worry about the regulars on nights like this."

"May I speak to your residents?" Cassie asked. "I'll be cautious… and kind."

Michelle smiled and nodded, wary eyes watching her as she made her way into the room. Some of the people ignored her completely, wrapped up in their own world. For a moment, Cassie wondered what would need to happen in her life for her to end up using such a place. Frighteningly, it probably wouldn't take much.

On the edge of the makeshift dining area, she found who she was looking for, having not expected Mark to be there, she'd found the next best thing. One of the women eyed Cassie's approach, whispering something which made her companion glance in her direction before lowering her gaze again.

"Hello, ladies," Cassie said, coming to stand before them. Only one met her eye. She was older than her friend, perhaps in her thirties, but it was hard to tell. Her dark hair poked out from beneath her woollen hat, hanging to her shoulders in natural curls. She had a tanned complexion with a solitary silver nose stud and immaculate white teeth that showed as she smiled broadly. Her friend didn't look up. Cassie had her pegged as a twenty-something, slim and blonde, although wearing multiple layers of thick clothing. "I'm looking for a friend of yours," Cassie said. "May I join you?"

"You're police, right?"

Cassie nodded. "DS Knight," she said, producing her ID and pulling out a chair. The second woman stared at her, her expression stern and fixed. "I'm looking for Mark."

"What's he done?"

Cassie smiled reassuringly, shaking her head. "Nothing. I'm worried about him."

"You'd be the first."

"He seems like a nice guy," Cassie said. "I like him."

"He is a nice guy."

So far, it was only the brunette who seemed willing to speak, her friend was staring at a half-empty cup of tea, cupped with both hands before her.

"Do you know where I could find him?"

The brunette shrugged. "Not really."

"It's unusual for him not to come here though, right?" Cassie glanced towards the door. "Particularly on a night like this, yes?"

She nodded. "It's going to rain later. I can feel it."

Her words sounded hollow, distant.

"Not a time to be outside."

"You can spare me the guilt trip or the manipulation," the brunette said, eyeing Cassie fiercely. "I lived with an expert at it for years… and you're not a patch on him. I'm not stupid."

Cassie cleared her throat. "Okay… what's your name?"

She stared hard at Cassie, seemingly taking her measure and relented, allowing her guard to drop, if only a little. "Julie."

Cassie smiled warmly. "Okay, Julie. I don't know Mark and I am looking for him regarding something I'm working on, but I think he can help me. And that's why I need to speak to him."

"Help you with what exactly?"

"I think Mark knows a witness… someone who may have seen a murder. And this person, if they saw what I think they saw, is in real trouble."

Julie sat back, glancing sideways at her friend

who cocked her head. It was as if something unsaid had passed between them.

"Is Mark helping you find this guy?"

Cassie inclined her head. "He was, yes." Julie nodded, sniffed but didn't say anything. Cassie thought she was about to be dismissed. "And, you see, the thing is if this witness is in trouble, then anyone around them is also likely to be in danger too."

"Now you mean Mark?"

Cassie nodded. "I do."

She waited patiently, letting the words sink in. Julie bit her bottom lip and shrugged.

"I don't see what we can do about that. We don't know where he is. The last time we saw him, he was talking to you."

Cassie exhaled deeply. "I'm not trying to get you to grass him up for anything. I really do only have his interests at heart, but I do need to find him." She thought about threatening the two women with arrest, for obstructing a police investigation. It might prove fruitful in time, but she didn't feel like she had time to play those games, choosing to rely on sincerity. "Please. Do you know where he goes during the day?"

Julie held Cassie's gaze, sighed and shook her head. "Sorry."

"Well, I hope you can live with yourself if something happens to him."

"That's not fair," Julie said.

"Yeah, well life isn't!"

"A fact I'm well aware of," Julie hit back.

"He goes to his gran's."

Cassie was taken aback. These were the first words the blonde girl had said. She still couldn't bring herself to make eye contact, and her voice was almost lost among the general hubbub in the room.

"Mark goes to his grandmother's? What, her house?"

The girl nodded. "She lives here in the town. Mark visits her during the day, but his family are not to know. They wouldn't like it."

"I see. And do you think he's there now?"

She shrugged. "He's not supposed to be there at night."

"Can I have the address?"

AVENUE ROAD WAS LOCATED at the edge of Hunstanton town centre. On one side of the road were a mixture of Victorian detached and semi-detached properties with 1960s-built bungalows opposite them. The house was in darkness as Cassie approached the door. The curtains of a front-facing bay window were open allowing her to peer into the darkness, but no one seemed to be home. She rang the bell and waited. There was no response from inside. Stepping back, Cassie looked at the upper two floors, but they too were in darkness.

Footsteps behind her made her look round and a man walked up the path to the neighbouring property. Cassie caught his attention. Brandishing her warrant card, she inclined her head towards the house.

"Do you know if your neighbour is likely to be home?"

"I should think so. She's pretty much housebound these days." He was concerned. "Is everything all right?"

Cassie glanced at the house. "Housebound you say?" He nodded. "When did you last see… sorry, what's her name?"

"Eleanor." His forehead creased in concentration. "You know, I've not seen her in days. The carers come and go. I see their little van parked outside."

"But you haven't seen Eleanor yourself for a while?" He shook his head. "How about anyone else coming or going?"

The man thought about it. "Her daughters are here quite a bit. As are her carers… but I don't recall anyone else."

"Would you notice?"

"Oh yes. We keep an eye out for her, and my wife works from home." He pointed to the front room of their house. "And the office is right there, so she would see."

"I have to say… I am a bit worried. I don't suppose you know how I can get into the house to check on her, do you?"

He looked pensive, glancing at his own house. "Well, my wife does have a key… for emergencies. Is this...?"

"An emergency?" Cassie nodded. "It might well be that you'll be saving a life."

"I should probably check with the family."

"Time is pressing."

He frowned, his eyes flitting between Cassie and the house.

"I suppose you are the police… I'm sure it will be fine. Give me a sec and I'll find the key for you."

He hurried indoors, returning a couple of minutes later with a key on a ring. He passed it to Cassie and she went to the door.

"Should I—"

"No need," Cassie said. "I'll give you a shout if I need to."

Reluctantly, he agreed and watched as she unlocked the front door and entered. Inside the house all was silent with the ticking of an antique clock in the hall the only sound. The house felt cold, very cold. Houses like these must be almost impossible to keep warm, particularly in the current financial climate and spike in energy prices.

"Hello!" Cassie called. "Eleanor? It's the police."

The house was three storeys tall and very narrow but seemed to stretch back some way. Cassie passed two downstairs reception rooms, both in darkness, and then left the long hall and entered a rear sitting room. Light spread under a closed door from the next room beyond a large open fireplace located at the centre of this one. She guessed she was in a rear extension added at some time in the past. There were fewer period details the further she walked.

Knocking on the door, she eased it open, blinking as the artificial light struck her eyes. Half expecting Mark to be sitting in the kitchen, she was surprised to see a figure sitting in front of a television with her back to the door. It was an evening quiz show and the volume was ear-splittingly loud.

Cassie entered, feeling a wall of heat strike her. There was an oil-filled radiator plugged in to her right and it was kicking out a lot of heat. The woman, presumably Eleanor, was sitting in a wheelchair, a blanket across her legs. To her left was an upright chair with a knitted blanket lain across it, where a black and white cat was curled up, studiously watching Cassie's approach.

Eleanor noticed the cat rather than seeing Cassie and she turned to her. If she felt alarmed by her presence, she didn't show it. Instead, she smiled warmly.

"Hello, dear," she said.

"Eleanor?"

"Yes, of course. Who were you expecting?"

Cassie smiled, glancing around for evidence that someone else was present. She didn't see any.

"I'm sorry to interrupt your quiz," Cassie said, "but I'm looking for Mark." Eleanor's smile faded and she seemed confused. "Is he here?"

"Well, he was..." she said, absently fingering her necklace. "Earlier on, but he's not here now."

She seemed fearful. Cassie came closer, the cat warily watching her. Cassie reached out and the cat allowed her to scratch the top of its head.

"You're a pretty little thing, aren't you?" Cassie said.

Eleanor smiled again. "He's a great judge of character."

Cassie took a chair from a small dining table in the corner, setting it down next to Eleanor. "Mark is your grandson, isn't he?"

She giggled. "No," she said, conspiratorially. "That's just what we call one another. I'd love to have a grandson like Mark, but I'm afraid I hardly ever see my own."

"And so, Mark is... who to you?"

Her eyes narrowed, the fear returning. Cassie took out her identification. "Don't worry, I'm the police."

Eleanor visibly relaxed, reassured by authority. "He does all sorts for me, Mark. He's a good boy."

"All sorts?"

"Yes... shopping... running errands and the like." She reached out and took Cassie's hand in hers. Her touch felt light, reflecting the frailty that was obvious by her appearance. "My carers are lovely, and they do much for me, but they are so busy. They're in and out in three quarters of an hour."

"How often do they come?"

"Twice a day, morning and evening." She glanced at the clock mounted in the kitchen. "They'll be here anytime between now and ten o'clock to help me to bed."

Cassie glanced at her watch. "That's a bit vague."

"Sign of the times, young lady. They'll get here when they can."

"What about your family. Do you see them often?"

"Not as much as I'd like... but they do come to see me. My daughter will telephone every day."

"Local, are they?"

"Oh yes. Hunstanton girls, both of them."

Cassie smiled, reading the pride in Eleanor's smile. "And what do they think of Mark?"

"Oooh... you can't tell them Mark has been here. They would be very, very angry."

"That's okay," Cassie said, tapping the end of her nose. "It'll be our little secret too."

Eleanor beamed at her.

"Has Mark ever brought any friends to visit you?"

"Friends? No," she said, thinking hard. "At least, I don't recall."

The doorbell rang, Cassie noting a green light flashing from a device plugged in on the kitchen worktop, but Eleanor didn't react. A few moments later two women entered the kitchen, surprised by Cassie's presence.

"Hi, Eleanor, sorry we're a little late…"

Cassie rose and showed them her identification and both women seemed concerned for their client's welfare. Cassie waved it away. "We were just chatting. Don't let me get in your way."

One of the carers set about heating a meal in the kitchen for Eleanor to eat while the other moved to speak with her. Cassie moved aside to enable them to work. Loitering in the kitchen, she watched the two carers working with incredible speed and efficiency.

"Do you both always see to Eleanor?" Cassie asked the one cooking.

"Most of the time, unless we just get too busy. Then someone else comes around."

"Have you ever found someone else present?"

She stopped what she was doing momentarily,

looking at Cassie. "Other than her daughters, June and Mary, no. Why do you ask?"

"Just curious," Cassie said, although the woman didn't seem to believe her.

"And you come at this time every day?"

"It depends on what our clients need on the day, but we aim for between seven and ten in the morning… and between five and ten at night."

"Five would be a bit early to put someone to bed, wouldn't it?"

She shrugged. "We have more clients than we can possibly manage," she said, lowering her voice. "We'd like to be here for a lot longer, but… it is what it is, you know?"

Cassie nodded and excused herself. This was a large house for one person to live in. Clearly it had been a family home for a long time and an elderly, infirm occupant who spent most of her days alone would make an easy target for an unscrupulous person. Mark hadn't struck her as one such person, but his relationship with this woman struck her as odd. Perhaps it was benign; a place to stay during the day to keep him off the streets in exchange for the odd errand and providing a lonely person a bit of company.

She couldn't see it, not really. However, being very much aware of her own rampant cynicism, she couldn't rule it out. Standing at a set of French doors overlooking the rear garden, Cassie spotted a string of lightbulbs suspended above a small patio and spying a light switch to her left she flicked it on, illuminating the garden. It was narrow, mirroring the width of the house, but it was deep bearing in mind how close to the town they were. Expecting to see light cast from the rear of the properties on Westgate which ran broadly parallel to Avenue Road, she was surprised to see how few overlooked the garden. The buildings on Westgate were large, some were hotels, and they appeared small from her vantage point.

"I'm just popping out back," she said to no one in particular. The doors were unlocked, and she stepped out, closing them behind her to try and keep the heat in. The string of bulbs crisscrossed the patio and were attached on one side to the boundary fence, shared with neighbours, and on her left to a brick outbuilding which likely formed the original outside toilet and coal shed, although a lighter shade of brick suggested this had been extended at some point in the past. Cassie made her way down the garden. Reaching the end of the outbuilding, she found another set of French doors on the end. These were wooden, single glazed and in a poor state of repair. Net curtains hung on the inside of the doors, the room in darkness, and the nets only helped to shroud the interior from prying eyes.

Trying the door, she found it unlocked. Tentatively pushing the door open, she illuminated the interior with thc light on her mobile phone. Stacked against one wall were several dozen canvasses. Shelving lined the walls and upon them were assorted sizes and types of plastic boxes, jars and baskets. Eleanor, or someone close to her, must have been an artist at some point. The beam of light scanned the room settling on the far corner where she saw a number of blankets and a couple of sleeping bags scrunched up in a pile. Besides these she found food wrappers and a couple of plastic water bottles. Someone had been sleeping here.

Backing out of the room, she made her way down the garden and beyond the reach of the exterior illumination, relying only on the light from her mobile. At the end of the garden she found a wooden gate. It opened out onto a narrow, unmade lane that offered access to the rear of properties on Westgate and Avenue Road, explaining why the former seemed so far away. A handful of cars were parked to the side flush with the boundary fences or walls of their owners' properties, barely leaving room for anyone else to get through. However, with precious little on-street parking to the front, residents made the most of what space they could find.

Going back into the garden, she called Tom, just as her eyes caught sight of something else leaning against the wall in the dark, a mature clematis overhanging it and hiding it from a casual glance.

"Hi, Cassie. What have you found out?"

"Well, I think I know where Mark has been spending his time during the day, doing his Good Samaritan piece for an old lady, but that's not all that's interesting here." She switched to the camera function and took a quick snap. "I'm sending you something."

There was a brief moment of silence as the picture was sent over Hunstanton's weirdly patchy mobile coverage and then Tom received it.

"Well, I'll be damned," he said. "It looks like you were right. Mark knew more than he was letting on after all."

"Long gone now though," Cassie said, looking over her shoulder at the entrance to the lane. "You could slip in and out of a house on Avenue Road without anyone being any the wiser."

"So, now we're looking for Mark as well as Terry?" Tom asked.

"If you find one, I suspect you'll find the other," Cassie said, regretfully. "I'm heading back in." She hung up. Taking a deep breath, she cast one more lingering glance at the old bicycle leaning against the wall in Eleanor's garden and had to conclude that their investigation had now shifted from locating a potential witness to finding two suspected murderers. Both of whom were used to being ghosts in modern society. They'd have to find them soon or else they might never track them down.

Before she left she was going to insist on a family member staying with Eleanor or taking her to their home. If Mark was making a run for it, he'd be unlikely to return to Avenue Road. He was far too savvy to risk it, knowing Cassie would track him there sooner or later. Even so, Eleanor clearly trusted him and Cassie couldn't take the risk.

CHAPTER TWENTY-FOUR

TAMARA OPENED the front door to find David standing in the porch with a white carrier bag in one hand and a bottle of red wine in the other. She pointed at the wine.

"I said I'd be working tonight."

He grinned. "Who says it's for you? I need something to wash this down with," he said, holding the white bag aloft. She could see takeaway cartons stacked inside. "Come on, this'll get cold if we don't get into it."

She made way for him to enter, closing the door after him and hurrying to catch him up as he made his way into the kitchen.

"Sorry about the mess—"

"Oooh…" David said, standing at the threshold and looking over the piles of clutter that dominated the island as well as the dining table beyond it, "I see you've… tidied."

Tamara slapped him on the back of the head, walking past him. "We can always eat on trays."

He rolled his eyes at her but didn't comment. Setting the bag down on the floor, he looked around searching for something. "Your parents took those mangy felines with them, didn't they?"

"Yes. We are a moggy-free house now."

"Good. I'll leave the food on the floor until I've cleared space on the table," he said, looking at the floor and then Tamara. "It's probably cleaner down there anyway."

Tamara smiled ruefully, wagging a pointed finger at him. "It's a good job I like you, Professor White."

"Like me?" he said, feigning offence.

"Yes… I… like you," she repeated, smiling.

He leaned forward, pointedly making eye contact. "And I… like… spending time with you."

"Touché," she said. "You clear space and I'll get plates and open the wine and so on." He nodded, scratching his forehead as he contemplated what he would do with everything on the table. "Did you have any luck with Terence Westfield?"

"I did, yes… after a fashion." He stopped, put his hands on his hips and turned to her. "You're going to have to get a grip on all this, Tamara. I mean… I'm starting to think you have something wrong with you."

She chuckled. "Are you sure you want to pull on that particular thread?"

He angled his head and frowned. "Probably not."

"Westfield?"

"Oh right, yes. I spoke to a couple of people in the faculty who remember him."

"And?"

"Spoke highly of him," David said, resuming his monumental task of finding space. "Seriously. You need to sort this."

"It's in hand," Tamara said as he stared at her, mock-wincing. "Honestly. I have a plan and have my best assistant on it. Now, Westfield!"

"Yes, as I said, good chap. No one had a bad word to say about him. He was odd though which, let's face it, for us academics isn't in itself… odd."

"Odd in what way?"

David thought on it. "Amiable and well liked, but he was a bit of a loner. He was married and had a child… a daughter, I think they said, but he never brought them along to any of the social events, Christmas parties, summer drinks… that sort of thing."

"Do they know what happened to him?"

David shook his head. "Not really."

"How did he come to leave the university?"

"Oh, that I can tell you. He had some kind of breakdown. They were a little vague on the details. To be fair, it was a very long time ago. Something happened in his personal life, some tragedy, and he just couldn't cope any more. Went to pieces, the poor man."

"Eric seems to think his wife and child died."

David looked perplexed, then smiled, happy to have found the surface of the dining table. "Can't say that anyone could confirm that, I'm afraid. I'd have thought they'd have remembered if that was the case but," he shrugged, "what do I know?"

"I don't believe it!" Tamara said. David looked at her and then followed her eyeline out of the kitchen window.

"What is it?" he asked just as Francesca, Tamara's mum, appeared at the patio doors. She tried the door but found it locked, so she knocked on the glass, pointing at the handle, an excited smile on her face.

David crossed to the door and opened it for her. Francesca came in, shuddering and hoisting a large laundry bag onto the dining table in the space David had only recently cleared. He frowned but said nothing. Francesca cast a disapproving look around the room, tutting.

"I thought you were going to clean this up?" she said to Tamara, leaning towards David, "If you want to keep a good man, you have to be good at keeping house." She nudged David in the ribs, winking. David flushed, glancing at Tamara in a silent plea for help.

"Mother, I thought you were going to help me find a cleaner. Did you have any luck?"

"I did, Tammy dear. I went through the local newsletter and I made a note of telephone numbers advertised on the community information boards in both the community centre and supermarkets. From there, I've interviewed three prospective candidates over the telephone."

Tamara was thrilled. "That… is good. Thank you."

"One of them came across so, so well that I couldn't not employ her!"

Tamara smiled. "That's great! I'm sorry I doubted you, really, I am." Francesca seemed genuinely pleased to hear her say so. The two had a somewhat fractious relationship at the best of times. "You didn't call about it, so I figured you hadn't made progress, Mum. So… when does she think she can start?"

"Oh, sorry, Tammy. I meant I employed her for our house; your father and me. Unfortunately, none of them I spoke to turned out to be suitable for you."

"Ah-hah… why not?"

"Well, they only work in Sheringham, Tammy. None of them would come this far out." She smiled apologetically, shrugging slightly. "There's nothing I can do about that, is there?"

"So… that's it?"

"Well," Francesca said, indignant, "what do you expect me to do?"

"How about interview cleaners who *aren't* only based in Sheringham… where you live. You could try that."

The comment threw her mother, who stared at her blankly. It was a logical conclusion to reach, but her mother had an expression of utter bewilderment. She did what she usually would do in a scenario like this and quickly changed the subject.

"I brought your laundry back!" She pointed at the bag on the table.

David looked at Tamara, stifling a laugh. "Your mum still does your washing for you?"

"No, my mum lets herself into my house and takes my laundry without asking," Tamara said.

"I didn't use my key today though, did I?"

"And taking things without consent is actually called theft."

"Only if I don't intend to return it," Francesca said, wagging a finger at her. That was all Tamara needed, her mother quoting the law at her. "What's that smell? Is it Chinese?"

"Thai," David said.

"Oh, I love Thai food," Francesca said.

Tamara was ready to send her mum packing but

didn't get the chance, interrupted by her phone ringing. It was the station.

"Evening, Tamara. I'm sorry to trouble you, but it couldn't wait."

Tamara recognised the voice of the duty inspector.

"That's okay, what is it?"

"We've found a body and I think one of your team will need to take a look at it as soon as possible."

TAMARA PARKED her car at the top of the rise just before Butterfield Meadow came to the roundabout connecting it to the A149 leading into Hunstanton. The roundabout was constructed to facilitate the several hundred new homes built on the south side of the town in recent years. The road swept down from the main coast road cutting across a section of no man's land before going into the housing estate. It was in this patch of ground where Tamara and Cassie met PC Marshall. A fire engine was parked behind his patrol car, flashing lights on both vehicles flickering in the night as the fire brigade crew gathered their equipment together to pack it away.

"Evening, Ma'am," PC Marshall said, smiling a greeting to Cassie.

"What do you have for us?" Tamara asked.

"This way," he said, climbing over the simple wooden fence lining the embankment and gesturing for them to follow. Once over the barrier, they descended down a steep grass-lined slope to the meadow. The developers had made an effort to landscape this section of the development planting new trees as well as placing log piles to encourage local wildlife to return there, post construction.

The development was closer to sea level than much of the town and a bridge was constructed to bring traffic from the A149 on the Heacham side rather than filter it through the existing infrastructure. This patch of land, worst-case scenario, could flood. It was unlikely to be tidal, the sea defences of the town did spread this far along the coast, however water running off the hillside could pool in this place, hence the need for the raised road with a culvert beneath to carry away prospective flood water. It was here that PC Marshall led them.

He stopped at the entrance to the culvert, pointing to a mass in the centre and only visible with the aid of a torch. He handed his to Tamara.

"A passing motorist spotted smoke and stopped to investigate. He called the fire brigade thinking it was kids mucking around with fireworks or something."

Tamara exchanged a glance with Cassie and they both stooped to enter the culvert. It was five feet in diameter, and they found traversing the interior easier than expected. PC Marshall followed a couple of paces behind. As they moved closer, it was apparent the mass was a body. It was wrapped in a twill material, similar to decorator's dust sheets, but they were no longer cream but were blackened and charred.

"The station officer reckons the poor sod was doused in an accelerant… petrol or similar, before being set alight," Marshall said.

Tamara covered her mouth. The odour of charred flesh made her stomach turn. The sight of it did little to alter that. Cassie coughed, covering her mouth as well.

"Any ID?" Tamara asked.

"No, Ma'am. He's not carrying anything. I mean, I'm assuming it's male because of the size of the hands. The face… well… it's pretty grim."

Cassie edged closer, using a handkerchief, she lifted the edge of the material to see beneath. "Can you put a bit of light on it?"

Tamara didn't want to see the vivid details but did as requested, aiming the beam at the human remains. She fought the revulsion threatening to make her retch. Cassie cursed.

"What is it?" Tamara asked.

"You see the hand," she said, pointing at the victim's blackened hand. Part of it wasn't seared as badly as the rest; the skin still partially visible where the forefinger met the thumb. Tamara could see what looked like an imprint or stain.

"What is it?"

"A tattoo," Cassie said. "A swallow in flight."

"You've seen it before?"

She nodded. "It's Mark. We've found Mark."

"So, if this is Mark," Tamara said, looking straight at Cassie, "where the hell is Terry?"

CHAPTER TWENTY-FIVE

Tom stared at the information boards willing a detail to leap out at him. Something they'd missed in all of this. Mark Oatley, a homeless man, who'd lived around Hunstanton all of his life largely without incident had been found dead. His body the victim of a crude cremation. Only time would tell if that was the result of an amateurish attempt at disposal or merely to try and destroy evidence. It didn't make sense. None of it did.

"The scenes of crime team are on their way to Butterfield," Eric said, hanging up his desk phone. "Pathologist is on standby-by for when the body ships. Dr Paxton will work through the night if necessary."

"Good," Tom said without looking round, frustration building. "What is Terry's connection to Mark, besides the fact they live on the streets?"

Eric frowned, shaking his head. "I can't see one. They are different age and social strata. Mark left school at sixteen and has jobbed around as far as I can see from his HMRC tax records. He's certainly never worked in academia or geology."

"Perhaps they've lived near to one another in the past?" Tom asked and he saw Eric wince. "I know, it's a reach, but why would Mark put himself out for Terry. He's likely been hiding him at Eleanor's house this past week, but why? Why take that risk if Terry has witnessed a murder—"

"Or committed one," Eric said. "If Cassie is right and Mark helped Terry kill Simon Shears." Tom glanced at him, gesturing for him to continue. "Well, Simon could take care of himself. He was a bouncer, so he was probably pretty handy with his fists. There's no way old Tramp Terry could take him down in a one on one. Someone was holding Shears while another attacker stabbed him." He shrugged. "Why not Mark?"

"Because it doesn't make any sense."

"Does it have to?" Eric asked. "Make sense, I mean? Sometimes people kill people… and at this time of year they get desperate. A robbery gone wrong?"

Tom took a deep breath. "People don't become

killers like that out of nowhere. The attack on Shears was absolutely savage, but why would Shears be out there in Fring? He wasn't out walking, not with a four-hundred-pound pair of shoes on."

"Meeting them there?"

"Likely," Tom agreed. "But the question stands; why?"

Eric's brow furrowed and he glanced at Danny who was sitting alongside him, chewing on the end of a biro. He shrugged.

"I might have something," Kerry said. All eyes turned to her as her fingers flew across her keyboard in front of her. She nodded to herself, smiling. Spinning her chair to face the room, she indicated the screen with her thumb. "Sarah Roper's maiden name was Dunston, her mother Caroline. Interesting thing is that Dunston was Caroline's maiden name. She changed her name back to her family name when she divorced."

"Well, I hope you're going somewhere with this because all that just made my head hurt," Danny said.

Tom's eyes narrowed. "So, who did she divorce?"

"Terence Westfield," Kerry said, her eyes shining. "Which makes Katy Roper—"

"Tramp Terry's granddaughter," Tom said quietly, his eyes darting to the information board detailing the search for Katy.

"Which means…" Eric said, "that Katy is with him?"

"Explaining why Terry left his bicycle at Eleanor's house on Avenue Road," Tom said, turning back to them. "It is certainly possible, and if Simon Shears was grooming his granddaughter, it would give him a motive to kill."

Danny sniffed. "Any paedo comes after my family, he's a dead man."

Tom looked at him and Danny squirmed in his seat. "Theoretically… hypothetically speaking, obviously."

Tom rubbed at his chin. "It's a motive but it doesn't help us find him though."

"Where would he go?" Eric asked. "He was staying at the yard in Fring but that's off limits because we've been there and it's now a crime scene."

"The same with the shelter," Tom said. "Terry can't go there because he must know that sooner or later we would come looking for him there. Mark provided him a safe haven and when he got wind that Cassie was directly looking for Terry, he fled to warn him."

"Hey," Danny said, "if Katy is with him – even now – after all this… he couldn't keep her on the street. I mean, it's absolutely Baltic out there," he said, thumbing towards the window. "Maybe Terry is used to sleeping rough and has some resilience but we're talking about a fifteen-year-old girl."

"His old house?" Kerry suggested. Tom thought that a strong possibility. Up until now, Terry had only paid it a brief visit if that was who the neighbour saw loitering outside.

"If he has Katy with him and feels he has no other option, then they might go there. It's true."

"But who killed Mark?" Eric asked. "Do we think Terry would do it to cover up his involvement?"

"Maybe Mark threatened to come to us," Danny said.

Tom shook his head. "He has been reluctant to do so up until now. Why would he change his mind?"

Danny shrugged. "Feeling the net closing in?"

Tom frowned. "Maybe... but something still feels off in all this."

Eric's mobile rang and he checked the screen, contemplating declining the call and leaving voicemail to pick it up. However, it was from the boat yard in Blakeney. He answered.

"DC Collet." Eric listened, his eyes widening. Snapping his fingers to get everyone's attention, he put the call onto speaker and he laid his mobile on the desk. "It's the owner of the Blakeney boat yard where Karl Roper works. Mr Briggs," Eric said, raising his voice, "please could you repeat what you just told me?"

"Um... yes, sure. I was just locking up to go

home and I found the petty cash tin has been emptied, so I thought I'd better see what else is missing."

"And?" Eric asked, expectant.

"One of our boats is missing. It is due to be laid up for the winter but was still in the water while the client decides what he wants us to do with it."

"Mr Briggs, this is DI Janssen. When do you think the boat was taken?"

"This afternoon," he said emphatically. "It was there when I ducked home for a couple of hours and gone when I returned. As was Karl."

"Is Karl's car still parked in the car park, Mr Briggs?" Eric asked.

"Yes."

"And do you have any cameras on site?"

"Of course. I checked the footage before I called you, but the hard drive is missing. I think whoever took the cash and the boat also took the footage of them doing so."

"Karl hasn't returned to site?" Tom asked.

"N-No… you don't think Karl has… I mean, Karl has worked for me for years. He's broken bread with my family in our home. He is almost like a member of my family. Why would he do this to me?"

Tom looked at Eric, slowly nodding. "Because family is important, Mr Briggs." The comment was wasted on the man without more context. "Tell me,

Mr Briggs, what type of boat has been taken and how much cash is missing?"

"It's a Cetus Dory 17… a flat-bottomed, shallow draught boat, ideal for group fishing trips. That sort of thing. Cash wise?" he said, blowing out his cheeks. "No more than a couple of hundred, but I don't really keep track of it until my accountant starts asking for receipts, you know?"

"Dorys are ocean-going capable, aren't they?" Tom asked, scouring his memory and picturing the likely composition of the boat.

"Coast hugging, certainly… or they can be launched from something larger, if necessary, like a schooner, if you're fishing in deeper waters."

"Single outboard motor, easy to navigate rivers and waterways, but you wouldn't want to be caught in rougher seas, right?"

"Perfect for Norfolk, Detective Inspector. You know your boats."

Tom smiled. "Thanks, Mr Briggs. I'll have someone come by tomorrow and take a statement if that's okay?"

Eric thanked him for calling and hung up. Tom looked around the room.

"Katy's father, Karl Roper, has stolen a boat and a fistful of cash on the same night his ex-father-in-law is most likely on the run."

"And we know Karl has been lying about when he last saw Katy," Eric said. "Why that particular boat? He's not going to sail to France or Norway in it, is hc?"

"No," Tom said, gravely, "but he could get them out of Norfolk when he thinks we'd be watching the roads and transport hubs. A few hundred pounds won't go far, but it's something."

"So, we're back to square one?" Danny asked.

"Not quite," Tom said, jabbing a pointed finger at Eric. "Why that boat?" He turned and crossed to the information board, tapping the map where Westfield's family home was circled. "Smuggler's Lane. It's called that for a reason. The lighthouse at Hunstanton guides you into the shore. The sea is shallow all along the coast from Old Hunstanton through to and beyond Holkham fourteen or so miles away. When the tide goes out, it drops off for a quarter of a mile, or more, some days."

"The perfect landing place for a shallow draught boat," Eric whispered. "Just like back in the day when the smugglers used to avoid the Customs and Excise officers."

"Miles of coastline with nothing but sand dunes, wildlife and wind to accompany them. That's where they'll be," Tom said. "But maybe not for very long." He glanced at the time. It was approaching ten o'clock. "Low tide is right on us. Karl won't have been able to come in close to the shore, so they'll have quite a trek across the sand to reach the boat. That gives us time if we leave now."

"Shall we gather as much uniform as possible to come with us?" Eric asked.

"No, we don't want to spook them with the lights and sirens. The ground is too open for us to cover every place they could slip through. We'll have them hold back until we get eyes on the targets and then they can move in." Tom reached for his mobile to call Tamara. "Come on, let's get moving."

THE PROBLEM the team had was that there were only two approach roads that brought them anywhere near to Smugglers' Lane. Arriving en masse would leave them hopelessly exposed to being seen, so they had to park in the nearby Caley Hall Hotel and make their way down under cover of darkness. At this time of the night there was minimal movement from the locals. The rain had been on and off throughout the day, changeable weather was forecast along with an increasing sea breeze. The conditions were far from ideal to be at sea, even close to the coast, in a dory boat. Many fishermen had been killed over the years due to the inherent instability of such flat-bottomed boats when used at sea, perfectly fine in clement conditions, but hazardous in others.

If this was the plan to escape the pursuers, then things were getting desperate.

Reaching the end of Smugglers' Lane, Tom and Eric moved towards the house and Tom silently detailed Danny and Kerry to wait at the gate, keeping a watch over the house in case anyone tried to flee. Tamara and Cassie were on their way, but they would go to the nearby golf club to meet up with the gathered uniformed officers. Once Tom gave the signal, they would move in, either on the Westfield family home or descend towards the beach. Even though the path from the house to the shore was clearly marked, the open expanse of sand dunes stretching along the coast offered numerous places for Karl to beach the boat. In all likelihood, he would come close to minimise the time it would take to hike over the wet sand to reach it.

Tom and Eric climbed over the gate as quietly as they could, skirting the tree-lined boundary to circumvent the house and see if anyone was visible inside before breaking cover to get closer. The clouds parted and a near full moon illuminated the grounds around the house in silverly light. Tom cursed under his breath. If they moved from the trees they were likely to be spotted almost immediately.

No light emanated from within the property and as soon as the moon was partially obscured by cloud cover, the two detectives scampered across the open ground to the house which they did without incident. Hugging the walls of the house, they made their way around it, peering into every window. At the rear they found a reception room with a broken pane of glass in one of the French Doors. The door was pulled to, but not closed and Tom felt his chest tighten. He signalled silently to Eric they were going to enter and Eric nodded his understanding. The hinges protested as Tom opened the door, shrieking as it moved aside. It sounded like nails on a blackboard and in the dead of night, it carried. There was nothing he could do about it though.

Eric followed Tom inside, a half step behind him. A full bank of cloud blocked the glow of the moon and as they moved deeper into the house, the darkness became all encompassing. Regretfully, Tom produced a torch and angled the beam around them as they progressed through the house. Cleared of all furniture, the property felt eerie and abandoned. Eric tapped Tom on the shoulder, pointing at the wooden floor. Tom cast his light down and he could see footsteps passing through decades of settled dust. These were recent, steps on top of steps. Lowering to his haunches, Tom examined them. Even a cursory inspection offered two distinct sets of footprints, one large and another smaller, narrower, most likely wearing trainers. A grown man and a girl perhaps?

These footprints were themselves disturbed by another, larger set. The tread pattern suggested they were boots, wide and heavy with deeper patterned soles. Most likely these were combat boots or similar. He put fore and index finger to his eyes and then pointed at these prints to ensure Eric understood what he was seeing. Eric's stern expression meant he got the meaning and they moved on. In a front reception room they found evidence of someone having been there recently. Empty crisp packets, chocolate wrappers and pre-made sandwich boxes were in a pile in one corner.

The stairs creaked under their weight; with over a century having passed since they were installed, it wasn't surprising. However, the upstairs didn't appear to have been utilised recently and Tom had to conclude that whoever had been here had already left. They hurried downstairs and back out into the night, joining Danny Wilson and Kerry at the end of the driveway.

"Nothing," Tom said, looking to his left and the path heading down to the beach. "Let's go."

The four of them set off at a run, but kept a gentle pace, slowing a few minutes later as they reached the unmade Golf Course Road. Crossing the road, the track cut through the golf course to where a line of beach huts stretched to both left and right among the dunes. The lifeboat station was a few hundred metres to their left beyond a line of houses. These were set back from the track and with little streetlighting anyone could pass through here unobserved. Tom knew Cassie was waiting nearby for his signal, and the temptation to flood the beach with as many officers as possible was almost overwhelming but he decided to stick to the plan, encouraging his small team to press on.

The clouds parted again as they crossed the open fairway via the sandy path making their route easier but opening them up to being spotted. Tom figured they would be focussed on their departure point rather than anyone following on behind them. After all, this was a one-way trip. The course was fenced off to the public beside the path they were on, with only one opening to reach the huts and the beach beyond them. They reached the huts. From here they could make straight for the beach or turn left or right and follow the path in either direction.

Tom gathered them together. "Right, Eric and I will go straight for the beach. Danny, take Kerry and head to our right a hundred yards and then you too cut left and make for the beach." Holding up his police radio, he waved it at them. "Mobile reception is pathetic the further out from the town we go, so if you see anything give two transmission clicks on the radio. Clear?"

They all nodded. Eric looked to their left.

"What about that way?"

"I'm betting Karl wouldn't beach the boat anywhere near the RNLI station. It'd draw too much attention. But at the same time, I shouldn't think he'll stray too far from Hunstanton, figuring he'd need the lighthouse to navigate by."

Danny looked skyward. "That moon keeps helping out though."

Tom shook his head. "It wasn't forecast. He'll stick to the plan. He has to."

"Why?" Kerry asked.

Tom inclined his head and smiled. "Because if I'm wrong, then we'll never catch them."

CHAPTER TWENTY-SIX

Kerry moved off with Danny in tow and Tom signalled for Eric to stick to the path. To his left, the moonlight reflecting off the black metallic paintwork, Tom spied a Land Rover Defender parked up behind one of the beach huts. The fact it was there was not unusual. The sandy path running to the rear of the huts, and parallel to the golf course, was accessible to 4x4 vehicles with an access point near the course clubhouse. To be there at night though surprised him.

Hurrying to catch up with Eric, they passed between the brightly coloured beach huts and clambered up the soft incline of the dunes to look down upon the beach. Keeping low so as not to be seen, both men knelt and scanned the immediate area. The sea was a long way out, the roar of the water audible but evidently some distance away. When the cloud cover allowed they caught glimpses of the white froth of the breakers as they crashed onto the beach.

Tom was grateful for the moonlight now. Without it, they would be searching in the pitch black, reliant largely on chance to find their quarry. Unable to see any boats anchored or beached, they descended to the beach proper. Moving left would bring them closer to houses, the lifeboat station and beyond those the hotel on the edge of Old Hunstanton and the lighthouse beyond. The natural barrier after these were the rocks beneath the cliffs, the former notorious for wrecking more than a few ships in their time. No, they would need to head to their right, working towards Danny and Kerry.

A keen route for ramblers, dog walkers or horse riders, the path along the coast was well marked. However, when the tide was out the open expanse created by the receding waters made it easy to avoid people all together and walk out over virgin sand. The shifting sands were crisscrossed with channels gouged out of the seabed by the retreating tides, creating sand bars cut off by water channels whose depths varied greatly. Navigating these in the dark would be treacherous. Tom was banking on this being widely known, especially by locals. Hopefully, Terry and Karl would keep their route to the water simple.

Tom led Eric towards the waves. They would then follow the shoreline until they came across the boat. This was risky because they would be seen, but the only way they could remain covert would be to keep close to the dunes. He judged the water was more than a quarter of a mile away, so that was impossible. The location of Tamara and the support team began to cause some consternation. They'd been traversing the beach for almost fifteen minutes, progressing around the coast. In daylight they would have likely covered more ground but the going was slow, particularly when the clouds rolled. Fortunately, the high wind meant frequent bouts of illumination.

Tom heard his radio crackle with two clicks, the indication that Danny and Kerry had made contact. Tom raised a hand and Eric dropped to his haunches alongside him.

"Go ahead, Danny." The volume was set to low for obvious reasons and the noise from wind and waves made it hard to hear the voice amid the distortion. "Say again."

"We have eyes on the target," Danny said. "Kerry says we're at the nature reserve bank. Do you know where that is?"

Tom knew. Roughly a few hundred metres ahead of them was a natural sand bank. It would flood with a high tide but spent enough time above the water for vegetation to grow and was a haven for wildlife, so much so that it was fenced off to stop the public from crossing it.

"I do. What can you see?"

"Two males… no, wait, I see a third."

"Katy?"

"Negative. Too large. This is another man approaching from the north on foot."

Tom was surprised. He expected to see Karl, Terry and perhaps Katy, but a third man made him anxious.

"We're moving to intercept—"

"No, wait for us!" Tom hissed into the radio but there was no reply. He looked at Eric who was already on the same page and the two of them got up and began to run, all thought of caution thrown aside. Kerry and Danny would be outnumbered facing at least one person they believed to be a killer, perhaps two.

Grateful for the parting of the clouds, Tom and Eric splashed through a knee-high tidal rivulet to reach the raised bank on the other side, stumbling as they clambered up it. The nature bank was to their right, a well-known landmass but it was also more than one hundred metres long and bearing out towards the sea. Unsure of where they would find their quarry, they were forced to slow down.

"Gun!" a voice shouted over the radio which was followed by the discharge of a shotgun round. Both Tom and Eric threw themselves to the ground, Tom landing halfway into a tidal pool. He cursed.

"Are you okay, Eric?"

"I'm all good," Eric said from the dark, somewhere to his left. It was time to call in support, but he'd dropped the radio. The moon reappeared and he saw it lying in six inches of water at the bottom of the tidal pool.

"Damn it!"

With Danny and Kerry in danger, he couldn't stay where he was. It didn't seem as if the shot had been aimed at them, but it was close. Lifting himself up, he took advantage of the additional light, spotting a boat bobbing among the breakers. Several figures were involved in a tussle, but he couldn't make out whether any of them were his officers.

"Are you with me, Eric?"

"I'm with you," Eric said, although not as confidently as he might hope, but who could blame him. They were up and running a moment later, closing the distance between themselves and the small group. Tom could make out two men wrestling over something, a third was thumped in the side of the head and he fell into the water. From Tom's right he caught sight of two more figures sprinting across the open ground, Danny and Kerry. The two men staggered back and then separated, one of them bringing the barrel of the shotgun to bear.

"Police!" Tom yelled and the figure spun towards the sound and both he and Eric dived to the ground as another blast from the gun discharged, only this time it was at them. Tom felt a distortion in the air around him as the buckshot passed by, either that or his imagination created the mental image. It didn't matter. If it was a double barrel then the gun was now empty, but if not, then there could be another three shots left in it. Either way, he was up and running once again. The clouds shrouded them in darkness once more with only the white-caps of the water punctuating the darkness. He could sense Eric nearby, hear him breathing hard, but he couldn't see him.

More shouts came, followed immediately by a scream. He heard Kerry demand someone back off, but a high-pitched shriek emanated out of the darkness; one that could only be female. The fear gripped him and he redoubled his efforts; hearing Eric running alongside him, he knew he'd done likewise. And then they were into the fray. Someone threw a fist at Tom, a glancing blow to the side of his head. His momentum carried him forward, knocking his opponent off his feet. They both landed in shingle. Tom rolled and came to his feet, his target struggling to rise just as Eric hurled himself on top of the figure and they both went to ground.

The moon reappeared but of the gun or the man

wielding it, there was no sign. To his right he saw Kerry struggling on to her knees clutching the side of her head, disoriented. "Where's Danny?" he shouted but she looked at him with a blank expression, likely suffering a concussion. Looking to the water, he saw a figure attempting to get into the boat only to see another bearing down on him. The second man was carrying the shotgun.

Seeing Eric overpowering and securing one combatant, Tom broke into a run, closing the distance between himself and the boat in quick time. The tide had turned and it was now coming back in at speed. Tom splashed through the water. The noise of the wind, the breakers crashing onto the beach and the boat around them, meant no one heard Tom coming. Using the shotgun as a club, the second man swung it and the butt struck the individual trying to get aboard the boat. He screamed, lost his grip and pitched backwards into the surf.

Not content with that strike, the attacker set about the stricken man in the water, smacking him in the water repeatedly with the gun. Tom clattered into him, but without any real momentum, his pace slowed by the depth of the water coming almost waist high now. He was big, strong and easily a match for Tom and the two struggled for supremacy. Any thoughts of identifying himself as a policeman were lost as the two were locked in a struggle. It was clear to Tom that his survival was of little interest to the man he grappled with.

A wave broadsided them and Tom lost his footing, finding the water sweeping his legs out from under him, he went down backwards into the water. The fall happened so fast he didn't manage to take a lungful of air, instead breathing in the sour taste of saltwater through mouth and nostrils. Powerful hands forced down upon him and he felt the cold metal of the gun pinning his chest to the seabed. He wrestled to break free, kicking out with his legs but they failed to make contact, merely thrashing around in the water.

Panicking, Tom struggled, his lungs burned and all around him was darkness. All of a sudden, he was free, the restraining pressure holding him under disappeared and he burst to the surface gasping for air just as another wave struck him sending him back under. His coat and multiple layers acted as a drag and he floundered, trying desperately to right himself. Rolling to his front, he tried to find purchase with his boots in the mix of soft sand and shingle beneath him. Coming up once more, only this time the waves breaking upon his back, gave him a chance to draw a solid breath of fresh night air. He coughed violently, spewing sea water out of his lungs in an involuntary motion.

Looking around he peered through the darkness, seeing a figure hunched over something in the water barely ten feet away from him. Tom could hear screaming above the sound of the sea, only this time it wasn't born of fear or physical pain but a guttural, ferocious scream of wanton blood lust. Hurrying through the surf, Tom grabbed the individual who spun to face him, eyes wide, blood pouring from a wound to his forehead. He grimaced, staring at Tom with those wild eyes, but there was no aggression aimed at Tom, no attempt to attack him. The man's energy was spent, his breathing coming in ragged gasps.

Tom looked down to see a man's body floating at their feet, lying on his back staring up at the night sky, lifeless. It was Tony Shears, Simon's brother. He had a firm hold of the man before him, his grey hair and beard were wet through, water dripping from him. He wavered and for a moment Tom thought he was about to stumble or pass out. Tom supported him, holding him upright. He stared into Tom's eyes, lifting a shaking hand, he pointed at the boat threatening to drift away from them. It must have been pegged out as those boats didn't come with any way to firmly secure them at anchor, the incoming tide tearing it free.

"My… my granddaughter," the man said in a flat, monotone voice.

"Get out of the water," Tom said, tentatively releasing his hold on him and pointing back to the shore which was already a fair distance away from them now and getting further away by the minute. Terence Westfield teetered on the brink of falling over, each wave threatening to knock him into the surf, but he turned and made a good fist of making for the safety of the beach. Tom had to secure the boat. Wading through the water towards it, he grabbed the line that had been tethering it to the shoreline. It was hanging loose now, whether it had worked itself free on the tide or been cast off to make their escape prior to Tony's arrival, he couldn't say.

Red and blue lights flooded the darkness now as Tamara's back-up units raced along the beach to reach them. Eric or Danny must have summoned them. *Danny*. He still hadn't seen him. He pushed the detective constable's fate aside, the boat slamming into him as the tidal surge drove it at him. He gasped, the wind knocked out of him, but he held on. Here, the water was already mid-chest height and he found it difficult to maintain a firm grip on the boat and keep his solid stance in the water. Pushing off the seabed with as much might as he could muster, Tom levered himself up and over the lip of the boat with the aid of the rail, landing unceremoniously and falling against the centre console housing the steering and motor controls.

The boat was side on to the incoming tide and the waves were picking up, the dory bobbing around on the swell like a cork. To the rear he saw two bags and a jumble of clothing alongside the outboard motor. He had to start that engine and beach the boat as quickly as he could. Crawling to the stern, the jumble of clothing moved and a face appeared out of the darkness, screaming at him, abject terror in her eyes. Tom hesitated. He didn't have time for this but the girl was terrified, staring at him like a cornered rat.

"I'm a policeman!" he shouted but another wave, larger than any that came before it, slammed into the port side, seawater spilling over the rim and threatening to capsize the boat. Tom lurched to the rear and set about starting the motor. It was the third pull that fired the engine into life and he hurried back to the central console, increasing the power and steering the boat out into deeper water, fearful of colliding with his colleagues nearby in the water. Once he was confident he'd likely cleared anyone wading to shore, he angled the craft towards the lights on the beach and gunned it. The engine roared and the bow rose in the water as they bounced through the breakers beaching at speed moments later. The impact threw Katy forward but Tom used his own body as a cushion to break her fall, the two of them clattering to the deck and sliding towards the bow.

The engine stalled as they ran aground, the deafening roar of the motor gone, a weird silence followed. No longer screaming, Katy leaned into

Tom, clinging to him like a frightened animal much as Saffy would do when she'd woken from a nightmare. Tom wrapped his arms around her, drawing her to him and the two of them lay still on the floor, the teenager's head pressed firmly against his chest.

"You're safe now," he whispered into the mass of hair pressing against his chest. Katy Roper began to cry, softly at first but then she allowed herself the release of all the pent-up emotion and she wept openly. "It's all over, I promise. You're safe now."

CHAPTER TWENTY-SEVEN

Tom met Alice in the police station lobby. She rushed to him, dropping the holdall containing his change of clothes and flung her arms around him, gripping him with a ferocity that caught him off guard. Encircling her with both arms, he whispered in her ear.

"It's okay. I'm all right."

She clung to him and he wondered if this was a symptom of her wider anxiety stemming from recent events. "What if I'd lost you?"

He moved her back a fraction so he could look into her eyes, smiling. "I'm okay. I just got a little wet."

She held his gaze, and it was clear she didn't believe him.

"Cassie said there'd been a shooting."

He looked over his shoulder, imagining Cassie in the ops room. "Did she now? Everything's fine—"

"And the others, Eric—"

"We're all fine," Tom said, sweeping the hair away from her eyes. "We're all wet…" he looked her up and down, "as are you now."

Alice laughed nervously, stepping back from him and seeing her jumper was damp to the touch. "Yes, so I see."

"Where's Saffy?"

"Dad is watching her. She was asleep when I left, but they'll probably be watching cartoons and eating cake when I get back."

"They've taken to each other, haven't they?" Tom said, picking up the towel he'd cast aside when Alice ran to him.

Alice nodded. "Let's see if he sticks around."

"Maybe he will."

"I doubt it. The man never lasted the course before, so why would he now?"

"People change. They want to make amends…" Tom stopped, distracted.

"Tom? What is it?" she asked.

Shaking himself out of deep thought, he smiled. "Just thinking. Thank you for bringing these over," he said, reaching for the bag. "It's too cold for a dip in the sea."

"And everyone is all right?"

He nodded. "Kerry and Danny took a whack each for their troubles, but paramedics reckon it's just a concussion for Kerry. Danny will stay in hospital overnight just for observation.

"Sounds bad."

"Cassie said he's already whining at the nurses, so I reckon he'll be all right. They'll probably kick him out before breakfast."

"What actually happened?" Alice asked.

Tom sighed. "That's what I need to find out." He gave her another hug and they kissed before she withdrew.

"You'll call me later?"

"You should go to bed. I'm going to be here for hours yet, but I'll send you a text when I know what time I'll be home." He knew she would worry, even though he was safe and sound back at the station. If she woke during the night, the message would offer her some comfort. "Get some sleep."

Hurrying to the locker room, Tom quickly changed and returned to ops. Tamara was deep in discussion with Cassie and Eric when he approached.

"Update from the hospital, Danny's scan shows no damage to his skull, so it looks like he'll be fine," Tamara said.

"No damage?" Cassie asked, inclining her head. "Maybe it will have helped?"

Eric smirked.

"What about our Katy?" Tom asked.

"We're moving her to The Shelter. Both of the foster parents will meet her there. She'll have to stay with us until we sort this out, but then they'll take her back to theirs."

The Shelter was the nickname for the centre used to interview and process vulnerable victims of crime; be they victims of abuse, domestic violence or sexual assault. It was a regular house from the exterior and equipped as such inside, but with secure facilities to protect the victims and to give them a more comfortable environment for interview or medical assessment.

"Terry and Karl?" Tom asked. He had been taken to hospital along with the others to be assessed, under his highly vocal protest, but the staff from the RNLI who'd been dispatched to a holding pattern out at sea in case the boat got into trouble insisted on him going to hospital. He'd inhaled a lot of seawater and the concern around secondary drowning was stark; the formation of clots in the lungs due to the build-up of fluid irritating the lung lining. Given the all clear, he'd come back to the station where Alice was already waiting to see him.

"Eric thumped Karl after he took a swing at you," Tamara said.

"Oh, that was him, was it?"

Eric nodded. "He's quite a scrapper for a wiry bloke."

"And so Rocky, here," Cassie said, pointing at Eric, "knocked him spark out!"

Tom arched his eyebrows at Eric who flushed.

"Terry Westfield is downstairs in an interview room," Tamara said.

"Has he said anything?" Tom asked.

Tamara shook her head. "Only to confirm his name for the custody sergeant at detention—"

"And to ask after his granddaughter," Cassie added. "He's genuinely concerned about her."

"How is Katy?"

Tamara frowned. "Shaken up. She's barely said a word either."

"Are we going to find out what this has been all about?" Tom asked. "I'd like a crack at Terry. He's the one person at the centre of all of this and everyone else revolves around him. I'd like to bring Eric in with me."

Eric cocked his head. "Why me?"

"Because you've met him before. It might reassure him a little."

Eric seemed unconvinced but nodded.

Tamara agreed. "Let's get on to it then."

TERRY WESTFIELD SAT in the interview room dressed in white coveralls and a pair of sliders given to him in exchange for his wet clothing. Those clothes were already earmarked for forensic analysis in the Simon Shears murder; however, the seawater was likely to have destroyed any trace evidence that may have been present. He looked gaunt, haggard. His hair was dry now but still looked lank and greasy. The same could be said for his thick beard, unkempt and thinning, as was the hair atop his head. The skin on his face was deeply lined and weathered, clinging to his bone structure offering an almost skeletal appearance.

The price paid for decades of sleeping rough.

"Terry, I'm Detective Inspector Janssen," he said, sitting down. "This is DC Collet."

Terry's eyes narrowed as he looked at Eric who seemed uncomfortable under the scrutiny. "I know who you are," Terry said to Tom. "You brought my Katy to safety." Tom nodded and Terry's gaze shifted to Eric. "You, I recognise… but I don't know where from."

Terry's voice was clear and articulate, quite the contrast to what one might expect when looking upon him for the first time.

"We've met," Eric said. Terry sat forward, cupping his hands together on the table before him. "But it was a long time ago."

Terry smiled, revealing brown teeth and receding gums. "You must have been very young, Detective Constable…"

"Collet," he said, awkwardly. "But most people just call me Eric."

"Eric." Terry's brow furrowed and he concentrated, trying to recall their meeting. He shrugged, shaking his head. "No, I can't place you, but I meet all manner of people on my travels."

"As I say… it was a long time ago."

Eric glanced nervously at Tom who started the interview. "Just a quick reminder of your rights, Mr Westfield."

"There's no need, DI Janssen. I'm well aware of my situation."

"You have waived your right to legal counsel, Mr Westfield. Does that stand?"

"Indeed it does, and please, after everything I've experienced in my life, I prefer to be Terry. It's much more… comforting. Mr Westfield reminds me of who I once was… and I'm not that man anymore."

His tone sounded in many ways regretful, but there was more to it than that. Tom couldn't quite put his finger on what that was though. Perhaps it would come to him.

"Why do you live the way you do, Terry?" Tom asked. Terry met his eye and Tom felt he was studying him. "Sleeping rough… travelling around the county on your bicycle?"

Terry shrugged. "I'm presuming you have done at least a cursory examination of my past, Detective?" Tom nodded. "Good, then we don't have to waste time with the preamble." He spread his hands wide and then theatrically placed them palms down on the surface of the table. "So, what is it you really want to know?"

Tom took a breath. Terry stared at him hard, expressionless.

"I want to know why a respected academic, a family man, walks out and to all intents and purposes, drops out of society?"

"Ah… you find that odd?"

"For some, no I don't. For you, very much so, yes."

Terry smiled, but it was forlorn. He sighed. "My life, on the face of it, was incredibly successful, Inspector. But, as it is with many of these things, appearances can be deceptive. I met the most beautiful woman in the world one day, Caroline. Her smile could light up the darkest of days." He looked at Tom. "For me, at any rate. My parents were not keen… but I defied them, choosing my own path. This is a character trait I would repeat time and time again."

"What didn't your parents like about her?"

He scoffed. "Nothing about her personally. They got on very well, but…" His expression clouded "Caroline had her own darkness. One that she couldn't shake whenever the Black Dog came to visit."

"She suffered with depression?" Tom asked.

Terry nodded. "She was a paranoid schizophrenic, Inspector Janssen. Very troubled… and that made life difficult in many ways, not least for Caroline herself. You see, times may well have changed, but when *we* first got together, diagnosis and treatments of such an illness were hard to come by, particularly in deepest Norfolk."

"She was treated?"

"Yes… we did our best, managed her condition with all the enthusiasm we could muster. The brighter days were the best of my life, Inspector. They really were."

"And the darker ones?"

Terry lowered his eyes to the table; he was absently wringing his hands at this point.

"We coped," he said quietly. "For a time, things improved. So much so that we decided to start a family of our own."

"Sarah?" Tom asked.

He looked up at Tom and smiled. "Yes, Sarah… she was a blessing to us both and, for a time, life bumbled on. I thought we were over the worst of it. My career was taking off and Caroline… took to motherhood like a duck to water. For a time…" He whispered the last.

"It didn't last then I take it?"

He shook his head. "The change was mild at first, but incrementally things seemed to deteriorate. In hindsight, it was clear but I was so busy with my work at the university I failed to see what was happening at home. The incidents were increasing in their frequency... and my strategy for coping wasn't keeping pace." He sank back in his chair, staring at a nondescript point on the wall, deep in thought. "You know, it's little Sarah who I feel sorry for. She was alone with her mother... often... too often, looking back. And little did I know that Sarah was equally afflicted... like mother, like daughter. I should have seen it."

"I'll bet that put strain on the marriage?"

"Oh... it did, it really did; the marriage, the family... my own mental health." He looked at Tom ruefully. "I had your chaps out on many an occasion. Sometimes I called you... sometimes it was the neighbours responding to the screaming... the violence."

"Caroline was violent?"

He nodded slowly. "Frequently. I would put myself between her and our daughter... take the blows." He looked down at the table. Tom could see the whites of his knuckles showing as his hands were so firmly clasped. "I became very adept at hiding the injuries... the bruises. Coming up with all manner of tales with which to explain away the damage to anyone who asked, but," he lifted one hand and tapped his temple with fore and index finger "I couldn't hide the damage up here. One day," he sighed, "it all caught up with me."

"This was when you had a breakdown?"

"I believe the nurse labelled it as a mental episode, at the time." Terry frowned. "Around the same time, Caroline deteriorated… and took her own life." His eyes gleamed, clearly revisiting a painful memory. "And I never forgave myself."

"You couldn't hold yourself responsible for that."

"Had I been there, Inspector… I wouldn't have allowed it to happen, but I wasn't there. I was… oh, what difference does it make now. I was in an institution… and as such, I was unable to care for my wife or my child."

"Sarah was taken into care, wasn't she?" Tom asked. Terry nodded. "Did you try to get her back when you came home?"

He shook his head but didn't make eye contact. "I wasn't fit to be her parent. How could I cope with a troubled child, a child grieving her mother no less? A child who needed a father… and all she had was a broken shell of a man."

"It must have been difficult," Tom said.

"That's what I told myself, Inspector." He raised his head, meeting Tom's eye. "I told myself she was better off without me… but that was a lie. The first of many that I told myself. Excuse after excuse, all repeated for one reason and one reason alone; to aid in absolving me of my responsibilities." He inhaled deeply, his expression stern. "You asked me why I live the way I do? That's why, so I don't have to live the life I should be living. I can go from place to place, whenever I choose to and no one will place a burden on me that I do not care for."

"Some might say that's selfish," Eric said, an edge to his tone.

"And they would be quite correct, young Eric. I am selfish. Heartless, others might say."

"You're not heartless," Tom said.

"Oh no?"

"No," Tom said. "I don't believe so."

"Here we are, having only just met, and you think you know me?"

"Katy," Tom said.

Terry fixed his eye on Tom, slowly sitting back in his seat. He nodded stoically. "Yes… Katy."

"How did you come to be in touch with her?"

"I found her. I've kept an eye on my family in recent years, as I've come and gone. Sarah struggles, I know that. I kept my distance for a long, long time but… she reminds me so much of her mother. Recently, I tried to bridge the gap between us."

"How did that go?"

Terry chuckled but without genuine humour.

"About as well as one might expect. Or deserve, I should add."

"And she told you about Katy?"

"Yes." Terry was melancholy. "I had missed out on so much... her birth... those younger years when a child adores the adults around them." He looked at Tom and Eric in turn. "Do you have children?"

Tom didn't answer, preferring to keep the focus on Terry's life but Eric nodded.

"Then you'll know, Eric, when that little face lights up... it makes your entire life seem worthwhile, doesn't it?"

Eric looked away.

"And Sarah told you about your granddaughter? What did she say?"

Terry's expression clouded. "She told me she was in care, that they didn't see one another unless it was under supervision. It upset me, I must say."

"That she was in care?"

"Yes, but I wasn't angry with Sarah. I mean, how much of a hypocrite would that make me? No," he said firmly, shaking his head, "I saw what had happened to Sarah. What my abandonment of her has done to that poor child. My cloak of selfishness was cracked... and I wanted to see her... Katy, to help if I could and, dare I say, to make amends."

"Did it go well?"

"Better than with her mother, that's for sure. It

took time, but there was willingness on both sides. You see, Katy is very grown up for her age. She can see that what one does in the past is not as important as what one does in the present or, indeed, could do in the future."

"You built, what, a relationship?"

"We did… although it took time."

"And she confided in you," Tom said. "About Simon Shears and what he was up to?"

Terry averted his eyes from Tom's, silently shaking his head.

"You see, we are confident we have a lead on what Simon was up to," Tom said, "but as to how far along he was in his plans, we do not know. What we're trying to figure out though, is how Simon Shears wound up dead at your father's old place of business… where you have been staying?"

Terry looked back at him, anger burning in his eyes. "Hmm… it is a mystery."

"I think now would be a good time to stop with the lies, Terry," Tom said. "You lied to yourself for years, to your family. You wanted to make up for abandoning your family in the past and now, with what Simon was doing to your granddaughter, you decided to make amends, to protect Katy. And to that end, you murdered Simon."

"Simon Shears was absolute scum. Him and his low-life brother," Terry snarled. "Scum of the earth, those two."

"You murdered Simon and put his body in the boot of a scrap car, didn't you? And that is why Tony Shears came after you tonight with a shotgun. He knows it was you as well."

Terry shook his head, eyes clamped shut.

"It's okay, Terry. There was plenty of forensic evidence at the scene. We took your DNA earlier and we can cross reference that with samples from Simon's body. We don't need your confession. The science won't lie to us. What I want to know is who helped you. Mark Oatley?"

"Mark? He's got nothing to do with any of this."

"He provided you with a hiding place for the last few days at Eleanor's house. He's involved."

Terry sat forward, pointing at Tom. "Mark is a decent lad. He has done nothing wrong, so you should leave him out of it."

Tom and Eric exchanged a glance. "We can't do that, Terry," Tom said. "Mark's dead."

Terry's face dropped. He stared at Tom, as if trying to judge his sincerity. Then he looked at Eric who nodded.

"Mark's… he's dead?"

"You didn't know, did you?"

Terry shook his head, his mouth still open.

"How?"

"Someone killed him," Tom said quietly, "and

then they set him on fire. Most likely, they were trying to conceal evidence."

"Oh... no," Terry sank his head into his hands. "He was such a gentle boy, so kind and willing to help."

"Why would someone hurt another person close to you, do you think?"

"That must be how he found us... at the beach."

"Tony Shears?"

Terry nodded. "He came there to kill me..." He looked up at Tom, imploring him with his eyes. "To kill all of us."

"You asked for Karl's help to get away?"

"We did. Katy begged him." Terry took a deep breath, glancing up at the ceiling, as if looking to the heavens for support, before lowering his gaze to Tom. "They have been in touch. It's all secret. Katy knew her mum wouldn't support the two of them having a relationship and... who knows what social services would say. They chose to keep it between them. In a year or so, Katy would be able to make her own decisions. She would be an adult. As it turns out, the fact no one knew Katy and her father had formed a bond was a good thing." He glanced at Eric. "Until you came calling anyway."

"I should imagine he didn't take kindly to what Simon was doing to his daughter either. That's the truth, isn't it? Simon was abusing your granddaughter and you and he, her father, had to put a stop to it. The two of you lured him out to Fring and you killed him."

"No, no, no… it wasn't like that," Terry said. "Not like that at all. I just wanted to talk to him, make him see what he was doing was wrong." He shook his head. "It all got out of hand."

"Why didn't you come to us?"

"Because we didn't trust you to do the right thing," Terry snapped. "You haven't in the past!"

"So, you took the law into your own hands?" Tom countered.

"Vengeance is mine, and I will repay, says the Lord."

"Pardon me?"

"Deuteronomy, Inspector," Terry said, "although, admittedly, I am somewhat paraphrasing. Vengeance is not for me to deliver. Simon would face the wrath of God at the appropriate time. I wanted to protect my granddaughter, that's all."

"You're saying you didn't take part in killing him. You killed his brother Tony with your bare hands," Tom said. "I watched you do it."

"That was self-defence. I will face the judgement for what I did, I truly believe that." He held up a pointed finger. "However, I also believe my actions this night saved *both* our lives, wouldn't you agree, Inspector Janssen?"

Tom ignored Terry's question, pressing home his own line of inquiry.

"Was it self-defence when you killed Simon, too? The murderer will have Simon's DNA all over them. It was a particularly vicious killing, one that a jury will find hard to believe was entirely a result of self-defence."

Terry stared at Tom, his expression a mask of control and totally unreadable. He slowly closed his eyes, his lips pursed. He nodded.

"For the benefit of the recording," Tom said, "Terry Westfield has just nodded. Please can you tell me what you meant by that gesture?"

Terry took a deep breath before he released it slowly and met Tom's eye. "I did it. I killed Simon Shears. I dumped his body in the boot of that old car and then I took his car and parked it elsewhere."

"Where did you take it?"

Terry drew himself upright. "I parked it in a pub car park." He shook his head. "I don't remember which one." He sat forward, meeting Tom's eye. "Simon Shears was an animal. He had it coming… and I would do it again in a heartbeat."

"And you decided to kill Simon Shears by yourself?"

Terry hesitated, it was only a fraction of a second, a micro expression, but enough for Tom to spot.

"That's right. Someone needed to deal with him, seeing as you lot weren't going to."

"So, let me be clear," Tom said. "You lured Simon Shears out to the yard where you ambushed him, murdered him by stabbing him repeatedly with a knife, and then you concealed his body?"

Terry fixed his eye on Tom, and almost sneered as he nodded. "Yes. That's it exactly."

Tom and Eric exchanged a glance and Tom looked up at the camera mounted on the wall in the corner of the room, knowing Tamara would be watching from an adjoining room. He nodded almost imperceptibly, and then concluded the interview.

CHAPTER TWENTY-EIGHT

Tom left Eric in the interview room with Terry, stepping out into the corridor to find Tamara already waiting for him.

"What do you make of that?" he asked her.

"He is very self-deprecating. I think he's intelligent enough to know he's cornered."

Tom leaned against the wall, pressing the heels of his palms into his eyes, feeling the drama of the day's events catching up with him.

"It's a strong confession," Tamara said. "He's articulate… and it is unforced."

"Except he's playing the role of two men," Tom said. Tamara arched a single eyebrow. "Dr Paxton believes two people attacked Simon Shears."

"So, Terry is willing to take the fall?" Tamara asked. Tom shrugged. "Uniform have just brought

Karl Roper back from the hospital," Tamara said. "We have him ready to interview."

"Right," Tom said.

"Are you up to it? I can always have Cassie sit in with me if you'd rather—"

"No, no," he said, holding up a hand to reassure her he was up for it. "It's just been a long couple of days."

"Tell me about it. Once we're through here, I have to pick up the pieces at home." He looked at her quizzically. "I left David at my place eating a Thai meal with my mother."

Tom sucked air through his teeth, shaking his head. "Poor chap."

"I know," Tamara said, smiling. "He doesn't deserve me." She pointed at a door along the corridor. "Interview Room Two."

Tom entered the room. Karl Roper looked up at him, with an impassive expression. Cassie was sitting in a chair opposite, arms folded, staring at Karl, unflinching. Tom couldn't help but think it was a good thing she hadn't been a medical professional because her bedside manner would be awful. She was, however, quite adept at unsettling interviewees.

"Karl," Tom said, pulling out his chair and sitting down. "I'm Detective Inspector Janssen."

"You're the guy who got my daughter to shore safely tonight."

"That's correct. I am."

Karl tipped his head towards Tom. "Thank you. Tony got the better of me… if you hadn't been there…"

"Well, we were," Tom said, "and a lot of bloodshed could have been avoided if you'd come to us earlier."

Karl shook his head. "It wasn't my call to make."

"So, whose was it?"

He remained tight-lipped, looking away.

"We can get all of this wrapped up tonight quickly, Karl," Tom said. "We have a detailed statement along with a confession in relation to Simon Shears' murder—"

Karl sat upright, wagging an accusatory finger at Tom. "Now you look here, you can't have this done and dusted without even speaking to me! What the hell is going on here?"

Tom's curiosity was piqued. He'd expected to get very little out of Karl. Even so, they didn't need much from him as Terry had already given them the details, Tom having witnessed Terry drowning Tony Shears as well earlier that night.

"This isn't a stitch up, Karl," Tom said, "and we're more than willing to listen to your side of events."

"Yeah, well…" Karl said, relaxing a little, the tension dissipating from his posture, "that's good."

"Is there anything you'd like to say before we get into it?"

Karl stared hard at him, focussed. "I guess it's over now and it's time to clean the slate."

"I'm listening."

He took a deep breath, controlling the release and laying his hands flat on the table before him. Momentarily biting his bottom lip, Karl held Tom's gaze.

"I killed Simon Shears."

Tom held the eye contact, sensing Cassie's glance sideways at him.

"You did?"

"That's right."

Tom nodded slowly, tapping his index finger gently on the table, thinking hard.

"How did you kill him?"

"I stabbed him in the chest… over in Fring," Karl said, "and I dumped his body in the old scrapyard."

"That's interesting, Karl."

He looked at Tom suspiciously. "What is?"

"Terry Westfield has already confessed to the murder of Simon Shears, no less than twenty minutes ago."

Karl's mouth fell open, his brow furrowing. "Well… I wouldn't believe anything that man tells you."

"How well do you know Terry?" Tom asked.

Karl's eyes flitted between Tom and Cassie. Was he taking their measure? Tom couldn't be sure.

"Terry?" He shook his head. "Hardly know him at all. Until Katy brought him to me, I'd never met him, only heard about him through Sarah and, more recently, Katy."

"You mean, you didn't see him in the scrapyard the night you murdered Simon Shears?"

Karl closed his eyes, concentrating. "There was a lot going on."

"I can imagine," Tom said, the intrigue growing. "So, you first met Terry… when?"

"Earlier today," he said. "I knew he was with Katy, looking after her. They'd been together for a few days. I'm not sure how many."

"She told you that the other day, when you were seen together outside the convenience store in Blakeney?" Karl looked at Tom, surprised. "That's right, we have you and Katy on camera talking to one another. It looked heated."

Karl nodded. "It was. She was worried… frightened about Tony Shears and what he might do."

"You know Tony?"

Karl snorted. "Everyone knows Tony! He's a piece of work. If you're not scared of him, then you damn well ought to be."

"She was running from him?"

"And his brother," Karl said. "But I took care of him."

"So, you said. Tell me, how many times did you stab Simon?"

Karl stared at him momentarily before shrugging. "I don't recall."

"You don't recall? Care to hazard a guess? I mean, it's not every day you kill someone. At least, I hope not."

Karl shook his head.

"Five? Ten times? More?"

"I guess so… maybe ten to fifteen times… but I don't remember. It could be more or less."

"And did you strangle him as well?" Cassie asked.

Karl looked at her. "I did what I had to do. Nothing more, nothing less. What else do you want me to say?"

Tom sat back, folding his arms across his chest. "I'd like to hear the truth."

"Well, I just told you the truth," Karl said defiantly. "There's nothing else to say about that."

"And tonight? Stealing a boat from your place of work and—"

"To get my daughter to safety, any way I could. I feel bad for taking the boat, but I didn't have time to come up with anything else."

"You said it wasn't your call to come to us," Tom said. Karl nodded. "Then whose call was it not to, Terry's?"

Karl shrugged, looking down at the table. "Maybe?"

"You don't recall?" Cassie asked, mockingly.

Karl glared at her, then laughed, a dry and humourless sound. "Yeah. That's right. I don't."

Tom fixed him with a stern look. Karl didn't flinch.

"I don't believe that you're being honest with us, Karl."

He glared at Tom now. "I don't care what you think. You can charge me now because I have nothing else to say."

Sitting back in his seat, Karl looked up at the ceiling, arms crossed. The interview was over. Tom looked at Cassie who raised her eyebrows as if to say she had nothing.

"Right," Tom said. "Wait here and I'll make sure custody has a cell allocated for him."

Tom got up and went to the door, feeling Karl's eyes on his back. Leaving the room, he waited for Tamara to come out from where he was sure she'd been watching the interview. She arrived moments later, cocking her head, she exhaled heavily.

"What on earth was that about?"

Tom thought about it. "Let's put him in a cell. They can both stew on it for a while until we can get to the bottom of it."

"Which of them is telling the truth?"

"Maybe they both are," Tom said, "or neither."

Tamara looked puzzled.

"I think I know, but somehow I don't think either Terry or Karl is going to help us."

A few minutes later, Tom opened the door to the interview room where Eric sat patiently with Terry Westfield. Tom beckoned for them both to stand.

"Eric, take him down to the custody suite. We'll be bringing Karl Roper down there in a minute as well."

"How is Karl?" Terry asked.

"He'll be all right. No major damage," Tom said as both men stepped out into the corridor. He gestured with an open palm the way Terry needed to go. Eric joined them. "I'll be right behind you," Tom said to Eric who nodded, taking hold of Terry's arms and handcuffing him. Eric then led Terry away.

"YOU'RE A GOOD POLICEMAN, ERIC," Terry said as they walked together down to the custody suite.

"You think so?"

"I do, yes. I'm not sure I would have been so brave to charge into the darkness when a man is waving a shotgun around."

"It's my job," Eric said, smiling, appreciative of the compliment.

"Very courageous."

They passed through into the custody suite, Eric signalling to the sergeant that they were heading to the cells. He acknowledged Eric with a wave.

"Cell number three, if you please," he said, and Eric gave him a thumbs-up.

The block housed only a half dozen cells and none of them was presently occupied. The door to the cell was open and Eric stood aside to let Terry enter. He turned to face Eric who unlocked and removed the handcuffs.

"Well, it's nice of you to say, but I might not be one for much longer."

"A policeman?" Terry asked. Eric nodded silently. "Why ever not? It suits you."

Eric frowned. "My other half… she wants me to leave. We're separated."

"And that's because of the job?"

Eric nodded. "I think if I stay doing it, she'll not come back to me and I miss her. I miss our son. I'd do anything to have them come home."

"And if you quit, you believe she will? Come back, I mean?"

"Yes, I think so."

"And will that solve your marital problems?"

Eric shrugged. "I don't know. Maybe."

Terry cocked his head. "And maybe not. The problem isn't your job, Eric. Take it from me, a man who believed his devotion to his work helped destroy his life. The job is part of who you are, what makes you the person you are today."

"If you say so."

"I do. You are the sum total of everything that has happened to you, your life experience, good and bad. Without it, you would be someone completely different. Maybe you would be in one of these," he said, rapping his knuckles on the open cell door and walking into it.

"I sincerely hope not," Eric said. Standing at the entrance to the cell, looking along the corridor back into the custody suite, he saw people milling around but no one was paying him any attention. He was unsure of whether to go through with what he wanted to do, his confidence ebbing away the longer he stood there.

"Is something on your mind, Detective?"

Eric swallowed hard, his mouth and throat were dry. Terry had sat himself down now on the thin, blue plastic-covered mattress with his back against the cell wall, hugging his knees before him, concern etched on his face. But it wasn't concern for himself.

"Um… I wanted to speak with you before you leave here," Eric said. "I'm not sure I'll get another chance."

"I'm intrigued. What is it you want to say?"

Eric didn't want to make eye contact, but he forced himself to. "You remembered my face… or you said you did. And… I wanted to talk to you… about something."

Terry slowly nodded, keeping a watchful eye on Eric. "I remember you, Eric. I do. That's the thing about working in teaching… you see so many young faces come and go. One has to remember them. Not always the names, but I can always recall a face, the features, mannerisms… the look. It is something of a skill, and I recall that look on your face, similar to the one you have now. The same one you had when I spoke to you in town a few years ago. You were new in your uniform, all shiny shoes and bursting with pride. Do you remember?"

Eric took a breath and nodded. "I do. We have spoken several times over the years."

"Yes, I know. The look in your eyes that first time I saw you in uniform that day. I saw the same look that night all those years ago… the shame… when you and your friends threw those stones at me." He fixed his gaze on Eric who buckled under the scrutiny. "A gang of schoolchildren… bored… seeking excitement, or so they thought, and taking advantage of a vulnerable old man who wasn't hurting anyone, let alone them."

"I… I… don't know what to say."

"You all ran away when I fell, and it was only you who stopped."

"I thought… you might be hurt."

"Aside from a cut to my forehead, only my

pride, Eric, and my dignity of course." Terry smiled. It seemed genuine. "A man is judged by what he does in this life, but sadly not by what follows with the same level of temerity. You've done the right thing, DC Collet. You've committed yourself to something larger than you, and what you do *means something* now." He nodded approvingly. "Most people will not see it for what it is, or for how much of you is sacrificed in the pursuit of those higher goals. Do people treat you strangely?"

"Some do, yes. It comes with the uniform, I think."

"They will fear you. Perhaps some people will shun you. But it counts, Eric, what you do every day counts for something. Never underestimate that."

"I don't want to make excuses for what I did…"

"No, quite right that you shouldn't, Eric. That is a sign of a weak mind. You must take responsibility for your actions, always."

"Do you think I should resign?"

Terry smiled warmly. "That's not for me to say, Eric. Only you can make that decision but be sure that you are making it for the right reason."

"I shouldn't make a life-changing decision to please someone else?"

"If you feel it is the right decision then that is exactly what you should do. However, if you don't truly believe it, then to do so will eat away at you…

like a cancer and one day, many years from now, your angst surrounding that decision will pour out of you like poison. It will be what discolours your soul."

Eric frowned. "Poetic."

"Devastating. You have one life, Detective Constable Collet. Live it without regret, and if that does not fit in with the woman you've chosen to spend your life with," he said with a brief shrug, "then perhaps you have chosen badly."

Eric contemplated those words, his forehead creased in concentration.

"I'm sorry," he said. "For what we did to you."

"I know you are, Eric," Terry said, smiling. "I know it."

Eric smiled awkwardly, feeling self-conscious. Backing out of the doorway, he made to close the cell door only for Tom to appear leading Karl Roper with a firm grip on his upper arm.

Tom stopped at the entrance to the cell. Karl looked past Eric, making eye contact with Terry. He offered him a curt nod in greeting and Terry smiled warmly back at him.

"Just so the two of you are aware," Tom said, "I'm impressed by your commitment to protect the one you love, but I'm afraid it will be for nothing."

"What?" Karl asked. "What are you talking about?"

"Oh… the two of you haven't discussed it then? It's not part of a wider scheme?"

Karl looked at Terry who seemed equally confused. As was Eric, judging by his expression.

"The two of you, both confessing to the same murder and claiming to have acted alone muddied the waters," Tom said. "But then I got to thinking, what would be the reasoning behind making such a claim? What is so precious to the two of you that you would be willing to ruin your own lives in order to protect it? The only thing the two of you have in common… Katy."

Karl's expression shifted from confusion to anger and he tried to wrestle his arm free of Tom's grip. It was to no avail. Tom stared at him. "I don't know whether Terry lured Simon to the breakers' yard with the intention of killing him or if Simon followed Katy back there and it was a spontaneous action by a frightened teenager." He looked between Terry and Karl. "At some point I hope one… or both of you will tell us the truth of what happened that night, saving Katy from having to maintain this farce."

Karl struggled against Tom's grasp. "I did it!" he hissed. "Do you hear me? It was me, not her."

Tom shook his head, gesturing for Eric to open the cell door opposite. Tom steered the still protesting Karl into the cell and pulled the door closed. Karl threw himself at the door, kicking at it and screaming.

"You bastard! I did it. It was me!"

Tom turned to see that Terry hadn't moved, still sitting with his knees up to his chest, his eyes glazed over. "Anything from you, Terry?" he asked.

Terry Westfield blinked and he looked up at Tom.

"The sins of the fathers are visited upon the children," he whispered quietly. Tom sighed, closing the cell door.

"Bloody hell!" Eric said quietly. "Are you sure?"

"We'll run the forensic comparison tests on the DNA recovered from beneath Simon Shears' fingernails," Tom said. "If I'm right, that should be conclusive enough to put her at the murder."

"Damn."

Tom placed a supportive hand on his shoulder. "Call it a day, Eric. It's been a long one."

CHAPTER TWENTY-NINE

THE LODGE in Old Hunstanton was quiet. No doubt it would pick up once the patrons arrived for dinner or a few drinks in the evening. For now, Hunstanton CID had the place almost to themselves. Tom was at the bar when Alice arrived with her father and Saffy in tow. Saffy bounded up to Tom and threw her arms around him, as was customary when she hadn't seen him for several days.

"Can I have an ice cream?" she asked him.

"Saffy, it's barely above freezing outside."

The temperatures plummeted once the stormy weather passed, but the team didn't mind. They were all pleased to have a resolution in the cases they'd been working. Even if the end result was somewhat bittersweet. The DNA tests returned an inconclusive potential match to Katy Roper and with her father, Karl, and her grandfather sticking to their stories regarding who carried out the mul tiple blows that assisted in Simon Shears' death, the Crown Prosecution Service was currently at an impasse in terms of who to charge with the murder. Terry would be charged with manslaughter regarding the death of Tony Shears, but a successful argument could, and most likely would, be made for mitigating his actions as justifiable self-defence. Tom was willing to speak on Terry's behalf.

Katy herself, diagnosed with a form of PTSD would undergo therapy, but in the meantime the case progressed. Unless she was willing to open up, the two men would likely stand trial. The investigation team believed Terry had restrained Simon, but they all found it difficult to believe it was a premeditated attack. However, as Tamara pointed out, it wasn't for them to decide. Tom was pleased it was out of their hands as to who would be tried for the crime. Regarding Mark's grisly murder, it was clear to the team that Tony Shears had followed the same path to find his brother's killer as they had, abducting and then torturing him into revealing the whereabouts of Terry Westfield. That was the only explanation for Tony being at the beach that night to intercept their escape. With Tony dead as well, they had to accept they'd never know for sure but it was a reasonable conclusion to draw.

"I'm sorry," Ian said, approaching the bar. Alice

detoured to say hello to the team, Cassie giving her a massive hug. "I told her I'd get her some ice cream."

"How about hot chocolate?" Tom asked. "Marshmallows and whipped cream. The Lodge is legendary for it."

"If I must," Saffy said, feigning disappointment before bursting into a broad smile.

"Are you staying for a bit longer?" Tom asked.

Ian shook his head. "I've booked a flight home for the day after tomorrow."

"Oh!" Saffy whined, bringing a smile from her grandfather.

"But I'll be back next month, I promise. Perhaps sooner, depending on how it goes with… you know?" he said, referring to his ex-wife and Alice's mum. She was still fighting, even improving but it really was a matter of time now. The promise to return placated Saffy at least. Ian inclined his head. "I have a few things to sort out at home, but I'll come back and stay a little longer. Not with you," he said quickly to Tom, offering his hands in surrender. "I wouldn't want to outstay my welcome."

Tom was relieved. He seemed to be a nice enough chap, as far as Tom knew, but the tension was still there between Ian and his daughter. Tom did not want to be caught in the crossfire.

The drinks Tom ordered were lined up on a tray

and Tom excused himself. Ian ordered for Saffy, himself and Alice. Tom walked through to the lounge bearing the drinks. He set them down and Alice gave him a hug. Danny Wilson entered from the other side of the bar making a beeline for the table. He smiled and nodded a greeting to Tom before tossing a small yellow plastic box onto the table, catching everyone's attention.

"All right," he said, pointing at the box, "which one of you sods taped a banana air freshener to the underside of my desk?"

Everyone burst out laughing.

"Gits! Every single one of you," Danny said, then caught Tamara's eye, and then Tom's. He flushed. "Not you, obviously… sorry." His embarrassment only made everyone laugh more.

Kerry picked up her and Eric's drink, passing his to him and then indicated for the two of them to step away from the group. Once out of earshot, she absently scratched the side of her head. Eric felt awkward.

"Eric, did you tell Danny that I'm… that I like women?"

Eric coughed, averting his eyes from her gaze. "Um… I might have said something like that… but… sorry—"

She reached out with one hand and placed it on top of his free hand, squeezing it gently. "I'm not interested in Danny," she said. "I've only ever been interested in you."

"Oh," Eric said, feeling his neck and face getting warm.

"It's just..." she frowned, "I think you're still very much in love with Becca." She forced him to meet her eye, angling her head into his eye line. "And I'm not going to play understudy... at least not right now."

Eric coughed again. "Right. Yes, of course."

She pointed past him towards the door. Eric turned and saw Becca in the lobby, George in her arms. His heart leapt. He hadn't seen either of them in over a week. Becca smiled and came over to him, Kerry was forgotten and she drifted away, which very much emphasised her point. Not that Eric noticed her leaving.

"Hello," Becca said timidly.

"Hi," he replied, trying to hide his joy at seeing them. George beamed at his father and Eric looked at Becca. "May I?"

"Of course."

Eric set his drink down on the nearest table, and then took his son into his arms. George squealed in delight as Eric bobbed him up and down.

"You're getting big, little man!"

"He is. I can't carry him for long these days without my arms going numb," Becca said.

"How did you know we were here?"

Becca didn't get a chance to answer, Cassie appearing at her shoulder. She winked at Eric and gave Becca a quick hug. "Nice to see the family together."

"Yes, it is," Eric said, looking at his estranged wife.

"Don't mind me," Cassie said. "Aunty Cass just came to grab a minute with the wee man."

Reluctantly, Eric passed him to her and he was mildly disappointed to see George react to Cassie's touch as much as he had his own. Cassie sauntered away with a grinning George, taking him to see the others. Eric felt suddenly self-conscious, standing alone with Becca. She seemed to be feeling the same, shifting her weight between her feet.

"Eric… I've started seeing someone."

His face must have instantly dropped because she reached out, gripping his forearm, panic stricken.

"No, not like that," she said, lowering her voice. "A therapist. The GP put me onto her. He thinks I'm suffering from postnatal depression." She smiled awkwardly. "I-I don't know why he thinks so… I mean, I've been such a delight to be around this past year or so."

Eric laughed, relieved. "I've been thinking. About what you said before… about me and the police," Eric said. "I've been thinking… and I think you're right—"

"No!" she said. "I wasn't right. All you've ever wanted to be is a policeman, and I'm not going to take that away from you."

"But I'll find something else—"

"Find what else?" Cassie asked, whirling back up to them, George laughing maniacally as she swirled him around.

"A new job," Eric said.

"Oh no you don't, DC Collet," Cassie said pointedly, passing George back to him. "You are not leaving me with… with… that," she said, pointing at Danny. "Banana-man is a no go."

"Don't worry, he's not leaving," Becca said.

"Well, maybe not yet," Eric replied. "But we'll see." He looked at Cassie who smiled. "What is it with Danny anyway? He kind of reminds me a bit of you."

"Me?" Cassie said, arching her eyebrows.

"Yeah, he's like a slightly less aggressive, less masculine form of you."

Cassie nodded, smiling. "Eric, that's the nicest thing you've ever said to me."

"I try."

She looked at Danny, watching him regaling the group with his attempted take-down of Tony Shears, the one that saw him knocked unconscious in the surf. It appeared to be a Herculean effort, judging by how he was re-enacting it for the audience.

"He's nothing like me," Cassie muttered. "I mean, maybe before I matured… and was cultured."

"Cultured, you?" Eric asked, laughing.

"Yes, Eric. Cultured." She playfully slapped him on the back of the head. "I'm getting the drinks in." She looked at Becca. "Are you stopping for a bit?"

Becca glanced at Eric and smiled. He returned it. "Yes, I'm stopping."

"Excellent. I'll get the drinks then."

"I'll get them," Eric said. "I don't need one, so I'll just get—"

"Nah, I've got it. The usual for you two, seeing as you can walk home from here?" She waved away Eric's protests. He still had a full glass. "We're celebrating. Especially the two of you."

Both of them nodded and Cassie went to the bar, ordering more drinks. When the barman had them lined up in front of her, Cassie pointed to Tamara. "It's on her tab, right?" The barman nodded and Cassie took the drinks over to Eric who gratefully accepted them. Cassie left the three of them together, returning to the main table.

Tamara broke off from her conversation with David and nudged Cassie's arm. "Why do I think you had something to do with the two of them meeting up today?"

"The world works in mysterious ways, T," Cassie said.

"That's God."

"Say again?"

"It's God who works in mysterious ways, Cass."

"Well," she shrugged, "I've been called far worse!"

FREE BOOK GIVEAWAY

Visit the author's website at **www.jmdalgliesh.com** and sign up to the VIP Club and be the first to receive news and previews of forthcoming works.

Here you can download a FREE eBook novella exclusive to club members;

Life & Death - A Hidden Norfolk novella

Never miss a new release.

No spam, ever, guaranteed. You can unsubscribe at any time.

Enjoy this book? You could make a real difference.

Because reviews are critical to the success of an author's career, if you have enjoyed this novel, please do me a massive favour by entering one onto Amazon.

Type the following link into your internet search bar to go to the Amazon page and leave a review;

http://mybook.to/JMD-dead-to-me

If you prefer not to follow the link please visit the sales page where you purchased the title in order to leave a review.

Reviews increase visibility. Your help in leaving one would make a massive difference to this author and I would be very grateful.

BOOKS BY J M DALGLIESH

One Lost Soul

Bury Your Past

Kill Our Sins

Tell No Tales

Hear No Evil

The Dead Call

Kill Them Cold

A Dark Sin

To Die For

Fool Me Twice

The Raven Song

Angel of Death

Dead to Me

Blood Runs Cold

Life and Death ***FREE -** visit jmdalgliesh.com

Divided House

Blacklight

The Dogs in the Street

Blood Money

Fear the Past

The Sixth Precept

Dark Yorkshire Books 1-3

Dark Yorkshire Books 4-6

Audiobooks

In the Hidden Norfolk Series

One Lost Soul
Bury Your Past
Kill Our Sins
Tell No Tales
Hear No Evil
The Dead Call
Kill Them Cold
A Dark Sin
To Die For
Fool Me Twice
The Raven Song
Angel of Death

In the Dark Yorkshire Series

Divided House
Blacklight
The Dogs in the Street
Blood Money
Fear the Past
The Sixth Precept

Dark Yorkshire Books 1-3
Dark Yorkshire Books 4-6

Printed in Great Britain
by Amazon

44796773R00231